ACCLAIM FOR THE WRITING OF MATT BRAUN

"Matt Braun has a genius for taking real characters out of the Old West and giving them flesh-and-blood immediacy."
—Dee Brown, author of *Bury My Heart at Wounded Knee*

"Matt Braun is a master storyteller of frontier history."
—Elmer Kelton

"Braun takes the big men, the complex personalities of those brave few who were pivotal figures in the settling of an untamed frontier."
—Jory Sherman, author of *Grass Kingdom*

"Matt Braun is one of the best!"
—Don Coldsmith, author of the Spanish Bit series

"Braun blends historical fact and ingenious fiction . . . A top-drawer Western novelist."
—Robert L. Gale, Western biographer

St. Martin's Paperbacks Titles
by Matt Braun

YOU KNOW MY NAME

(previously published as ONE LAST TOWN)

MATT BRAUN

St. Martin's Paperbacks

You Know My Name was previously published under the title *One Last Town*.

YOU KNOW MY NAME

Copyright © 1997 by Matt Braun.

ISBN: 0-312-97245-8

Printed in the United States of America

St. Martin's Paperbacks edition/August 1999

St. Martin's Paperbacks are published by St. Martin's Press, 175 Fifth Avenue, New York, N.Y. 10010.

10 9 8 7 6 5 4 3 2 1

TO

THE MEMORY OF

BILL TILGHMAN

A MAN OF VALOR FOR ALL TIME

CHAPTER 1

Tilghman stared out the window. The car sped over a hill past a country cemetery, the granite slabs framed against a dingy autumn sky. He saw the graveyard flash by, fallen leaves swirling around the headstones, yet these were fleeting images. His thoughts were far down the road, centered on the Ku Klux Klan. He wondered what they would find in Okmulgee.

The sun was a hazy globe in the distance, slowly cresting the horizon. Their destination was a closely guarded secret, and they were already some miles east of Oklahoma City. Except for their escort, no one knew where they were headed, or that they meant to confront the Klan. Those were Tilghman's instructions, agreed to before he would accept the assignment. The governor deferred to him on matters of security.

The rolling plains were stark, a great sea of grass gone tawny with early frost. The highway was as empty as the land, and the three cars in the convoy roared along at top speed. All of the vehicles were unmarked, but the lead car and the one in the rear were packed with state troopers. The center car was a four-door Buick, larger than its escorts and somewhat less crowded. Besides the driver, and a trooper in the shotgun seat, the only other occupants were Tilghman and the governor. Neither of them had spoken in several miles.

"You're awfully quiet, Bill." The governor finally broke the silence. "Not borrowing trouble, are you?"

"No need to borrow trouble," Tilghman replied. "We'll likely find all we want in Okmulgee."

"You're still convinced we'll have problems?"

"Things have gone too far for the Klan to back off now. I just suspect they'll turn out in force."

"By God, let them! We have to put a stop to this terrorism, once and for all. I mean to convince them I'm serious."

Governor Martin Trapp was scrappy as a terrier, and known for his temper. Like Tilghman, he had participated in the great land rush of 1889, and watched old Oklahoma Territory grow to statehood. A lawyer by profession, he had first entered politics in 1907, and gradually made his mark in the Democratic party. By the fall of 1924, two years after being elected governor, he was locked in a struggle for political survival. The Klan had challenged his authority to rule in Oklahoma.

"Don't get too feisty," Tilghman advised him. "You need to keep a cool head today. Otherwise things could go to hell in a hurry."

"Yes, of course," Trapp said, still fuming. "I understand the gravity of the situation. I'll restrain myself."

"Just follow my lead whichever way it goes. We want to bring you back in one piece."

"I'm counting on your reputation to put the fear of God into them. You're probably the only man in Oklahoma the Klan respects."

The governor's praise was a simple statement of fact. Tilghman was seventy years old, his brushy mustache and unruly thatch of hair long since turned gray. But he was still tall and hard, with cold blue eyes, broad through the shoulders. Curiously, his fame was undiminished from the old outlaw days, in the 1890s, when he'd served as a deputy U.S. marshal. In later years, he had also served as sheriff of Lincoln County and chief of police in Oklahoma City. A legend, he was known to every schoolboy in Oklahoma.

Special assignments from a series of governors had transformed him into a figure of mythical proportions. A year ago, he'd tracked a fugitive to Mexico, ending in yet another shootout, and the killing merely added luster to his reputation as a manhunter. He was acknowledged across all of Oklahoma as the one lawman who never failed. A gunfighter of the old school, who, come hell or high water, always got his man. In a land that prided itself on such things, it was the highest accolade.

Martin Trapp was no different than previous governors. When there was a tough job to be done, whether revolting convicts at the state prison or the Ku Klux Klan, he called on Bill Tilghman. Though he was some fifteen years younger, he had grown to manhood during the era of the horseback marshals. In his view, Tilghman was the one lawman from old Oklahoma Territory who had made the transition into the twentieth century. Their relationship was one of mutual respect.

"Troubling times," he mused now. "All the hatred and violence, and for what? I find myself wishing for the old days."

"Yeah, it's a different world," Tilghman agreed. "Horse thieves and train robbers took pride in their work. Not much pride in whipping a man half to death."

"We have to somehow turn the tide, Bill. If we fail, the Klan will all but own Oklahoma."

A recent Klan flogging had brought the situation to a head. The latest in a rash of atrocities across the state, the one in Okmulgee had been particularly brutal. The governor had finally drawn the line and declared war on the secret brotherhood. Through the attorney general he had ordered a grand jury empaneled at the Okmulgee courthouse. He demanded indictments against known Klan leaders. Tilghman was more concerned with the governor's safety.

"Stay right on my coattails," he said. "I doubt you've got many friends in Okmulgee."

"You think the Klan can bully people into accepting mob rule in place of law?"

"Governor, the Klan's already got them bullied. Otherwise you wouldn't have me along as your bodyguard."

The statement was a hard truth. A mood of isolationism had swept the country after the World War, and with it a resurgence of bigotry. Three years past, during the Great Red Scare, some seven thousand suspected Bolshevists had been jailed without warrant, and many deported without judicial process. A year later Congress enacted a bill to protect the racial purity of America.

Immigration of Europeans was limited severely, and banned altogether for Asians. This hotbed of jingoism, fueled by evangelist preachers, provided a fertile climate for the rebirth of the Ku Klux Klan. In keeping with the antics of the Roaring Twenties, the KKK flaunted itself with bold provocation. Yet for all its bizarre regalia and absurd rituals, the movement expanded rapidly across America. By 1924, the membership was estimated at five million, with one hundred thousand members in Oklahoma alone. The political apparatus of at least seven states was dominated by the Klan.

Oklahoma had thus far kept the State House free from entanglement. But the Klansmen controlled many rural areas, justifying their methods with a call to patriotism. Okmulgee was one among many such towns, where law-abiding citizens were fearful to speak out. The recent flogging had provided all the pretext the governor needed, and he meant to use it as an object lesson for the rest of the state. By appearing personally, Trapp would demonstrate that neither he nor Oklahoma could be intimidated by a gang of hooded thugs. That was the message.

Tilghman saw it in somewhat simpler terms. To him, the Klan was the bastard child of weak law enforcement.

The collusion of local and county peace officers allowed the KKK to exist, and grow. In Chandler, where he owned a horse ranch, he had been instrumental in nipping the movement at its very roots. Klan organizers were visited by Tilghman and the sheriff, and none too gently persuaded to move along. Word got around that it was a mistake to try recruiting members in Lincoln County.

The story was picked up by newspapers around the state. In interviews, Tilghman advocated extreme measures to stamp out the violence; as the most famed lawman in Oklahoma, he became an overnight symbol of the anti-Klan forces. Chandler experienced none of the terrorism that became commonplace elsewhere, and that seemed to make his case. His already formidable reputation took on added authority.

To Tilghman's way of thinking, the governor should have acted sooner. But he subscribed to the adage better late than never, and he was pleased that Trapp had asked him along. The sun was high when the cars entered downtown Okmulgee, and he steeled himself to the task. Over the years he had faced many mobs, and he knew that surprise gave him the edge. On a visceral level, it felt almost like old times. He was ready for anything the Klan had to offer.

A crowd of several hundred men was gathered in front of the courthouse. When the caravan rolled to a halt at the curb, Tilghman stepped from the Buick and a low murmur swept over the throng. His tall-crowned Stetson, and the ivory-handled Colt jutting from beneath his suit jacket were trademarks that brought instant recognition. He was known here as he was known throughout the state, for he had often gone hunting outlaws in what was once the land of the Five Civilized Tribes. There were many in the old Creek Nation who had reason to remember his deadliness in a fight.

One swift look of appraisal was enough to confirm Tilghman's earlier suspicions. There were no hoods or white robes, but the faces before him were filled with bitterness and hate. These were Klansmen, and clearly, their leaders had brought them here to intimidate the grand jury. All in all, it was an impressive show of force, and only slightly more than he'd expected. He stared back at the crowd with an impassive expression.

Governor Martin Trapp stepped out of the car. His face was known as well, and the men gathered there abruptly turned from a crowd to a mob. A dark, muttering growl erupted, and the hate on their features quickly changed to rage. Before anyone could react, the state troopers formed a wedge, with the governor tucked in the middle. Tilghman took the lead, walking straight ahead, and bulled a path through those who failed to step aside. He led the way up the worn marble steps, and a moment later the governor's party disappeared into the courthouse. The Klansmen, not yet recovered from their shock, were left staring at the door.

Inside, the building was strangely silent. The troopers' boot heels echoed through the corridors with a ghostly clatter. Still in a wedge, they marched down the hallway and halted before the county attorney's office. Tilghman motioned for the troopers to wait and followed the governor through the door. The outer office was empty.

A voice sounded from an inner office. When they came through the door, a weedy man with blinking eyes looked up from the telephone on his desk. He quickly replaced the receiver on the hook.

"Governor Trapp?" he said, clearly startled. "I'm Horace Green, the county attorney. I was just trying to get you on the phone."

"Were you?" Trapp said. "To what purpose?"

"I need some help here. I had to dismiss the grand jury."

"By whose authority?"

"I had no choice," Green said weakly. "That mob out there had them scared to death. They weren't about to indict anybody."

"What about the sheriff?" Tilghman asked. "Couldn't he protect your jurors?"

"The sheriff took off," Green said. "Him and all his deputies. The whole courthouse is empty."

"Bastards!" Trapp cursed roundly. "We'll just see about that. Let me use your phone, Mr. Green."

Green stood by, nervously eyeing Tilghman, while the governor called the state capital. After a short, blustery conversation, Trapp slammed the phone down. "Your problem is solved," he announced. "I have instructed the attorney general to place Okmulgee under martial law. The National Guard will arrive here by tomorrow afternoon."

"Martial law?" Green looked dazed. "You're occupying the town?"

"Indeed I am. Reconvene your grand jury and get me those indictments. Otherwise, start looking for a new job, Mr. Green."

"I'll try my best, Governor."

"Don't try," Trapp ordered. "Do it!"

Nodding to Tilghman, the governor walked out. In the corridor, he shook his head. "What do you think, Bill? Will it work?"

"I think the Klan will fold when they see the National Guard. You'll get your indictments."

"We'll put the Kluxers out of business yet. Mark my word."

The state troopers again formed their wedge. Tilghman led the way and they came out the courthouse door in a tight phalanx. They were greeted by a strident chorus of catcalls and jeers, which quickly turned to the ugly bloodlust of a mob. The crowd surged forward, jostling and shoving to reach the front rank. Their faces were contorted with rage, screaming obscenities, their clenched fists raised in threat.

Tilghman went down the steps, directly into the mob, his stride deliberate. The crowd faltered, their gibes momentarily stilled, thrown off by his lordly air of disdain.

Then, suddenly, a man lunged out from the pack, grabbed for the governor. Tilghman's reaction was sheer reflex, and the old Colt appeared in his hand. He laid the barrel across the man's skull.

The man stiffened, blood spurting from his forehead. He toppled backward into the arms of the crowd, and an angry roar went up as the Klansmen collected themselves, on the verge of rushing forward. Tilghman brought the Colt level, hammer at full cock. His pale eyes stared down the barrel.

"Stand fast! I'll shoot the first man that moves."

The mob froze as it turned to marble. Behind Tilghman, the troopers had drawn their pistols, fully prepared to back the man who led them. Absolute silence descended on the crowd, particularly those in the front rank, the ones closest to the guns. For several moments, it was as if the world had stilled in sound and motion. Abruptly, commanding instant attention, Tilghman wagged the barrel of his Colt.

"I want you boys to clear a path. Keep your heads and nobody will get hurt. Stand aside—now!"

The Klansmen split apart as if cleaved in half. Tilghman moved through their ranks, staring with icy calm into the eyes of those he passed. The silence held and the mob watched, spellbound by the menace of a gray-haired old man, as the troopers followed him to the curb. Quickly, he shoved the governor into the Buick, then waited until the troopers were in their own cars. He kept the snout of his Colt trained on the crowd.

"Goddamn you, Tilghman!" someone shouted in a coarse voice. "Don't you never come back to Okmulgee!"

Tilghman found the man, fixed him with a look. His mustache lifted in a slow smile, and he stepped into the Buick, slammed the door. The lead car pulled away from the curb, and the convoy turned west from the courthouse. Martin Trapp let out his breath in a gusty sigh. He glanced back through the rear window.

"There for a minute, I thought we wouldn't get out alive."

"Well, like they say, close don't count. We got lucky."

"Hardly luck," Trapp observed. "I'm glad you were along, Bill. I think I owe you my life."

Tilghman smiled. "All in a day's work, Governor."

CHAPTER 2

The ranch was located on Bell Cow Creek, three miles northwest of Chandler. A hawk veered slowly into the wind and settled high on a cottonwood as Tilghman drove into the compound. When he shut off the engine, the old Ford coughed and sputtered, then finally died, and he stepped out. He stood for a moment brushing road dust from his suit jacket.

Neal Brown, his foreman, walked over from the stables. "You oughta get yourself a horse. That tin lizzie sounds like it's gonna croak any day now."

"Hello to you too, Neal."

Tilghman, who had no love for automobiles, would have much preferred a horse. He had left Oklahoma City early that morning and spent most of the day on the road. His rump felt galled from the pounding.

"So how'd it go?" Brown said. "You wipe out all them Kluxers?"

"The governor ordered out the National Guard. They should be hitting Okmulgee before sundown."

"Well, good for the gov. High time somebody boxed their ears."

Brown was short and wiry, with a quick smile and an uncanny way with horses. He had been with Tilghman since the land rush days, and over the years the ranch had developed a reputation for blooded stock and fine saddle horses. The operation was profitable, and whenever Tilghman was called out on assignment he knew the ranch was in good hands. Neal Brown had forgotten more about horses than most men ever learned.

"Anything need attention," Tilghman inquired. "Or have you got it under control?"

"Gawddamn place runs like a Swiss clock. I'm insulted you'd ask."

"Glad to hear you're on the job. Have one of the boys saddle Copperdust. Think I'll go for a ride later."

"Whereabouts you headed?"

"Wherever Copperdust takes me. I'll let you know when I get back."

Tilghman walked toward the main house. The compound was situated on a wide expanse of woodland, with cottonwoods along the creek and a grove of live oaks stretching westward for a quarter mile. A wide corral was centered in the clearing, with the stables near the stream and the bunkhouse below a stunted hill to the north. The terrain on all sides rolled away in lush grassland.

The main house was set off from the creek, shaded by tall trees, with a covered porch overlooking the western woodlands. Every time Tilghman came home from a trip, he was struck again by the peacefulness of the scene. He thought that was in large part due to Zoe, his wife of thirty-four years, and a woman with firm opinions about what made a house a home. Her hand was evident from the latticework on the porch to the flower gardens that bloomed in summertime. She brought a touch of grace to the whole affair.

Zoe stepped through the screen door as he moved onto the porch. "Welcome back," she said, kissing him on the cheek. "I can't say you look any the worse for wear."

"All pretty routine," Tilghman remarked. "We drove over to Okmulgee and drove back. Nothing much to report."

"Not from what I hear on the radio. They say the governor sent in the National Guard. That sounds rather ominous."

"Well, the Klan wasn't exactly cooperative. But all things considered, I reckon that's to be expected."

She laughed, gently mocking him. "You wouldn't tell me if there was a pitched battle. I have to depend on the newspaper, or the radio."

"Where'd you get a notion like that?" Tilghman said, playing along. "I always tell you . . . sooner or later."

"Later being the rule with you, Mr. Tilghman."

Her eyes sparkled with a mischievous glint. Tilghman thought she had changed little in all their time together. She was twenty years younger, what he'd once thought of as his child bride. But now, at age fifty, she still had the verve and spirit of a woman half her age. She was tall and statuesque, with extraordinary green eyes and exquisite features. Her auburn hair was flecked with random wisps of gray.

Tilghman often regretted that they'd had no children. Certainly, it wasn't from wont of trying; even now she still kindled a fire in his belly. Doctors were at a loss for an explanation, and they had long ago reconciled themselves to the fact. But Tilghman would have traded years off his life to have had a son or a daughter with her spirit. He thought it was the only thing missing from their marriage.

She put an arm around his waist as they turned toward the door. "Well, I'm glad you're back," she said gaily. "I won't have to find another beau for the dance."

Every Saturday night, when he was home, they attended a dance at the Elk's Club. Tilghman knew there were any number of men in town who would have welcomed the chance to squire her for the evening. He never let on, but he was curiously proud that other men coveted his wife. She was all too aware of their admiration, and enjoyed teasing him.

"Who'd you have in mind?" he said now, his expression deadpan. "Wally Tucker? Maybe Joe Thompson?"

"God forbid!" she said with a minxish smile. "They're much too old for me. I was thinking of someone younger."

"That what you do, when I'm off on business? Flirt with all the young bloods?"

"Actually, I had a tryst planned today. You've spoiled it by coming home."

"Next time I'll stay away longer."

"Don't you dare!"

She put her arms around his neck as they moved into the parlor. She kissed him full on the mouth, then pulled back, a wicked gleam in her eye. "We could have a tryst of our own tonight. Unless, of course, you're too tired."

Tilghman laughed. "We'll see who yells 'uncle' first."

"I assure you it won't be me."

"Ought to be quite a night, then."

Tilghman hung his hat on a wall peg beside the door. The parlor was decorated with frilly curtains and modern furniture upholstered in bright patterns. Her one concession was his old leather wingback chair, positioned before the fireplace. He crossed the room to the chair.

"Got the coffeepot on? I could use a cup."

"The coffeepot's always on for you. I won't be a minute."

Tilghman dropped into his chair. A folded newspaper was on the sidetable, and a headline caught his eye. He unfolded the paper, quickly scanning a story on the front page. The dateline was Chicago, and the story related the gangland slaying of three men, killed in a hail of machine-gun fire. His features creased with disgust.

Zoe returned with the coffee. As she handed him the cup, she saw the cloudy expression on his face. She took a seat on the divan. "Something wrong?"

Tilghman rapped the newspaper. "Al Capone and his

pack of hooligans. They gunned down three men in broad daylight.''

''Yes, I read about it. What's the world coming to?''

''Whole country's on a downhill slide. Has been since those damnfools in Congress passed Prohibition.''

''For someone who doesn't drink, you're awfully vehement.''

''A man in my line of work needs a clear head. I don't object to liquor for other folks.''

''I understand,'' she said. ''We have the Ku Klux Klan and Chicago has Al Capone. Different problems for different places.''

''Don't kid yourself,'' Tilghman told her. ''Oklahoma's crawlin' with bootleggers. They're just not so trigger-happy.''

''Perhaps our gangsters are more intelligent.''

''How so?''

''Well, I only know what I read. But it seems they operate more like the feudal lords of medieval times. Little kingdoms, so to speak, where no one infringes on the other.''

Tilghman liked her command of the language and her educated manner. She had graduated from the state university shortly before they met, and soon after that they were married. Apart from her attractiveness, her quick mind was one of the things he admired most. For his part, he had barely made it through grade school. His education was from the college of hard knocks.

''I like that.'' he drained his coffee cup. ''Medieval kingdoms in the middle of Oklahoma. Helluva note.''

''Would you like more coffee.''

''Think I'll take a ride. After Okmulgee, I need to clear the cobwebs. Just get off for awhile.''

Zoe understood. Her husband was a private man, rarely revealing his innermost thoughts to anyone but her. Yet, though it would have surprised other people, he was introspective as well, deeper than he appeared. More often than not, when he returned from an assignment, he saddled up and went for a ride almost as a matter of habit. He needed to be alone to sort things out.

A short while later, Zoe watched from the door as he rode west along the creek. He was dressed in range clothes, the old Colt strapped around his waist, sitting tall astride Copperdust. The stallion was his favorite mount, a barrel-chested bloodbay with speed and endurance. She thought he looked like a grizzled warrior aboard a winged horse.

Some distance upstream Tilghman reined to a halt on a low knoll. A brisk October wind whipped across the plains, fallow grass rippling in its wake. The rich scent of the land, the rolling, endless prairie, acted as a restorative on him. He took vigor from the raw vitality of space and sky, and with it, the vision to see things clearly. His mind centered on the Klan, and Al Capone, and a world somehow tilted off its axis. All of it seemed a far cry from old Oklahoma Territory.

A scant seven years ago Americans had marched off to war in the belief they were fighting the war to end all wars. Yet they quickly discovered that there was nothing chivalrous about the poison gas and machine guns found in the trenches of France. Instead there was a brute savagery in the killing that suggested humanity's end. On the day Armistice was declared something over ten million people had lost their lives.

Upon returning from the Western Front in 1919, the doughboys came away with their faith shaken. In a flush of patriotism they had marched off to fight the Kaiser, but never again would they believe in flags or parades. The hell of modern war had proved too much, and their reaction was one of massive cynicism and a retreat into apathy. The War to End All Wars became a sham, and the postwar millennium, rather than a new dawning, became a dirge. America turned its back on the world.

A generation of cynics decided to party rather than mourn. The ferment of the Roaring Twenties, born among the skyscrapers of New York, swept westward across the plains. To some, the very fabric of America seemed threatened. But the masses wanted escape, not worry. By the millions, they queued up each week to watch Douglas Fairbanks and Mary Pickford, Charlie Chaplin and Fatty Arbuckle. For them the flickering image in a darkened theater was the reality, and the world a gargantuan joke. A joke to be toasted with ribald scorn.

Toast it they did. The Volstead Act made Prohibition the law of the land. Yet no one aside from fundamentalists and idealistic reformers took it seriously. Tens of thousands of speakeasies sprang up across the country, and the ubiquitous hip flask became a mainstay in American culture. Whiskey flowed as never before, smuggled in by rumrunners, dispensed by bootleggers, and served with cordial equanimity at the neighborhood speak. America wallowed in a sea of booze.

To Tilghman, there was double-edged humor in national Prohibition. Old Oklahoma Territory had been wide open, with saloons on every corner and pop-skull whiskey the drink of the day. Yet on the day of statehood, in 1907, Oklahoma had gone dry, and far from a novelty, the bootlegger had become an institution. Oklahomans had a headstart on the rest of the country, and with passage of the Volstead Act, speakeasies swapped their former notoriety for a newfound status. Suddenly it was a barrel of laughs, almost respectable. Flaunting the law became one of life's more humorous pastimes.

All humor aside, Tilghman often wondered if he'd outlived his time. By 1924, horseback marshals were a thing of the past, and the automobile had shattered the isolation of rural America forever. Yet, for all the disruptive influences of motion pictures and the motorcar, it was the magic of radio which at last toppled an insular and outmoded way of life. A flick of a switch brought instant access to the outside world, and suddenly the planet shrank to the size of a man's living room. The impact on the backlands was felt throughout America.

Oklahoma, no less than the rest of the nation, was

profoundly changed by radio. People clustered around their sets in the evening and sat mesmerized by the talking box. In a way, it was as if they were eavesdropping on the world, and even better, their neighbors. The news was pithy and fresh, sometimes bizarre and frequently shocking, and phrased in such a way as to make it highly repeatable. Moreover, today's news was reported today. Yesterday was already in the past.

Thinking about it, Tilghman was reminded that he was no longer the bearer of news. Zoe had known about Okmulgee and the Klan, and the National Guard, even as he was rattling along in the Ford from Oklahoma City. He felt at odds with the radio, just as he felt himself a stranger in the Roaring Twenties. He had adapted to change, and he could manage as well in the modern world as the next man. But he often found solace, and welcome retreat, on the hinterlands of the ranch. He sometimes yearned for the days of the horseback marshals.

The sun heeled over to the west, and Tilghman suddenly awoke from his woolgathering. He joshed himself for slogging around in deep thoughts, and drifting into reverie of times long gone. By the grace of God, and a fast gunhand, he'd made it into the twentieth century. He wasn't convinced that motion pictures or radio, or for that matter, the automobile, made things better. But he had lived to see it, and that was a damn sight better than the alternative. All in all, it could have been worse.

Shortly after dark, when he walked into the kitchen, Zoe was taking a tray of biscuits from the oven. She turned, watching as he unbuckled his gun belt, and blew a damp lock of hair off her forehead. She looked at him with quizzical humor.

"Well, Mr. Tilghman, did you solve all the world's problems?"

Tilghman chuckled. "I'm still working on it."

CHAPTER 3

On Saturday night the courthouse square was packed. Chandler was the county seat, as well as the hub of trade for outlying farmers and ranchers. People came to town on Saturday to sell produce, restock supplies, and visit with their neighbors. For most, it was the social event of the week.

Every parking place on the square was jammed with trucks and automobiles. The stores stayed open late on Saturday, and the sidewalks were thronged with people. Tilghman and Zoe arrived shortly after nightfall, entering the square from the north road. Some twenty thousand people resided in Lincoln County, and from all appearances, fully half of them had come to town. The night was off to a rousing start.

Tilghman was behind the wheel of Zoe's Packard. One of the more expensive cars on the road, the interior was plush, with a mahogany dash board, and the outside was painted a lustrous midnight blue. He'd bought it for her birthday, a replacement for a smaller Ford that had seen better days. She reveled in the power of the engine, and often made excuses for shopping trips to town, merely to get out for a drive. He rarely set foot in the car except for the Saturday night dance.

Traffic was heavy on the square. Tilghman kept the car in first gear as they crept by the courthouse and an array of shops and stores. The Packard was a familiar sight, and people on the sidewalks waved and called out his name. Years ago, he had served two terms as sheriff, and he was easily the most respected man in Lincoln County. Everyone took pride in the fact that the foremost peace officer in the history of Oklahoma was a member of their community. He had refused countless offers to seek higher public office.

The Elk's Club was a block east of the square. A large stone building, the club contained meeting rooms, a private though illegal bar, and a banquet room that was converted into a dance floor on Saturday nights. The membership was composed of the county's leading citizens, bankers and merchants, doctors and lawyers and politicians. They came there to socialize, and talk business, and hear the latest gossip. For the most part they were affluent and influential, concerned with the affairs of the day. The weekly dance was a time to celebrate their good fortune.

The band was playing "Japanese Sandman" as Zoe and Tilghman came through the door. As it was every Saturday night, the club was jammed with Chandler's prosperous set and their offspring. Couples dipped and swayed, gliding across the dance floor, and the bar was doing a lively business. Prohibition in Lincoln County, as with most of Oklahoma, was overlooked wherever business and civic leaders gathered. The sheriff, who routinely raided speakeasies, wisely avoided the Elk's Club. His discretion once again proved that some men were more equal than others.

Tilghman checked his hat and Zoe's wrap at the cloakroom. Her hair was upswept tonight, and she wore a silk crepe dress that accentuated her slim figure. They moved through the crowd, pausing to exchange greetings with friends, working their way toward the dance floor. The band swung into "Margie" and Tilghman took her in his arms, quickly caught the beat of the music. For all his gray hair, there was still ginger in his

step, and he led her smoothly into the number. She
smiled happily.

"You look especially handsome tonight, Bill."

"Funny thing," Tilghman said wryly. "I was just
thinkin' you're the prettiest woman in the place. Guess
we're a matched pair."

She laughed. "I would hope so, after all these years.
Of course, you might like me better if I were a flapper."

"I like you just the way you are. A woman ought to
look like a woman."

Zoe shared the sentiment. The younger generation,
both men and women, were joined in a revolt of manners
and morals. Upon returning from the war, two million
doughboys were infected with the eat-drink-and-be-
merry-for-tomorrow-we-die spirit. The war matured
them too quickly, and their torn nerves required the emo-
tional stimulants of excitement and whiskey and fast living. Their elders acted as though nothing had changed,
as if everyone still lived in a Pollyanna world. But the
veterans found the old morality to be antiquated, and
dull.

American girls came under the same influence. Their
own revolution was accelerated by the suffrage movement and the growing independence of women. Like
their brothers, they rejected the starchy, outdated customs of an older generation. They drank, experimented
with sex, and in a mood of disillusionment, explored
everything forbidden them by a moral code they could
no longer tolerate. The double standard still existed, but
it was fast disappearing. Within the past year the so-
called flapper had ceased to be an oddity.

The band segued into an earsplitting Charleston.
Tilghman cocked one eye, shaking his head, and led Zoe
off the dance floor. As they moved away, it occurred to
her that the era of the flapper was not confined to big
cities. She watched the daughters of friends rush to the
floor with their partners as the tempo quickened. They
wore short skirts, rolled their stockings below the knee,

and bobbed their hair in a shingle cut. Their breasts and hips were flattened to effect a boyish figure, and their faces were painted with an exotic blend of cosmetics. All in all, they presented a startling contrast to the bland, full-bosomed look of their mothers.

Their fathers simply looked mortified. Yet the craze had swept America, and girls in small towns were quick to imitate those in New York and Chicago. Not all the girls in Chandler were flappers; many still followed the customs of a saner time. But the number was growing, and despite their parents' protests, certain young women found it fashionable to flaunt themselves. Zoe sympathized with the parents, who seemed helpless in the face of what amounted to a cultural rebellion. To some smaller degree, she sympathized as well with the daughters, too impressionable for their own good. She thought they looked, and oftentimes acted, like tramps.

Wallace Tucker, the state senator from Chandler, and Mayor Leon Suggs were standing at the edge of the crowd. They were engrossed in conversation, and seemed oblivious to the wild gyrations on the dance floor. Zoe looked for their wives, and saw them seated at a table, staring daggers at some of the girls caught up in the beat of the Charleston. They appeared scandalized, and though they would never admit it, perhaps a little jealous. She decided not to join them.

Tilghman halted before the men. "Senator. Mr. Mayor. Good to see you."

"Well, Bill!" Suggs wrung his hand. "The man of the hour. Congratulations."

"I second the motion," Tucker added. "You and the governor pulled the rabbit out of the hat."

The grand jury in Okmulgee, under the protection of the National Guard, had indicted five Klasmen. An editorial in the *Chandler Herald* had lauded Tilghman for his role in bringing order to chaos. Tilghman was never comfortable in the limelight.

"Governor Trapp gets all the credit," he said. "The

National Guard was what turned the trick. Took lots of gumption to call them out.''

Tucker grinned broadly, glanced at Zoe. ''Your husband is much too modest. He needs to toot his own horn.''

''Oh, not really,'' she said slyly. ''The press always gives credit where credit is due.''

''Hear, hear!'' Suggs echoed. ''Everybody in Oklahoma knows Bill Tilghman was there.''

Zoe knew that Tucker and Suggs genuinely admired her husband. But she knew as well that they envied his close relationship with Governor Martin Trapp. She thought they sometimes saw him as a direct link to the state house.

''We were just talking politics,'' Tucker went on. ''We'd like your opinion on something, Bill. What do you think of Calvin Coolidge?''

Tilghman shrugged. ''Not the greatest president we ever had. But he's fair-minded toward business and he favors smaller government. I reckon we could do worse.''

''How do you rate his chances for re-election?''

A little over a year ago, when President Warren Harding died of a sudden illness, the then vice president, Calvin Coolidge, had moved into the White House. The presidential election was scarcely a month away, and there was some debate as to whether Coolidge would win a full term on his own merits. He was not a man of great personal magnetism.

''I suspect he'll win,'' Tilghman said now. ''He's honest, and he sticks to his word. Folks like that in a politician.''

''Good point,'' Tucker said, nodding. ''Integrity might yet be his salvation. I just wish he was more of a go-getter.''

''The world's full of go-getters these days. I think folks will vote for somebody they can trust. That's Cal Coolidge.''

Zoe thought her husband's simple wisdom went to the heart of the matter. Just recently, an Eastern writer had declared that Jesus was a hardheaded go-getter who had put together the greatest sales organization on earth. She considered the bizarre analogy in keeping with the ballyhoo and whooppee of the Roaring Twenties. But she suspected that the average people, voters in the heartland, would choose Calvin Coolidge. Trust was all too scarce a commodity in a time of bathtub gin and eroded morals.

Nor was she surprised that a state senator and the mayor were interested in Tilghman's opinion. He was a man of deep personal integrity, and his entire life had been devoted to upholding the law. When they returned to the dance floor, she was reminded that people valued his common sense wisdom, ordinary people as well as those in high places. She felt herself the luckiest woman in the room, and spent the rest of the evening in his arms, swirling around the dance floor. She was even amused by the antics of the flappers and their escorts, whenever the band played a wild, leg-kicking tune. Her husband seemed all the more the one constant in a merry-go-round world. Her anchor to what was real.

Later that night, on the way home, she scooted across the car seat. He glanced around as she snuggled against his arm. "I had a wonderful time," she said, hugging him. "I wish there were a dance every night."

Tilghman grinned. "Glad you enjoyed yourself. What was so special about tonight?"

"I don't know," she said dreamily. "It was just special."

"Well, there's always next Saturday night."

"Oh, that's too far away. A whole week."

"What the hell—!"

Tilghman jammed on the brakes. The Packard slowed to a halt, dust roiling off the dirt road. A short distance away, framed in the headlights, they saw a boy of ten or twelve. He was leading a saddle horse.

"What on earth?" Zoe said, staring through the windshield. "Isn't that Everett Johnson's boy . . . Bobby?"

"Yeah, looks to be."

Tilghman hooked the gear shift in neutral, set the hand brake. He left the motor idling as he and Zoe got out of the car and walked forward. The boy shielded his eyes from the glare of the headlights.

"Hello, Bobby," Tilghman said. "Out sort of late, aren't you?"

"My house went lame." The boy darted a glance at Zoe, then hurried on. "Stepped in a hole along about sundown and must've pulled something. I've been tryin' to get him home ever since."

"Well, let's have a look. Probably nothing serious."

Tilghman knelt down. The horse, a dun gelding, stood with the hoof of his right foreleg barely touching the ground. Gently, talking to the horse in a low voice, Tilghman probed from the postern upward. After a moment, his hands stopped, and he grunted to himself. He got to his feet.

"Bobby, it's not good. I'm afraid your horse broke his leg."

The boy paled in the headlights. "Will you help me get him home, Mr. Tilghman. Dad'll call the vet and get it fixed."

"Nothing a vet could do," Tilghman said softly. "Nothing anybody could do, Bobby. I'm sorry."

"I don't believe you! Scout's plenty tough, tough as they come. He'll mend just fine."

"Listen to me, son. Your horse is crippled, and he's in a lot of pain. You don't want him to suffer, do you?"

Bobby Johnson's eyes welled with tears. He pressed his face to the horse's velvety muzzle, and Zoe thought her heart would break. At last, his voice hollow, the boy looked at Tilghman.

"You sure he's got to be put down, Mr. Tilghman? Ain't there no other way?"

"Bobby, I know it's hard. But you've got to think of him. It's the only way."

Zoe took the boy by the shoulders, holding him closely, and walked him to the car. The youngster moaned in a tortured voice. "Oooh no, please . . . Scout."

Tilghman waited until they moved away, then began unsaddling the horse. When he was finished, he led Scout at a slow hobble to the edge of the road. He pulled his Colt, whispering in a soothing voice, and thumbed the hammer. Scout went down as the roar of the gunshot echoed through the night. He kicked once, then lay still.

Tilghman heard the muffled sobs as he approached the car. When he climbed into the seat, Zoe was holding the boy pressed to her breast, one hand caressing his head. She gave Tilghman a look of unbearable sadness, her eyes moist and glistening. Words failed them both, and as a practical matter, nothing either of them might say would console the youngster. As he drove off, it occurred to Tilghman that there was only one cure for a boy who had lost his horse. He decided to invite Bobby and his father over to the ranch.

Zoe held the boy cradled in her arms. She ran her hand over his hair, listening helplessly as he snuffled, trying to catch his breath, his tears dampening her dress. Everett Johnson's small cattle spread was a mile or so off the main road, and she was only vaguely aware when the car slowed for the turn. Her thoughts were on the youngster, his head close against her breast, his shoulders heaving as he struggled to control himself. She wondered what it might have been like to have a son. A fine young boy who loved his horse.

The sky was clear, ablaze with starlight. She stroked the boy's head, watching the glittery blink of distant stars, suddenly lost in her own reverie. Her deepest regret in life was that she had been unable to bear children, to give Tilghman a son. The emotion was one she normally suppressed, tucked away in some dark corner of

her mind. But tonight, holding the boy, she was flooded
with a sense of loss.

She wished she could wish upon a star, and make it
all come true.

CHAPTER 4

The night was illuminated in a coppery blaze by hundreds of flares. A forest of timbered derricks dotted the oil field; volatile casinghead gas had been piped into the air and set afire at each well site. The flares burned night and day, venting the gas skyward, and on a starlit night there was something spectral about the sight. The flames lit the countryside.

Seen from far away it was as if an army of towering giants stood shoulder to shoulder, torches in hand, bathing the earth in an eerie glow. But the illusion was deceptive, like the work of an evil madman, evoking a sense of the unreal only at a distance. Up close the derricks and spitting gas were all too real, ugly and smelly and clearly of this world. Cromwell just looked like hell on earth.

The oil field was largely deserted at night. Every evening, when dusk settled over the land, the roughnecks and roustabouts who worked the wells began a mass exodus into town. A skeleton crew of night watchmen was left to tend the wells, their main duty to keep an eye on the gas pipes. One pipe, left unlit for any length of time, could spread enough casinghead gas to ignite a firestorm. Oil fields had been burned to the ground by fire leaping from well to well.

Shortly after midnight a Dodge touring car drove out

of town. There were three men in the car, one driving, another in the passenger seat, and the third in the back. The one in the back was Turk Milligan, robust as an ox, with scarcely any neck, his head fixed directly upon his shoulders. A Thompson submachine gun lay on the seat beside him, within easy reach. On the floorboard, pinned beneath his feet, a fourth man lay unconscious. His throat worked in a feeble moan.

"Shut your trap!" Milligan idly stomped on his head. "Your big mouth is what got you here."

Dave Falcon, the driver, glanced in the rearview mirror "Gimme some directions here, Turk. Where you wanna go?"

Milligan leaned forward. He pointed off into the night. "Head for the west end of the field. I'll tell you where to stop."

The other man, Bud Shuemacher, looked around from the passenger seat. "Why go all the way out there? We could dump this asshole anywhere."

"You heard the boss," Milligan told him. "Our boy's just supposed to disappear. No witnesses, and no body found later. Got it?"

"So how you gonna make him disappear?"

"Don't strain yourself worryin' about it. I already got it figured out."

"Whatever you say, Turk."

"Keep your eyes peeled for night watchmen. We're lookin' for a spot where nobody's around."

A brisk October wind drifted across the oil field. On cold nights, Milligan knew that the watchmen usually made their rounds once an hour. The rest of the time, to stay warm, they took refuge in tool shacks near the wells. For tonight's job, all he needed was a few minutes with no one in sight. Then, quickly and simply, he would perform the vanishing act.

The man beneath his feet was Will Bohannon, the city marshal of Cromwell. Too honest for his own good, and stubborn in the bargain, he had refused to take payoffs.

Instead, determined to drive the racketeers from Cromwell, he routinely raided gambling dives and ginmills.
He refused to listen to reason, and he'd ignored a series
of threats meant to warn him off. The result, after being
dragged into a dark alley, was a one-way ride. He would
not return.

Milligan directed the car through a labyrinth of rutted
roads. On all sides oil derricks rose like smudged stee-
ples against the clear starry sky. The field stretched east
to west some four miles, and north to south almost three
miles. Even at night the wells pumped crude, and the
pounding clunk of equipment sent a steady, monotonous
roar across the landscape. At the western edge of the
field, the derricks began to thin out, scattered here and
there rather than butted one upon another. The glow
from the gas flares leeched out into the nearby woods.

"Pull over," Milligan ordered. "This looks good."

Falcon braked to a halt at the edge of the road. There
were three derricks clustered along a dirt track, and no
other wells within a hundred yards. The men climbed
out of the Dodge and stood for a moment searching the
night. The hiss of gas flares was punctuated by the clunk
of pumps, but there was no one in sight. Milligan waved
his arm.

"Just like I told you," he crowed. "Dead as a graveyard."

"That's a good one." Shuemacher laughed, then hesitated. "You was makin' a joke there, wasn't you,
Turk?"

"Yeah, Bud, I'm a regular goddamn comic. Let's get
our boy out of the car."

Falcon and Shuemacher reached into the back and
hauled the lawman from the floor. They dumped him on
the ground, and Shuemacher slapped him a couple of
times to bring him around. Will Bohannon groaned, then
rolled to his hands and knees, and slowly levered himself
erect. His pistol holster was empty and the badge on his
coat gleamed dully in the starlight. He wobbled, still

fuzzy from the beating he'd taken in the alley, and managed to catch his balance. He stared blankly at the men.

"What—" His voice broke, and he cleared his throat. "Why'd you bring me out here?"

Milligan laughed. "This is your send-off party, Marshal. Farewell and bye-bye."

"Jake Hammer's a bigger fool than I thought. You'll never get away with this."

"Think not, huh? Lemme tell you something, you fuckin' chump. You should've listened when the listening was good."

"Look . . ." Bohannon hesitated, steadied himself. "You boys kill me and you'll wind up in the electric chair. Let me go and we'll forget the whole thing. You've got my word on it."

"Hear that?" Milligan mocked him. "Mr. Toughnuts says we're gonna ride ol' sparky. How's that for laughs?"

Falcon gestured into the night. "You said this was gonna be quick, Turk. Maybe we oughta get it done with." He paused. "You know, before somebody comes along."

"Yeah, yeah." Milligan pulled a pistol from his waistband. He held it in his palm, grinning at the lawman. "We're gonna do you with your own gun. Ain't that the berries!"

Bohannon swallowed hard. "Think about it a minute, Milligan. You'll have the state police all over you for this."

"They'll have to find you first. But c'mon, lemme hear you beg. I'm a sucker for a hard luck story."

"Do it, for chrissakes," Shuemacher said crossly. "You talk all night and we will get caught."

Milligan riveted him with a cold look. "Here." He tossed Shuemacher the pistol "You're such a big, bad hardass. You kill him."

"Me?" Shuemacher protested. "Why me?"

"Teach you to keep your goddamn mouth shut, that's why. Go on, let him have it."

Shuemacher grunted something under his breath, then raised the pistol. Bohannon stared into the muzzle, a nervous tic jumping below one eye. A moment of dense silence slipped past, and the pistol belched a streak of flame. The lawman buckled at the knees, a splotch of blood on his chest, and toppled to the ground. Shuemacher walked forward and shot him in the head. His skull exploded in a mist of brains and bone.

"Satisfied?" Shuemacher said. "Think he's dead enough?"

Milligan shrugged. "Looks dead to me."

"So how do we make him disappear? What's the big secret you've been holdin' out?"

"You two bring him along. I'll show you a real trick."

Falcon grabbed the dead man's legs and Shuemacher took his arms. Milligan led them toward what appeared to be a pond, the surface slick and starlit. On closer examination, the pond proved to be a slush pit, some thirty feet deep, dug before the three wells were drilled. Oily sludge, a mix of earth and water and raw crude, was brought to wellhead during drilling and dumped into the slush pit. The result was a primordial swamp, thick with sludge from the wells.

"Give him the heave-ho," Milligan said, motioning to the pit. "Put some muscle into it and toss him way out there. I want him dead-smack in the middle."

The men swung the body back and forth, gaining momentum with the weight on each arc. Finally, on Milligan's command, they released the body on an upward swing and flung it high in the air. The dead lawman hit the slush on his back, one leg crooked at an angle. For several moments nothing happened, and they stood there, watching intently. Then the sludge parted, like the jaws of an oily maw, and slowly sucked the body into its depths. A single bubble popped on the starlit surface.

"Jeeez," Falcon said in hushed awe. "Don't that beat all. Fuckin' thing just . . . ate him."

"Told you, didn't I?" Milligan barked. "Nobody'll ever find the sonofabitch. That goo won't never let him go."

Shuemacher looked impressed. "You sure the hell convinced me, Turk. Never saw nothin' like it."

"Let's get our butts in gear. I wanna tell the boss."

The men trudged back to the car. A moment later, after the engine rumbled to life, the Dodge eased onto the road. Behind, the night once again claimed the isolated well site, the hiss of flames jetting skyward. Nothing remained to mark the passage of death.

A shaft of starlight rippled across the dark sludge.

Derricks were everywhere. Oil was more important than real estate and some of the timbered structures were even wedged between buildings. All across town there was a rhythmic thud, like mechanical heartbeats, as hungry pumps fed on the black blood of the earth. Hauled to the surface after millions of years, thick with the viscera of extinct beasts, the oil gave off a primeval stench.

Yet if the air was saturated with the cloying smell of crude, there was something vital, almost galvanic, about the town itself. In three months Cromwell had mushroomed from a sleepy backwoods village into a boomtown of ten thousand riotous fortune seekers. By truck and by car they were still coming, like worker ants drawn irresistibly to a cache of pungent riches.

Cromwell was a promoter's carnival. Lease hounds and catchpenny boomers and blue-sky bunco artists began gathering within days of the strike. Wildcatters sold stock to finance their drilling operations, and conmen, feeding on speculation, sold pipe dreams. Town lots went for twenty thousand dollars each, and in some sections an acre of land brought three hundred thousand dollars. One tract, only forty-five feet square and located near the discovery well, was capitalized at one million dollars.

The wages of sin also struck a bonanza. Oil men liked their pleasures raw and simple, and once the boom started there was a brisk trade in every vice known to man. Gambling dives and dance halls and bawdy houses filled with pajama-clad whores sprouted across town. These hellholes were crooked, especially the gaming joints, but they catered to oil magnates and roustabouts alike. A man could shoot a dime in a dice game while at the roulette table a high roller dropped a thousand on a single spin of the wheel. The losses, large or small, never seemed to dampen anyone's style. Cromwell was floating on an ocean of oil, there for the taking.

The Sportsmen's Club was the hottest spot in town. Jake Hammer, the owner, operated a rollicking speakeasy, with a trio of jazz musicians to set the tone. Toward the rear, through a door guarded by a pair of goons, a full-fledged casino was open to anyone with a taste for action. Hammer was a congenial host and a spiffy dresser, a thickset man with sharp eyes and a square jaw, his hair shiny with pomade. His origins were in question, some said Kansas City and others said Chicago, but everyone assumed he had a shady past. His gang of hooligans acted as though they owned Cromwell.

Turk Milligan came through the door a little after one o'clock. Falcon and Shuemacher, only a step behind, stopped at the bar for a drink. Hammer caught Milligan's eye, nodded, and led him into the casino. They moved past the gaming tables, crowded with players, and entered an office at the rear of the building. Hammer took a seat behind his desk.

"Everything go all right?"

Milligan bobbed his head. "Just the way you wanted, boss. Dumb fucker won't never be found."

"Good." Hammer lit a cigar, puffed smoke. "No one saw you?"

"Had the place all to ourselves. Went off real private."

"You always were reliable, Turk. Go have a drink, find yourself a woman. I'll talk to you tomorrow."

"Sure thing, boss. Just yell when you need me."

Milligan backed to the door, went out. Hammer sat for a moment, wreathed in smoke, savoring his cigar. At length, reaching for the phone, he placed the receiver to his ear. He jiggled the hook.

"Central switchboard. May I help you?"

"Operator, I want to call Wewoka. The number's 2836."

"That will be long distance, you know."

"Yeah, I know."

"Connecting your call now. Thank you, sir."

There was a tinny buzz as the call went through. After three rings Hammer heard a click at the other end. A voice came on the line. "Yes."

"Thought you'd want to know. Our friend got his bon voyage party tonight."

"Any problems?"

"No. Nothing to worry about."

"That's excellent news."

"Figured you'd be pleased."

"Good night, Jake. I'll be in touch."

The line went dead. Hammer replaced the receiver on the hook, tilting back in his chair. He took a long draw on his cigar and blew a smoke ring at the ceiling. His mouth curled in a satiric smile as he reflected on the vagaries of life, and death. Some men were like smoke rings.

Here one moment, gone the next.

CHAPTER 5

Three days later Everett Johnson and his son drove into the compound. They were there at Tilghman's invitation, extended the night he'd dispatched the boy's horse. Neither of them knew the purpose of the visit, for none had been given. But the elder Johnson felt it would be unneighborly to refuse.

Tilghman walked down from the house as they climbed out of the truck. He thought the boy still looked dispirited, though he was clearly trying to put on a brave front. Everett Johnson was a bear of a man, ham-fisted and broad, with features weathered the color of saddle leather. His smile was genuine but oddly diffident, for he'd grown up on tales of Oklahoma's most famous lawman. He extended his hand.

"Good of you to ask us over, Mr. Tilghman."

Tilghman accepted his handshake. "I'm glad you could come."

Johnson nudged the boy. "Bobby, mind your manners. Say hello."

"Hello, sir," the boy said, kicking at a clod in the dirt. "Thanks for havin' us."

"Why, it's my pleasure, Bobby. How are things since I saw you last?"

"Okay, I guess."

"Still a little down in the dumps, hmmm?"

"Well, maybe a little."

Johnson laid a paw on his shoulder. "He's a good boy, Mr. Tilghman. He'll snap out of it."

" 'Course, he will," Tilghman agreed. "Never doubted it for a minute." He glanced at the boy. "Like to show you something, Bobby. Get your opinion."

"Yessir."

Tilghman led them across the compound. He halted outside the corral, motioned through the rails. "That's what you might call my prize stud. His name's Copperdust."

The stallion was on the opposite side of the corral. He was barrel-chested, standing fifteen hands high, his hide glistening in the sun. Watching them, nostrils flared, he pawed the earth as though he spurned it and longed to fly. He suddenly whinnied a shrill blast, crossing the corral in a headlong charge, then swerved away an instant before colliding with the rails. His stance lordly, inspecting them, his eyes were fierce with freedom.

"Jiminey," the boy breathed, staring mesmerized at the stallion. "That's some horse."

Tilghman nodded. "I'd have to say, there's not many the equal of Copperdust. He's sired some of the finest stock in Oklahoma."

"Yeah, I'll bet he has."

"As a matter of fact . . ."

Neal Brown, as though on cue, led a two-year-old colt up from the stables. The young horse was frisky, snorting and kicking his heels, already broad through the chest. A blaze-faced bloodbay, he whickered in greeting, and Cooperdust snorted, stamping the ground. Brown stopped, holding the colt on a short lead.

"Bobby," Tilghman said, gesturing. "You remember my foreman, Neal Brown."

"Yessir." The boy ducked his head. "How do, Mr. Brown."

"Just fine," Brown replied. "Good to see you again, Bobby."

"Well now," Tilghman said, his expression quizzical. "Here's what I wanted your opinion on. What do you think of this colt?"

"He's a beauty." Bobby studied the colt a moment. "Was he sired by Copperdust?"

"I see you have an eye for horseflesh. No question about it, he's got his daddy's lines."

"Gonna be a big one, ain't he?"

"Not too big for you."

"Me?" A look of tense expectation came over the boy's face. "What d'you mean?"

"I mean he's yours," Tilghman said simply. "Break him gentle and he'll be a friend for life. Ncal will show you the ropes."

The boy's eyes went round with delirium. His father abruptly stepped forward. "Hold on now," Johnson said. "I appreciate what you're tryin' to do, Mr. Tilghman. But we're not ones to accept charity."

"No charity to it."

"All the same, we couldn't do it. You set a fair price on the colt and I'll buy him."

"He's not for sale," Tilghman said firmly. "This is a matter between friends—Bobby and me."

"Pa!" the boy pleaded, his face stricken. "C'mon, for goshsakes . . . please."

"Just won't do," Johnson said. "Sorry, son, but that's the way it is."

Tilghman drilled him with a look. "Are you a Christian, Mr. Johnson?"

"'Course I'm a Christian. What makes you ask a thing like that?"

"Then consider the colt a Christmas present. A little early, but that's neither here nor there. No good Christian would deny a boy a Christmas gift . . . would he?"

"Well . . ." Johnson faltered, aware of his son's gaze, and somehow certain he'd been outfoxed. "I suppose if you put it like that, I wouldn't have no objection."

"You mean he's mine?" Bobby whooped. "He's really mine?"

"All yours," Tilghman said with a grin. "You go along with Neal now. He'll get you and the colt started off right."

Brown handed Bobby the colt's lead rope. They walked away, with Brown already coaching him, the boy's eyes bright with excitement. Johnson watched after them a moment, shaking his head. He finally looked around.

"You snookered me pretty good there, Mr. Tilghman."

"Everett, why don't you call me Bill? No need to stand on formality."

"Well, anyway, I want to thank you. That's a fine thing you done."

"A boy needs a horse. No thanks necessary."

The men arrived early that afternoon. Their spokesman, Walter Sirmans, had called yesterday requesting a meeting. In the short conversation, though he'd been sparse with details, the urgency was apparent in his voice. They represented the Cromwell Citizens Committee, and he preferred not to discuss particulars on the telephone. Tilghman had agreed to meet with them.

There were four men. Sirmans, clearly the leader, was in his early forties, the owner of a dry goods store. The others were somewhat younger, businessmen who had followed the boom to Cromwell. Among them, they owned a lumber yard, a hardware store, and a pharmacy. The trait they all shared was a sense of apprehension, underscored by a severe case of nerves. They seemed to be sitting on the edge of their seats.

Zoe served coffee in the parlor. After she retreated to the kitchen, Tilghman looked around at the men. "Have to admit, you've got me curious. What can I do for you?"

Sirmans took the lead. "Are you familiar with Cromwell, Mr. Tilghman?"

"No more than what I read in the papers. I understand it's a pretty big strike."

"Yessir, it's big, all right. Engineers estimate there's forty million dollars in oil under the ground."

"Lot of money," Tilghman observed. "Sounds like you're in clover."

"Maybe too much so," Sirmans said dourly. "All that money has attracted an undesirable element. Gamblers, speakeasies, fancy women. You name it."

"Boomtowns draw a rough crowd. Never seen it fail."

"Three nights ago it got rougher than we expected, Mr. Tilghman. Our city marshal disappeared."

"Disappeared?" Tilghman inquired. "You mean he quit?"

"Some think so." Craig Thomas, the lumberyard owner, shifted on the sofa. "There's talk he just took off, lost his nerve."

"But you think otherwise?"

"We sure do," Thomas said. "Will Bohannon was a rough customer himself. He wouldn't have run."

"We think he was killed," Sirmans added quickly. "Probably buried somewhere he'd never be found. Not that we'll ever prove it."

Tilghman nodded. "Any idea who killed him?"

"A man by the name of Jake Hammer. Or at least, he would have ordered it. He's what you might call our local gangster. He runs things."

"Whiskey, women, gambling, all that?"

"So everyone in town says. There again, we'll never prove it."

"Has the sheriff investigated your marshal's disappearance?"

"That's a laugh," Owen Tippert, the pharmacist, said hotly. "The whole county's on Hammer's payroll. All except Judge Crump, the district judge. He's a straight arrow.''

"Cromwell?" Tilghman mused. "That's Seminole County, isn't it?"

"Unfortunately," Sirmans acknowledged. "Crooked-est county in Oklahoma."

"How so?"

Sirmans launched into a familiar tale of corruption. The World War had provided the impetus for the oil boom, and the automobile industry ultimately made oil the most profitable business in America. By 1924 there were ten million passenger cars on the roads, and fears of an oil shortage broke out. The search for new reserves accelerated, and wildcatters opened more than thirty fields in Oklahoma alone. Tulsa became the oil capital of the world, with several modern refineries operating day and night. Oil companies and wildcatters were riding an unimagined wave of prosperity.

Seminole County was but the latest backwoods area to experience a boom. After the discovery well was brought in, oil scouts and promoters descended on Cromwell in a frantic rush to lease choice locations. Hardly a day went past without reports of another gusher, and geologists predicted the pool would produce upwards of 455 million barrels. On the heels of the oil men was a tide of opportunists, legitimate and otherwise, and within weeks Cromwell became a rip-roaring boom-town. The amount of money that flowed from the wells was staggering, and the underworld crowd made vice a rough and ready form of free enterprise. County officials, susceptible to bribes and graft, rarely set foot in Cromwell.

"Corrupt to the core," Sirmans concluded. "Hammer's goons collect weekly payoffs from every speakeasy and gambling joint in town. Word's around that it's protection money—goes straight to the courthouse."

"Hammer owns the town," Tippert added. "Everybody knows he's the bootlegger for Seminole County.

His trucks supply liquor for all the ginmills.''

Tilghman considered a moment. ''What's the Cromwell Citizens Committee?''

''You're looking at it, Mr. Tilghman,'' Sirmans confessed. ''The four of us put it together in an effort to limit the vice trade. Everybody else was afraid to join.''

''Afraid of this Jake Hammer?''

''Well, like I said, we don't have any proof it's Hammer. But everybody knows he's the man.''

''So why have you come to me?''

''We need a marshal,'' Sirmans said earnestly. ''Somebody with savvy enough to deal with Hammer. We figure that's you.''

''How can you four hire a marshal?'' Tilghman asked. ''Who gave you the authority to appoint peace officers?''

''Cromwell's unincorporated, still wide open. No mayor, no city charter, nothing. We hired Bohannon and paid him out of our own pockets. We'll do the same with you.''

''There's lots of lawmen around. Why me?''

''You don't scare,'' Sirmans said. ''We read what you did to the Klan in Okmulgee. We know your reputation, Mr. Tilghman. You're the man for the job.''

Tilghman weighed the thought. ''I have to say it's an interesting proposition. When do you need an answer?''

''The sooner the better. We've got the makings of a good, solid town. But it's desperate for law enforcement.''

''Let me think about it. I'll call you in a few days.''

''I've got a feeling you won't let us down, Mr. Tilghman. Cromwell needs you.''

''I'll be in contact.''

After a round of handshakes, the men trooped out to their car. Tilghman stood in the doorway, watching as they turned onto the road and drove off. He found himself intrigued by the thought of bringing law to a boomtown, what was clearly a hellhole in the midst of anarchy. The last time he'd tamed a town was in Dodge City, in 1884, forty years ago. A lot of water under the bridge since then, but he told himself an oil town was no wilder than a cowtown. The one difference, perhaps the only difference, was in the new breed of outlaw.

America, in the throes of the Roaring Twenties, had spawned a phenomenon all its own, the underworld mobster. Prohibition had created a market worth millions of dollars and controlled exclusively by gangsters. Crime was now big business, a singularly dangerous form of business, conducted with brass knuckles and tommy guns. Still, the public wanted its booze, and people were content to watch the mobsters butcher one another so long as the corner speak never went dry. So the rackets grew and diversified, proliferating amid a climate of violence.

In that respect, Oklahoma was no different than the rest of the nation. The state couldn't boast an Al Capone or a Dutch Schultz, but mobsters no less than nature abhor a vacuum. The rise of oil boomtowns gave rise to backcountry gangsters, many imported from large cities, and every bit as modern as their eastern counterparts. For the most part, they divided the oil towns among themselves, and conducted their affairs without the tommy-gun sensationalism. But there were exceptions, and Cromwell seemed to be a case in point. The gangsters there apparently had no qualms about killing lawmen.

Zoe entered the parlor, moving to the doorway. She stopped behind Tilghman, placed a hand on his shoulder. He stared out into the afternoon sunlight, all too aware that she'd overheard the conversation from the kitchen. He waited for her to speak.

"Bill?"

"Yeah."

"You're not seriously considering it, are you? The job in Cromwell?"

"I told them I'd think about it."

"What does that mean exactly?"

"Why, I reckon I'll sleep on it. Give it some thought."

She turned, walking toward the kitchen. "Then I suppose it's true, what they say. There's no fool like an old fool."

Tilghman wasn't surprised that she'd got the last word. Nor was he all that offended by her choice of words. He had to admit she had a point.

CHAPTER 6

Tilghman drove to Oklahoma City the next morning. He planned to talk with the governor and inquire into the political innerworkings of Seminole County. He also intended to check out Walter Sirmans and the Cromwell Citizens Committee. There were two sides to any coin, and he'd seen only one. The other might prove revealing.

At breakfast, when he announced the trip, Zoe had made no comment. Life on the ranch began at first light, and by sunrise he was ready to leave. She walked him to the door, told him to drive carefully, and kissed him affectionately on the cheek. Her silence on the matter of Cromwell told the whole story. Nothing would alter her opinion.

The drive was some fifty miles, most of it on dirt roads. All morning, a rooster tail of dust in his wake, Tilghman was lost in deliberation. He was a realist, pragmatic in his assessment of men and events, and never more so than in regard to himself. He was seventy years old, no longer the man he'd been at forty. Yet he was still quick, and age had done nothing to dull the embers. He wasn't ready to quit.

All in all, he was willing to concede that Zoe had a point. A man his age had no business getting involved in a sinkhole like Cromwell. But he felt like an old war-horse whenever the bugle called, invigorated and charged with life, drawn to the sound of battle. A thought kept running through his head, and he found himself unable to set it aside. He'd been offered a chance that might never come his way again, and the temptation was overpowering. The chance to stamp out corruption and lawlessness, tame a town. One last town.

Tilghman entered the capitol building shortly after the noon hour. As he walked through the rotunda, a brilliant sun lighted the dome crowning the chamber. He paused, bathed in colors from the stained glass far overhead, staring upward. Unbidden, as though glimpsing the past, he was reminded of the great land rush, thirty-five years ago, in 1889. From that day onward, first in Old Oklahoma Territory, and after statehood, in Oklahoma, he'd worn the badge of a lawman. He saw no reason to quit now.

Upstairs, Tilghman went through the massive doors of the governor's office. In the anteroom, several legislators were huddled in conversation, awaiting their appointment, and he remembered he hadn't called ahead. The receptionist greeted him warmly, and called inside to announce his arrival. A few minutes later the governor's secretary, Mabel Clark, came out to get him. The legislators, reduced to silence, watched as she escorted him through the inner door. She laughed under her breath.

"Talk about bruised pride," she said. "They've been waiting an hour to see the governor."

"You sure he wants to see me now? Just slipped my mind to call."

"Oh, he's happy to let them cool their heels. How's Mrs. Tilghman?"

"She's fine," Tilghman said. "I'll tell her you asked."

"Be sure to give her my regards."

Martin Trapp rose from behind his desk. He leaned across with an outstretched arm as Mabel Clark closed the door. "Bill, good to see you," he said cordially. "Take a chair, make yourself comfortable."

Tilghman returned his handshake. "Sorry to drop in unexpected, Governor. Lots of people waiting to see you."

"They're here to lobby my support on legislation of some sort. All it will do is increase taxes anyway. Let them wait awhile."

"I appreciate your courtesy."

"Listen, I owe you," Trapp said lightly. "After we faced down the Klan, I got the support of the press across the board. That made all the difference when I sent in the National Guard."

"Well, sometimes," Tilghman replied, "the only way is to fight force with force. You did the right thing."

"I'm just thankful we got the indictments. But you're not here to rehash yesterday's news. What brings you to the capitol?"

"I've been offered a job. Some folks want me to take over as marshal of Cromwell."

"Cromwell," Trapp said, suddenly sober. "The state police tell me it's the worst of all the oil towns. Who offered you the job?"

"A fellow named Walter Sirmans. He's head of the Cromwell Citizens Committee."

"From what I hear Sirmans is a good man. I get a monthly report on trouble spots from the state police. Cromwell usually tops the list."

"Then you've heard their marshal disappeared."

"No, the next report isn't due till the end of the month. What happened?"

Tilghman quickly briefed him on yesterday's meeting. "According to Sirmans," he related, "the marshal was probably murdered. He thinks it's the work of the underworld crowd in Cromwell."

"I wouldn't be surprised," Trapp said. "These racketeers control every oil town in Oklahoma. They set themselves above the law."

"Sirmans says they *own* the law in Seminole County. Have your reports mentioned anything about that?"

"Yes, I'm afraid so. Wewoka is the county seat, and my sources indicate the courthouse is rampant with corruption. The sheriff—his name's Jim Bradley—has yet to assign a deputy to Cromwell. That alone makes him suspect."

"Yeah, it would," Tilghman agreed. "Way I get it, the town runs wide open. Gambling, liquor, whores, anything illegal. You'd think the sheriff would take an interest."

"As a matter of fact—" Trapp stopped, one eyebrow raised in inquiry. "Are you familiar with Judge George Crump?"

"Sirmans told me he's the only honest official in Seminole County."

"George and I are old friends. I plan to back him for a spot on the state Supreme Court. In any event, I spoke with him personally about Bradley, their sheriff."

"What'd he say?"

"There's no question in his mind that Bradley is on the take. Along with everyone else in the courthouse, including the county attorney. Without honest law enforcement, George's hands are tied."

Tilghman nodded. "A judge can't bring charges himself. That's the job of peace officers."

"All too true." Trapp studied him a moment. "Are you thinking of accepting the position?"

"Guess that's why I came to see you. Way it sounds, I'd be pretty much on my own. Except for Sirmans and his committee, nobody's bangin' a drum to clean up Cromwell. What's your opinion?"

"Where you're concerned, I'm somewhat biased, Bill. I believe you are the only man in Oklahoma equal to the job. In all the years we've known each other, I've never seen you fail."

Tilghman stared at him. "I detect a 'but' in there somewhere. You think I'm too old for the job?"

"Good God, no!" Trapp said emphatically. "I entrusted my own life to you in Okmulgee. Age has nothing to do with it."

"What does?"

"These mobsters are lower than the Klan or bank robbers, even common murderers. They are assassins in a game where life has no value. I hesitate to see you go in harm's way."

"I've been there before." Tilghman was quiet a moment, his gaze penetrating. "You want me to take the job, don't you?"

"Yes, I do," Trapp said frankly. "We need to set an object lesson for gangsters throughout Oklahoma. I believe you could accomplish that in Cromwell."

"And?"

"You always were too quick for me, Bill."

"Go ahead, what's the other reason?"

"In a nutshell"—Trapp spread his hands—"George Crump needs your help. Working together, I have every confidence you could expose the corruption in Seminole County. That would be quite a feather in his cap."

Tilghman smiled. "And help you put him on the Supreme Court."

"Politics is a rotten business, Bill. We often do things for all the wrong reasons."

"Well, whatever the reason, Cromwell's a damn good excuse. Nobody's above the law."

"One thing you can depend on," Trapp assured him. "You would have my support all the way. Since Cromwell's unincorporated, keep your state commission and let me appoint you marshal. That would make you the top law officer in Seminole County."

"I appreciate the offer."

Tilghman rose with a nod, walking toward the door. Trapp watched him, unwilling to leave it at that, and finally spoke. "Will you take the job?"

"I'll let you know, Governor. Soon as I know."

The door opened and closed, and he was gone.

* * *

Early that afternoon Tilghman braked to a halt on a street shaded by tall elms. The house was a modest stucco with green shutters and rose bushes bordering the porch. He crawled from the car.

A man was seated in a rocker on the porch, sunning himself. He was short and stout, his thinning hair gone white, thick jowls hanging over the collar of his wool sweater. His rheumy eyes followed Tilghman up the walkway, and his scraggly mustache lifted in a smile. His voice still bore the trace of an accent.

"Bill, good to see you, old friend. How you been?"

"Fair to middlin', Chris. How about yourself?"

Madsen stuck out a hand gnarled with arthritis. "I'm hunky-dory some days. Other days not so hot."

"You old reprobate," Tilghman joshed, gently shaking his hand. "I'll bet you've still got some get-up-and-go."

"Not the same any more, Bill. This porch about as far as I go."

Tilghman was always shocked when he came to visit. Thirty years ago Chris Madsen was a man of robust physique and unflagging spirit. A Danish immigrant, he had joined the cavalry and fought valiantly in the Indian wars. In 1891, he had resigned from the army, accepting a commission as a deputy U.S. marshal in Oklahoma Territory. Later, during the Spanish-American War, he had served with Teddy Roosevelt and the Rough Riders. Afterward, until his retirement in 1916, he had worked as a lawman throughout Oklahoma.

Madsen and Tilghman, along with Heck Thomas, had been dubbed by the press as the Three Guardsmen. Thomas, a transplanted Georgian, had first served as a railroad detective in Texas. He later rode as a deputy U.S. marshal, headquartered in Arkansas, and then transferred to Oklahoma Territory. Working together, the three lawmen had killed some thirty desperadoes, jailing four hundred more, and put an end to the old outlaw days in

Oklahoma. Afterward, Thomas served as chief of police in Lawton, until his health began to fail. He had died in 1912.

Tilghman remembered the camaraderie of those days with great fondness. In league with Madsen and Thomas, he had pursued outlaws from one end of Oklahoma to the other, and rid the territory of its lawless element. Today, seated in a rocker beside Madsen, he was saddened to see his old friend crippled by arthritis and reduced to walking with a cane. He found it difficult to believe that Madsen was seventy-three, only three years older than himself. The aged lawman looked spent and worn, a husk of his former self.

Still, for all his infirmities, Madsen was mentally sharp, a horseback marshal turned sage. Tilghman had come seeking advice from a man he respected, someone equally versed in the ways of renegades and stone-cold killers. He valued Madsen's opinion.

"I've been offered a job," he said casually. "Town marshal of a place called Cromwell."

"Yah, I read about it," Madsen said. "One of them oil towns, lots of gangsters and bootleggers. Worse than boomtowns in the land rush days."

"Well, the men we chased didn't have tommy guns, that's for sure. But what the hell, Chris, a thug's a thug. Things haven't changed all that much."

"You think that, you fool yourself plenty. These men today, they're quicker to shoot you down. Killing just part of their business."

Tilghman looked at him. "You saying I shouldn't take the job?"

"Damn right I say that," Madsen growled. "You was town marshal once, long time ago. Why you want to do it again?"

"I've been askin' myself the same thing. Guess it's hard to say no when good people ask for help. I was never one to turn a deaf ear."

"Time to get a little deaf. You're older now, Bill. Not

so quick on the draw. Let somebody else take the job.''

"Probably sound advice," Tilghman conceded. "I'll have to ponder on it.''

Madsen grunted. "You go to Cromwell, I think you get yourself killed. You ponder on that.''

Tilghman stared out into the street. A wayward thought surfaced, and he was reminded of Heck Thomas. He recalled that Thomas had suffered a long, grueling illness and a painful death. To a large extent, it seemed that Madsen was not all that different. A man ravaged by time and disease, slowly wasting away, waiting for death to rap on the door. Even worse, a man who had lost the will to struggle, and end it on his own terms. He thought there were better ways to go.

"You ever think of the old days, Chris?''

"What else I got to do, stuck in this goddamn rocker? I think of them days lots. Even when I sleep.''

"We had some high times, didn't we? You remember the shootout with Doolin and his gang? When we tracked them to that river crossing on the Cimarron?''

Bill Doolin was the most famous outlaw in old Oklahoma Territory. The legend of the Three Guardsman was born in part from a series of gun battles, ending in the deaths of Doolin and his gang. "Yah, I remember," Madsen said, his eyes suddenly clear. "Why you ask me about that?''

"I got to thinking about Heck. The last year or so, how he sort of withered away. Given a choice, maybe he'd rather have bought it there on the Cimarron.''

"Maybe." Madsen gave him a strange look. "I think you already made up your mind. You going to Cromwell, huh?''

"I'm leanin' in that direction, Chris. Leanin' strong.''

Tilghman drove away a few minutes later. He waved out the car window, his last impression of Chris Madsen that of a frail old man, consigned to a rocker in the sun. A man waiting patiently, perhaps anxiously, to die.

He told himself there was more to life than the safety of a rocking chair.

CHAPTER 7

Tilghman returned home early that evening. Lights blazed from the main house and the bunkhouse, and a pale moon cast shadows across the compound. As he stepped from the car, he realized he was stiff from a day of jouncing along washboard roads. He walked toward the porch.

Zoe met him at the door. She greeted him with a kiss, waiting while he hooked his hat and coat on wall pegs. Logs snapped in the fireplace, warming the parlor against the autumn night. He moved to the hearth, turning to face Zoe, hands clasped behind his back. Over the years he'd come to know her ways; he realized now she would never ask the question that hung between them. He spread his hands to the fire.

"Little nippy out there. The fire feels good."

She nodded. "We may have an early winter."

"Well, the geese are already headed south. Guess that tells the story."

"Have you eaten?"

"Drove straight through," Tilghman said. "Didn't take the time to stop."

"I made stew for supper. I'll warm it for you."

"Sounds good to me."

She went through the hallway to the kitchen. Tilghman moved away from the fireplace, his backsides toasted. Her curiosity was all too apparent, and he read anxiety in her face as well. But he knew she would wait him out, let him broach the subject in his own good time. Though he would have preferred tomorrow, he thought it unfair to put her off with awkward silence. She deserved to hear it tonight.

In the kitchen, Tilghman hung his gun belt over the back of a chair. The savory aroma of beef stew wafted from a black iron pot on the stove. Zoe was busy setting the table, and avoided his gaze as he walked to the sink. He ran water from the tap, briskly scrubbing his hands with a bar of soap. After rinsing off, he toweled his hands dry, moved to the table, and seated himself. Neither of them had yet spoken.

Zoc brought a plate of stew to the table. She returned to the stove, took biscuits from a warming oven, and served them on a separate plate. After pouring him a cup of coffee, she seated herself across the table. Tilghman broke a biscuit apart, slathered it with butter, and began eating. The stew was piping hot, rich with vegetables canned that summer from her garden. He nodded with appreciation.

"A man could get spoiled on your stew. Mighty tasty."

"You've been saying that for thirty-four years. I'd think you were worn out on my cooking by now."

"No," Tilghman said, munching a bite of biscuit. "I know enough to stick with a good thing. You and your stew."

She smiled faintly. "You still know how to flatter a girl too."

"Speaking of that reminds me. Mabel Clark said to give you her regards. Saw her when I called on the governor."

There was a momentary silence between them. Zoe understood that he had chosen an oblique way to work into the conversation. "I've always liked Mabel," she said. "Too bad we don't see her more often. How was the governor?"

"Top form," Tilghman said, pausing to swig coffee. "We had ourselves a good, long talk. I told him about this Cromwell offer."

"What was his opinion?"

"Turns out he gets a monthly report on Cromwell from the state police. Everything that Sirmans fellow told me was dead on the mark. Seminole County's a regular beehive of corruption."

She waited, thinking he would continue. When he speared stew meat onto his fork, she pressed ahead. "Did he try to discourage you from taking this job?"

"Nope." Tilghman chewed thoughtfully a moment. "Matter of fact, he was all for it. Wants to send me in there with my regular commission, Oklahoma State Marshal." He held her gaze. "That'd make me the top lawdog in Seminole County."

"Oh." She seemed to hold her breath. "What was your answer."

"I didn't say one way or the other. Figured I'd wait till I talked with Chris Madsen."

"How is Chris? Any better?"

"Worst I've ever seen him. He's gone downhill in a hurry the last few months. Damn shame."

"Yes, you're right," she said softly. "Chris was always one of my favorite people."

"Not many like him anymore. Good lawman."

"What was his advice on Cromwell?"

Tilghman chuckled. "You and Chris are of a mind. He thinks I'm too old to cut the mustard."

She watched him sop gravy with the last of his biscuit. Her voice was strained when she finally spoke. "You talk with the governor and you talk with Chris. But you haven't once asked my opinion. Why is that, Bill?"

"No doubt about where you stand. You've already made that pretty plain."

"And you've made your decision without me. Is that it?"

"Zoe, it's not a matter of with you or without you. There's some things a man has to decide for himself."

She stared at him. "You're going to Cromwell, aren't you?"

"Yeah, I am," Tilghman said without inflection. "I called Walt Sirmans from Oklahoma City. Told him I'd be there tomorrow."

"How could you, Bill? Don't my feelings mean anything to you?"

"No need to get upset."

"Of course I'm upset!" Her eyes spilled over with tears. "I'm the one who has to sit here and wait for the phone to ring. Wait for someone to tell me you've been killed."

"Hell, I thought you knew—I'm bulletproof. Nobody's gonna kill me."

"Don't make jokes! I'm in no mood for it."

Tilghman knuckled his mustache. "You've been waiting for that knock on the door since we got married. I haven't gotten myself killed yet. What's so different about now?"

"Are you serious?" she said with stark disbelief. "Good God, Bill, you're seventy years old! I wanted you to retire a long time ago. I still do."

"You'd have me sit in a rocker and wait for the supper bell, like Chris Madsen. No, I'm not about to retire."

"I didn't mean retire from *life*. You have a ranch, and the best horses in Oklahoma. Take the time to enjoy it!"

"I'm a lawman," Tilghman said stubbornly. "That's my line of work, not horses. Neal does just fine with the ranch."

"So you're determined to go to Cromwell?"

"Don't you understand, Zoe? I'm the one that got called. I've got to go."

"Then go and be damned. Don't give me a minute's thought! I'm just your wife."

Tilghman was taken aback by the fury in her voice. She pushed out of her chair, hurrying from the kitchen. In the parlor, she grabbed a shawl off the wall pegs and went through the door. The autumn night was crisp and chill, the moon high, flooding the compound with an umber glow. She wrapped the shawl tighter around herself, unnerved by her own anger, and deeper still, her fear. She was terrified that he would get himself killed.

Distracted, wondering that she'd rushed blindly from the house, she walked toward the stables. She took several deep breaths of cold air, tried to regain her composure. Oddly, she was more outraged than surprised by his decision, for it was much what she'd expected. He was first, last, and always a lawman, the ranch and horses hardly more than a sideline. On the day they were married, he had proudly worn the badge of a deputy U.S. marshal on the vest beneath his frock coat. And carried a gun into the church!

In fact, thinking back, she could not recall a day in their thirty-four years of marriage that he had not worn a gun. Or for that matter, a badge of one sort or another. Even in the midst of the Roaring Twenties, when men sported fedora hats and silk suits, he still wore cowmen's boots and a Stetson. And a gun, strapped on first thing in the morning, taken off when the day was done, as though it were an accepted part of normal attire. He was willful and set in his ways, a man of stubborn pride. Too old to change.

Her mind still in a turmoil, she wandered into the stables. She needed time to sort things out, to somehow construct a more convincing argument. Yet he was leaving tomorrow, and time was rapidly slipping away. A low nicker attracted her attention, and she paused at the stall of her favorite mare, Susie Q. The horse nuzzled her, snuffling softly, its breath like warm velvet. She pressed her face against the mare's downy muzzle, one arm looped around the strong, proud neck. As though hurt, and seeking comfort, she stood locked in a gentle embrace. Her eyes puddled with tears.

"Oh Susie Q," she murmured. "There has to be a way. There just has to."

"Evenin', Miz Tilghman."

Zoe jumped. She turned to find Neal Brown in the dimly lighted corridor between stalls. For more than three decades he had never once called her by her given name. He was shy around women, and his respect for her bordered on adoration. Long ago, she had reconciled herself to being an icon of some sort in his private thoughts. She swiped a tear off her cheek.

"You scared me, Neal."

"Never meant to," Brown apologized. "Just out checkin' things before I called it a night."

She knew that horses were his life. He had never married, and he devoted himself to the hundred or so brood mares and the stallions. He was a gentle man, unassuming, wise beyond reckoning about horses. She smiled tentatively.

"You must think I'm silly . . . talking to horses."

"No such thing. Horses are mighty good listeners. I talk to 'em all the time."

She glanced at Susie Q. "I wish they could talk. I need a few pearls of wisdom."

Brown's forehead knotted. "Anything wrong, Miz Tilghman."

"Something's terribly wrong." She hesitated, reluctant to bare her personal problems. Then, desperately in need of advice, she risked embarrassing herself. "Has Bill talked to you about this marshal's job in Cromwell?"

"After a fashion," Brown admitted. "Told me he'd been offered the job. Just before he left this mornin'."

"Tonight he informed me he's accepted the position."

"Well, that don't surprise me none. Figured as much when he told me about it."

"You did?" Zoe sounded confused. "Why would you think that?"

Brown shuffled his feet uncomfortably. "Like they say, leopards don't change their spots. He got the calling a long time ago. More'n forty years now."

"What do you mean . . . the calling?"

"I reckon it's like some men get religion. Only instead of a preacher, he got called to be a lawman. Sorta like he was ordained—to wear a badge."

"Are you saying it's a matter of duty? That he's somehow obligated?"

"More'n that" Brown observed. "When he's called, he feels honor-bound to go. Never yet seen him refuse."

"But, Neal . . ." She seemed bemused. "He's seventy years old!"

"Trouble is, he don't know that, Miz Tilghman. Ain't likely he ever will."

Zoe's thoughts all of a sudden turned inward. In an instant of revelation she saw what she had avoided until now, kept pushing back in her mind. Time lays scars on a man, and those scars might cloud his judgement while at the same time giving him wisdom about himself. The wisdom to know that a man's limitations are forever compensated by his strengths. Perhaps no greater proof existed than in the fact that he was leaving for Cromwell tomorrow. A boomtown controlled not by outlaws on horseback but by mobsters who rode in motorcars.

There was a sudden clarity to it all. Not unlike someone who'd heard the clock strike but had counted the strokes wrong. She realized that she was thinking of herself, not him. Her feelings and her fears were the thing uppermost in her mind. Which was not just wrongheaded and insensitive, but selfish. A man without pride in himself—and his place in life—was no man at all. She had to let him go.

"Thank you, Neal!" She kissed him quickly on the cheek. "You've made it all so clear."

"I have?" Brown blushed, rubbing his whiskery jaw. "What'd I say?"

"More than you could ever know!"

She hurried back to the house. In the kitchen, she found Tilghman seated at the table. He had cleared the supper dishes, and spread out before him were a Winchester carbine, a sawed-off double-barrel shotgun, and his old Colt .45. A ramrod in hand, he was methodically swabbing an oily patch though the bore of the Winchester. He glanced around as she rushed into the room.

"Whoa now, Nellie. Where's the fire?"

"No fire," she said, stopping beside his chair. "I simply thought you should hear the news."

"What news is that?"

"I've had a change of heart about Cromwell."

Tilghman laid aside the ramrod. "You're not sore anymore?"

"No," she said breezily. "You have my permission to go off chasing gangsters."

"You're a sackful of surprises. Why the change?"

"I had a long talk with Susie Q. She convinced me that men—like stallions—are obstinate creatures. A woman just has to overlook their hardheaded nature."

Tilghman cocked an eyebrow. "A mare treated you to all this weighty insight?"

She smiled brightly. "Susie Q is a deep thinker."

"That must have been some conversation. Wish I'd been there."

"Well, you weren't, and I see you have guns to clean. So I'll go pack your warbag. Anything special in the way of clothes?"

"The usual ought to do it. I'll probably take along a mackinaw."

"Yes, that's a good idea. The nights are getting chillier."

She touched him affectionately on the cheek, her eyes suddenly wistful. Then, without a word, she walked from the room. Tilghman broke open the shotgun and inspected the bore. Her abrupt change in mood left him puzzled, thoughtful. He idly wondered if he should have a talk with Copperdust.

The stallion might educate him in the ways of women.

CHAPTER 8

The rolling hills were dotted with stands of postoak and blackjack. Cromwell was situated some sixty miles east of Oklahoma City and forty miles southeast of Chandler. A narrow road traversed the terrain from the west, jammed with trucks and cars of every description. Everyone seemed to be in a hurry to get somewhere else.

Tilghman crested a low hill shortly before noon. Spread out before him was the oil field, stretching north and south on what was once isolated farmland. Timbered derricks, like spikes jutting from the earth, stood in stark disarray beneath a hazy sun. On first glance, the oil field was no different than those he'd seen across the breadth of Oklahoma. Cromwell was simply larger.

The pace of oil development seemed to him a frenetic symbol of the times. As he dropped down off the hill, hooking the old Ford into low gear, he was reminded that oil men were hardly new to Oklahoma. The first well drilled in Indian Territory was outside Muskogee, in the Creek Nation, late in 1884. At eighteen hundred feet it came in a duster and was abandoned, dampening exploration for a few years. Then, in 1889, a producing well was completed on Spencer Creek in the Cherokee Nation. It was thirty-six feet deep and pumped a half-barrel of oil a day. Scarcely an auspicious start.

That was the year of the Land Rush, and Tilghman

recalled that wildcatters continued to sink wells because everyone knew the oil was there. After the turn of the century, when war was declared in Europe, a demand arose for gasoline and fuel oil such as the world had never known. Prices boomed as America's reserves were drained, and new fields were opened all across the southwest. Curiously, when Armistice was declared on the Western Front, the demand for oil increased rather than diminished. Automobile and truck manufacturers became gigantic concerns during the war, and their expansion had a profound effect upon the oil business. Fears of an oil shortage broke out, and a whirlwind of exploration roared across the country. The race was still on to feed the gas tanks of a nation on wheels.

Cromwell was laid out on a T. Shawnee Avenue, which formed the cross of the T, stretched east to west not quite a mile. Tilghman entered town from the west, passing the lumberyard owned by Craig Thomas, and several oil supply warehouses. The street was clogged with flatbed trucks hauling equipment and trucks mounted with huge oil drums bound for distant refineries. The rank smell of raw crude permeated the town.

Tilghman was mildly surprised by the extent of construction. Buildings were wedged side by side, slapped together with ripsawed lumber, many of them two and three stories high. Up ahead, at the intersection, he saw Sirmans' dry goods store, and on the opposite corner Owen Tippet's pharmacy. He noted a hotel on the other corner, a nearby bank, and several dance halls. The boardwalks were crowded with men in rough work clothes, and automobiles, parked on an angle, lined the street. The town had taken on a look of permanence.

Three months ago, Tilghman reminded himself, all of this had been open farmland. A great deal had been accomplished in a short time, and as boomtowns went, he was impressed. At the intersection, he turned north onto Jenkins Street, which formed the leg of the T in the business district. The street ran several blocks, crowded with buildings, oil derricks towering here and there between structures. A few doors down from the intersection, he caught sight of the hardware store owned by Fred Wagner, the fourth member of the Citizens Committee. Farther down, on the corner of the next block, he saw the town marshal's office, with a sign hung over the door. He nosed the Ford into the curb.

The boardwalk swarmed with men. For the most part, they were roughnecks, who worked the derricks, and roustabouts, who performed manual labor. Their clothes were grimy, their hands blackened with oil, and many stood picking their teeth after lunch in one of the cafes along the street. Their workday began at sunrise and ended at sundown, with only a short break at noontime. They were hard men, made harder by work on the rigs, and few of them escaped without injury. A missing finger or a crushed foot was not unusual in the oil fields.

Tilghman stepped out of the car. As he closed the door, a commotion erupted catty-corner across the street. The crowd on the opposite boardwalk seemed to cleave apart outside a business establishment called the Sportsmen's Club. A roustabout, fighting his way backward into the street, was involved in a slugfest with two men wearing suits and ties. In the doorway, a third man, attired in a dapper double-breasted suit, watched the action with an impassive expression. A woman stood at his side.

The roustabout was outnumbered and outclassed. The two men in suits were skilled with their fists, clearly veterans of countless brawls. They maneuvered from either side, working in tandem, landing punches even as the roustabout tried to ward off their blows. Finally, staggered by an overhand right to the jaw, he dropped to his hands and knees. His opponents, warming to their work, started kicking him in the ribs and stomach. Tilghman was on the verge of intervening when the girl in the doorway ran into the street. She began pummeling the two thugs.

"Leave him alone!" she shrieked. "You're going to kill him!"

The thugs wavered under her assault. They glanced at the third man, still standing in the doorway, looking for instructions. He waved them off with a bored gesture. "Let the bum go. He's had enough."

The men laughed, brushing themselves off, and walked toward the club. As they moved away, the roustabout slumped forward onto the ground, his features masked with blood. The girl stooped down, reaching for him, when the man in the doorway called out, "All right, Josie, that's your good deed for the day. Let's get back to work."

The girl hesitated a moment, then turned away. She followed the men into the club with a look of barely disguised loathing. When the door closed, several onlookers stepped from the crowd and got hold of the roustabout. They dragged him to the boardwalk, waiting until his head cleared, and left him seated on the curb. His left eye was swollen to the size of a billiard ball.

Tilghman was surprised that none of the spectators had joined in the fight. He turned to a man standing near the fender of his car. "What was that all about?"

"Who knows?" the man said. "Poor stiff probably couldn't pay his bar tab."

"The Sportsmen's Club is a speakeasy?"

"That and a few other things. Got women and gamblin' too."

"Sporty, all right," Tilghman remarked. "Why didn't anybody jump in and lend that fellow a hand?"

"Them boys that whipped him was packin' rods. Nobody messes with Jake Hammer and his goons."

"Which one was Jake Hammer?"

"The one givin' the orders. He says frog and everybody squats. Why you askin' all the questions?"

Tilghman peeled his mackinaw aside. A badge was pinned to the pocket of his shirt. "I'm the new marshal," he said. "The name's Tilghman."

The man, who was crudely dressed, appeared to be a roustabout. He looked Tilghman up and down, noting the iron-gray mustache and hair, the boots, and the Stetson. His features wrinkled in an amused smile.

"You sure you ain't Wild Bill Hickok? Cromwell could use somebody like him."

"Tough place, huh?"

"This side of hell," the man said with conviction. "I wish you a lotta luck, Marshal. You're gonna need it."

"One last thing," Tilghman said, ignoring the comment. "Who was the woman involved in that ruckus?"

"Why, that there's Josie Rodgers. Ain't she a looker, though? Finest whore in town."

"Is she Hammer's woman?"

"Don't know and don't care to know. I never meddle in another man's business."

The roustabout nodded, moving off, quickly lost in the crowd. Tilghman stood staring at the plate-glass windows fronting the Sportsmen's Club. He thought it ironic that the marshal's office was directly across the street from Jake Hammer's headquarters. He wryly took it as a good omen.

Still musing on it, he crossed the boardwalk to the office. When he came through the door, he found a burly man, somewhere in his late thirties, seated behind the desk. A younger man, his face dotted with freckles, was tinkering with a coffeepot atop a pot-bellied stove. They had badges pinned on their jackets, and both of them carried holstered revolvers. The one behind the desk looked up with an oily grin.

"Well, well," he said, climbing to his feet. "You must be Bill Tilghman. Welcome to Cromwell."

Tilghman accepted his handshake. "You've got me at a disadvantage."

"Jim Bradley," he said. "Sheriff of Seminole County. Been an admirer of yours for years. Can I call you Bill?"

"Why not, Jim?" Tilghman was not impressed by the

amiable manner. He told himself he was in the presence of a crooked politician, rather than a lawman. "How'd you know I was getting in today?"

"Nothing much happens I don't hear about. Sirmans and his bunch have been bragging all over town."

"I didn't see any brass bands."

"That's rich!" Bradley said jovially. "I like a man with a sense of humor." He motioned toward the stove. "This here's Tug Sanders. One of my best deputies."

Sanders set the coffeepot on the stove. He moved forward with a feckless grin and an outstretched hand. "Honor to meet you, Mr. Tilghman. I growed up on stories about you chasin' outlaws." He pumped Tilghman's arm like he was trying to raise water. "Never figured I'd get to meet you in person."

Tilghman thought there was more here than met the eye. The deputy's greeting was somehow overdrawn, too effusive. He finally managed to extract his hand. "Glad to meet you, Tug."

Bradley and Sanders watched as he casually inspected the office. Apart from the desk and the telephone, and a small washroom, the place was bare as a monk's cell. A holding cage, with steel bars and a single door, occupied the rear of the room. There were no bunks in the lockup and the floor was poured cement. He jerked a thumb toward the cage.

"Looks more like a drunk tank than a jail."

"Does for a fact," Bradley said agreeably. " 'Course, that's mostly what you get here in Cromwell. Anything serious, we transport them over to the county jail."

Tilghman nodded. "How's your investigation going?"

"What investigation's that?"

"Will Bohannon, the former marshal. Wasn't he murdered?"

"Murdered!" Bradley rolled his eyes at the absurdity of it. "Bohannon was worthless as tits on a boar hog. Why would anybody kill him?"

"Guess that's the question, isn't it?"

"Way I see it, he just up and took off. Lazy devil wasn't never cut out to be a lawman."

"Maybe so." Tilghman let it drop. "Was this just a social visit, or have we got business? I want to look the town over."

"Little of both," Bradley said, lifting his chin in Sanders' direction. "I'm assigning Tug to the Cromwell office. He'll be a big help to you."

Tilghman saw where they were headed. Sanders was being installed as a watchdog, to report anything that might upset the sheriff's cozy arrangement with the mobsters. Which in turn would be reported to Jake Hammer.

"I've got no objections," he said. "Just so we understand that Tug answers to me and follows orders. Otherwise, you can keep him in Wewoka."

"Hold on now," Bradley said sternly. "I'm the law in Seminole County, and that includes Cromwell. A deputy don't take orders from anybody but me."

"You're welcome to the rest of the county. Starting today, I'm the only law in Cromwell."

"You'll play hell making that stick!"

"Don't bet on it," Tilghman said in a steady voice. "Governor Trapp assigned me here as a state marshal. That's all the authority I need."

"What?" Bradley looked dumbfounded. "You weren't hired by Sirmans and his crowd?"

"Tell you what, call the governor and check it out. I've got arrest powers anywhere in the state—or Seminole County."

"You monkey around in my county and there'll be trouble. You mark my word!"

Tilghman gave him a measured stare. "I was weaned on trouble, Sheriff. You mark my word."

Bradley went red as oxblood. He wheeled around, darting a shifty glance at Sanders, and marched out of the office. Tilghman turned, found the deputy watching him with a look of doglike bewilderment. He arched one eyebrow.

"What about it, Deputy? You along for the ride?"

"Yessir," Sanders said with a vigorous nod. "Whatever you say goes."

"I believe you were fixin' coffee."

"Yeah, I'd started to."

"I could use a cup myself. Go ahead while I get my gear out of the car."

Tilghman left him fiddling with the coffeepot. Outside, across the street, he saw Bradley hurry into the Sportsmen's Club. He chuckled to himself, amused by the thought of Bradley scurrying off to report that the Governor of Oklahoma, rather than the Citizens Committee, had brought him to Cromwell. He wished he were a fly on the wall.

On the street, he opened the trunk of the car. His Winchester and the sawed-off shotgun were wrapped in a blanket. He collected the weapons, stuffing boxes of shells in his coat pockets, and closed the trunk. As he turned, the carbine in one hand and the scattergun in the other, he caught motion in the window across the street. He saw Jake Hammer and Bradley watching him from the club.

A moment went by while he openly returned their stare. Then, hefting the guns, he rounded the car and walked toward the office. He thought it would not be long before he heard from Jake Hammer.

CHAPTER 9

Twilight settled over Cromwell as the sun went down behind a thick bank of clouds. Tilghman stepped out of the office, the badge now pinned to his mackinaw. He strode south along Jenkins Street.

Earlier he had dismissed Tug Sanders for the night. One reason was that he wanted Sanders to spread the word among oil men about Cromwell's new marshal. The other was that he intended to let the town look him over, and he was purposely alone. A brag of sorts, he nonetheless felt it had to be made the first night. He meant to show them that he was here to stay, that he was willing to accommodate anybody who thought otherwise. He was there to enforce the law.

Their workday done, the roughnecks and roustabouts flooded into town. By dusk, there were easily three thousand men on the streets, all in search of whiskey and women. As Tilghman moved along the boardwalk, they made way, watching him with open curiosity, almost as if they expected him to perform some bold and daring feat. Most of them hadn't been born when he'd killed his first man, but they knew the stories evoked by his reputation. Despite his age, they found the legend no less imposing in person.

A man with guts was no rarity in the oil fields. Yet this was something different, a special breed, perhaps the last of his kind. They were watching a genuine mankiller, a lawman of the old school, and for all his years, he still looked tough and hard as nails. They liked what they saw, the ramrod-straight manner, the no-nonsense cast of his eyes, the bulge of the Colt under his mackinaw. Even more they admired his audacity and his cool nerve, a one-man parade clearly meant to put the town on notice. They thought he had balls.

For all that, the roughnecks and roustabouts still wondered how long he would last. The grapevine was rife with rumors about Will Bohannon, the previous marshal, a man reportedly too honest for his own good. The word was he'd refused payoffs, incurred the wrath of the mobsters who ran Cromwell. On the oil rigs, there was the general consensus that he hadn't just disappeared, left town without a trace. The talk was that he had been killed, executed by the gangsters as a warning. Which made the new marshal all the more a curiosity, someone to watch. Based on his reputation, he wasn't an easy man to kill.

Tilghman regarded the oil workers with detached interest. They were merely spectators in a game that had little to do with rowdy drunks and barroom brawls. A greater risk had drawn him to Cromwell, just as danger had always exerted its pull on him in the past. He had accepted the assignment, deliberately pitting himself against organized mobsters, for reasons all his own. Times changed and men changed, and he readily admitted that no man was immortal. But he hadn't come to the oil fields to get himself killed. He was there for one last game. A game of wits with no rules. A game he'd never lost.

The streetlights came on as Tilghman approached the intersection of Jenkins and Shawnee. Across the way he saw Walter Sirmans through the window of the dry goods store. A courtesy call was in order, and he fended a path through the evening traffic. As he entered the door, Sirmans was wrapping a purchase for an oil field worker. The store stocked clothing of every description, from denim pants and overalls to dress shirts and ready-to-wear suits. Given the wear and tear of work on the rigs, he thought Sirmans probably did a good business. The customer passed him as he moved along the aisle.

Sirmans turned from the cash register. "Well, Marshal Tilghman, I heard you were in town. Wondered when you'd drop by."

"Waited till nighttime," Tilghman said, exchanging a handshake. "Figured that's when the real action starts."

"Yessir, things do get lively along about dark. What do you think so far?"

"I reckon it's about what I expected. You couldn't throw a rock without hitting a dive of some sort."

"Amen to that," Sirmans said glumly. "By last count, there were a hundred and three places selling alcohol, most of them with women. Not to mention brothels and gambling joints."

"Sounds about right," Tilghman commented. "A boomtown draws the vice crowd. Never seen it fail."

"Where will you start? Any ideas yet?"

"Well, first off, I'll get the lay of the land. Thought I'd scout things out tonight."

"I understand you saw Jake Hammer in action."

"Not much to write home about. Couple of his boys worked over a roustabout."

"Just you being there got his attention. He's already making his displeasure known."

"How so?"

Sirmans grimaced. "One of his goons—Turk Milligan—paid me a visit this afternoon. Hammer blames me for bringing you here."

"Does he?" Tilghman's eyes narrowed. "Were you threatened?"

"Milligan told me to mind my own business. Otherwise, in his words, I'll get my ass kicked."

"What's this Milligan look like?"

"A real tough customer. Heavyset, dark-features, with a neck like a stump post. Why do you ask?"

"I saw him this afternoon. He was one of the men who whipped that roustabout. He fights dirty."

"They all do," Sirmans said, with a nervous look. "I'm afraid you can't expect too much help from me. I've been put on warning."

Tilghman was hardly surprised. The good-intentioned men of the world, men like Sirmans, were quick to recruit others in the name of justice. But they were wary of dirtying their own hands, and easily frightened. He had seen it time and again over the last forty years. The moralists in life were seldom fighters.

"Don't worry about it," he said without concern. "I've never minded playing a lone hand."

"Say, that reminds me. Is it true what I heard about Tug Sanders? Word's around that Bradley stuck you with him."

"Besides being Bradley's spy, what else is wrong with him?"

"You name it," Sirmans said. "Don't be fooled by that Huck Finn look. He's a drunk, and a womanizer, and an all-around no-account. To top it off, he's Bradley's nephew."

"Nephew?" Tilghman appear amused. "Bradley keeps it in the family, hmmm?"

"I imagine he has to. Nobody would hire Tug to slop the hogs. He's just generally worthless."

"Well, maybe I won't have to worry about him spying on me. He doesn't sound too sharp."

"No, but he's Bradley's nephew," Sirmans countered. "And he's not altogether a simpleton. He just does dumb things."

"Worse comes to worse, I'll tie a can to his tail."

"How could you do that?"

"You forgot," Tilghman said. "I was sent here by the governor. I've pretty much got a free hand."

"Things work out for the best," Sirmans noted. "We

got you and we got the governor's support. We couldn't have hoped for more."

"Tell me that when the dust settles. I haven't yet arrested anybody."

"Yes, but the game's still early. You've only just got to town."

"Speaking of that," Tilghman said. "I need a place to stay. Any decent hotels in Cromwell?"

"The Regent." Sirmans pointed across the street, to the hotel on the corner. "Not as fancy as its name, but it's the best we've got to offer. Even has telephones in the rooms."

"Guess that's good enough for me."

A few minutes later Tilghman emerged from the store. That afternoon, when he'd driven into town, he had noticed an establishment next door advertising itself as Murphy's Dance Hall. He recalled a man and wife of the same name who had operated a dance hall following the opening Land Rush of Oklahoma Territory. That was in Guthrie, thirty-five years ago, and he had lost track of them as they moved on to other boomtowns. He thought it improbable that it was the same couple.

The inside of the dance hall was festively decorated with bunting and gaily-colored wallpaper. Japanese lanterns, which were strung overhead from wall to wall, lent the place an intimate atmosphere. A wooden balustrade separated the oil workers from the thirty or so young women who waited on the dance floor. The charge was a quarter a dance, and the men purchased tickets which allowed them entrance through an opening at the end of the railing. One ticket entitled them to ten minutes on the dance floor.

The girls were presentable if not attractive, and many of them had good figures. For the most part, they came from small towns across the Midwest, drawn by the lure of excitement in the boomtowns. Their features were rouged, their mouths painted in the fashionable beestung style with bright red lipstick. Their dresses were inexpensive and simple, cut low at the top and short on the bottom to show off their figures. On every ticket they received a commission of ten cents, and on a busy night a girl might earn five or six dollars. They were known throughout the oil fields as ten-cent-a-dance girls.

On a platform toward the rear of the room five musicians wailed away at the "St. Louis Blues." They were led by a glassy-eyed sax player, and the rhythm they produced evoked a mood of Jazz Age revelry. The roughnecks and roustabouts, with more enthusiasm than style, shoved the girls around the dance floor like a tribe of acrobatic wrestlers. No drinking was allowed on the floor, but the men outside the balustrade fueled themselves for the night ahead. They waited in line, swigging from pint bottles, their toes tapping to the music. Hardly a man among them would end the night sober.

Tilghman watched a moment, then walked toward the ticket booth. The woman behind the counter was stout and doughy, with chubby features and a pleasant smile. Even when she was younger, her motherly attitude toward the girls had earned her the nickname Ma. Her husband, a genial bruiser who policed the dance floor, was likewise known as Pa. From the old days, long ago in Guthrie, Tilghman recalled that their real names were Flo and Delbert. But in boomtowns across the Southwest they were known simply as Ma and Pa Murphy.

During a lull at the booth, Tilghman moved forward. "Evening, Ma," he said, tipping his hat. "Long time no see."

"Land's sakes!" Her eyes sparkled merrily. "I would've known you anywhere, Bill Tilghman. You haven't changed an iota."

"You always were a charmer, Ma. How's the world treating you?"

"Oh, I can't complain, and wouldn't anyhow. Del and me get along just fine."

Tilghman nodded toward the dance floor. "I see

you're still in the girly trade. Thought you would've gone respectable by now.''

"Look who's talking," she joshed him. "I see you're still sporting a star. Things haven't changed much since Guthrie.''

"A man does what he does best, Ma.''

"Yes, I heard you were the new marshal. Wish I hadn't, though.''

"Why's that?''

She glanced around, lowered her voice. "The boys who run this town are a rough crowd. Everybody just *knows* they killed the last marshal.''

"So I've been told," Tilghman said. "What's the sporting crowd think of this Jake Hammer? Anything on the grapevine.''

"Folks think he controls the booze traffic into Cromwell. And for that matter, the drug trade too.''

"Are you talking about cocaine?''

"Nothing else," she acknowledged. "Lots of dope fiends in the oil fields. Maybe it's all the loose money around. Anyway, it's big-time stuff.''

"First I've heard of dope." Tilghman considered a moment. "Any idea who sells it?''

"Curiosity killed the cat. I tend to my own knittin'.''

"Well, keep your ears open anyway. I'd count it a favor.''

She averted her gaze. "You're too straight for this dump, Bill. Stick around and they'll kill you too.''

Tilghman grinned. "Don't bet your bankroll on it, Ma. I'd hate to see you wind up in the poor house.''

"Just remember what I told you. You're no spring chicken anymore.''

"Yeah, but I'm a tough old bird. You'd be surprised, Ma.''

"I hope so, Bill. I surely do.''

Tilghman waved, turning toward the door. Outside, he patrolled east and then west along Shawnee. He was aware of the speakeasies, the drunken laughter, the eager looks of men rushing into bordellos. But these were vague images, for his mind was still focused on the words of Ma Murphy. Illicit liquor was one thing, but the dope trade was dirty business. Not one usually associated with rumrunners and backwoods mobsters. Which was food for thought.

Tilghman turned onto Jenkins Street. A block down, outside the Sportmen's Club, he saw Tug Sanders talking with the man he'd now identified as Turk Milligan. The deputy appeared to be drunk, swaying back and forth, his features slack. Milligan thumped him in the chest with a stiff forefinger.

"Enough of that," Tilghman said, halting a step away. "What's the problem?"

"Well, well," Milligan said in a surly voice. "Here's the old fart himself. I was just giving Tug a message for you."

"What's the message?"

"Haul your ass outta town, Buffalo Bill. Tonight wouldn't be none too soon."

Tilghman shrugged. "Or else?"

"Or else nothin'." Milligan raised a knotted fist. "Get out or get your butt whipped."

"Jake Hammer told you to deliver the message?"

"That's *Mr.* Hammer to you, old timer."

"All right, I've got a message for Mr. Hammer."

"What's that?"

The Colt seemed to materialize in Tilghman's hand. He laid the barrel across Milligan's skull, driving the bigger man to his knees. Then he struck him again, and Milligan collapsed onto the boardwalk. He left the man sprawled in a welter of blood, outside the door of the club. Holstering his pistol, he forcibly took hold of Sanders' arm. He marched him across the street.

Inside the office, Tilghman relieved Sanders of his revolver. The deputy drunkenly protested, but Tilghman grabbed him by the neck and waltzed him to the back of the room. He shoved him into the holding cage, slammed the door, and locked it. Sanders ricocheted off the wall and slowly settled to the floor. He passed out.

Tilghman seated himself at the desk. He tossed the keys in the drawer, then lifted the receiver on the phone. He jiggled the hook. "Central? Get me 5793 in Chandler."

A moment later Zoe came on the line. "Hello."

"Thought I'd give you a ring before it got too late. You miss me?"

"Of course I miss you! How are things there?"

"What with this and that, pretty routine. Just another day."

"You somehow make it sound dull. You wouldn't fib to me, would you?"

Tilghman smiled. "All's quiet in Cromwell."

CHAPTER 10

Wewoka was a small but thriving trade center. Located some fifteen miles south of Cromwell, the town's chief claim to fame was that it served as the county seat. Seminole County officials, accustomed to dealing with farmers, were now responsible for one of the largest oil fields in Oklahoma. A new prosperity rode on a crest of black gold.

The town revolved around the courthouse. All four sides of the square were jammed with shops and business establishments; even on weekdays, the streets were crowded with automobiles and trucks. The courthouse lawn, brown from autumn frost, encircled a granite structure vaguely Victorian in appearance. Tall windows in the building mirrored a bright morning sun.

Tilghman drove into the square shortly after ten o'clock. Beside him, suffering from a hangover, Tug Sanders sat slumped in the passenger seat. His eyes were bloodshot, and in the glare of sunlight, he winced from a pounding headache. A whiskery stubble covered his jawline, and his clothes were soiled and rumpled from a night in the holding cage. He looked like a bum fresh off a drunk.

On the square, Tilghman eased the Ford into a parking spot reserved for sheriff's deputies. He stepped out, closing the door, and stood waiting while Sanders gingerly crawled from the car. Several passersby, startled by Sanders' disheveled appearance, paused to stare as Tilghman led him up the walkway. Some were quick to remark that the deputy's pistol holster was empty.

Inside the courthouse, Tilghman marched him along a central corridor. Halfway down, they turned into the sheriff's office, where a secretary and another deputy were seated at desks. Tilghman appraised the layout at a glance, and continued on to an inner door at the far side of the room. He found Jim Bradley behind a desk littered with paperwork, talking to someone on the telephone. Bradley abruptly ended the call.

"Morning, Sheriff," Tilghman said, motioning to the door. "Brought you a present."

Sanders slouched through the door. He ducked his head with a shamefaced expression, halting before the desk. Bradley looked from one to the other, clearly bewildered, momentarily at a loss. His gaze settled on Tilghman.

"What's the meaning of this?"

"I arrested your deputy." Tilghman pulled a revolver from his waistband, placed it on the desk. "I took the liberty of unloading that."

"Who do you think you are, Tilghman? You can't arrest one of my deputies."

"Thought we got that straight yesterday, Sheriff. I hold a commission from the State of Oklahoma. I can arrest anybody I see fit."

"Like hell!" Bradley flared. "I won't stand for it!"

"Why, sure you will," Tilghman said with muted irony. "I'd wager you checked it out with some of your cronies at the statehouse. They told you I'm holding all the cards, didn't they?"

"What makes you think I know anybody at the statehouse?"

"You're a politician, Sheriff. No guesswork there."

A vein stood out on Bradley's forehead. "What's the charge against Tug?"

"Drunk and disorderly," Tilghman said evenly. "Hate to see a law officer make a public nuisance of himself."

"No such thing!" Sanders protested. "Just had a few drinks, that's all."

Bradley looked at him with disgust. "Shut your mouth unless you're spoken to. I'll tend to you later."

"One other thing," Tilghman interjected. "He was consorting with known hoodlums. That's a bad reflection on your office, Sheriff."

"I wasn't either," Sanders said feebly. "Turk Milligan and me was just talkin'. Nothing wrong with that."

Tilghman waited for a reaction. Bradley evidenced no surprise, and he thought that told the story. Jake Hammer had doubtless been on the phone within minutes of the incident last night. The sheriff's ears were probably still burning.

"I heard about Milligan," Bradley said, glaring at Tilghman. "But nobody told me you'd arrested Tug."

"How'd you hear about Milligan?"

"That's my business, Marshal. I hear lots of things."

"Then you know I whacked Milligan upside the head."

"What gives you the right to call him a hoodlum?"

"I hear things too," Tilghman said, deciding to deliver a message of his own. "Milligan works for Hammer, and everybody in Cromwell can't be wrong. They say Hammer's the boss of the rackets there."

"What!" Bradley involuntarily snorted. "Hammer's just a—"

Bradley cut himself short. He looked like he wanted to bite his tongue. Watching him, Tilghman got a visceral sense that all was not as it appeared in Cromwell. The sheriff had slipped, almost let a cat of some sort out of the bag. He tried for a note of casual interest.

"I didn't catch that, Sheriff. Hammer's just a . . . what?"

"A businessman," Bradley said lamely. "No different than other businessmen in Cromwell.''

''Yeah, maybe so,'' Tilghman replied with sardonic humor. ''Leastways if you're talking about liquor and whores and gambling.''

''Well, hell's fire, it's a boomtown! You expect me to bring it under control overnight?''

''What I expect from you is real simple. Keep Tug here in Wewoka and I'll drop the drunk and disorderly against him. That's the deal.''

''All right,'' Bradley said stonily. ''I'll send another deputy in his place.''

''No dice,'' Tilghman informed him. ''Your men aren't welcome in Cromwell. I'll handle things myself.''

''I'm the sheriff of this goddamned county! You can't post my deputies out of Cromwell.''

''I understand Tug's your nephew.''

''So what?''

''How many other relatives have you got on the payroll?''

''None of your damn business.''

Tilghman smiled. ''Do yourself and your relatives a favor. Leave Cromwell to me and stay out of my way. You've been officially advised.''

''You go to hell,'' Bradley's voice was flat and hostile. ''Nobody tells me what to do in my own county. I'll come and go as I please.''

Tilghman's smile darkened. ''Don't mess with me, Sheriff. You'll regret it.''

''Are you threatening an officer of the law?''

''I won't tolerate interference. Take it any way you want.''

Tilghman's cold eyes bored into him. Bradley felt a chill ripple along his backbone. ''I'll come to Cromwell any time I please. But—'' he hesitated, swallowed around his fear. ''I won't get in your way. You run the town to suit yourself.''

''Glad we could work things out, Sheriff. I'll see you around.''

Tilghman turned toward the door. As he went out, he heard Sanders start to whine. "Uncle Jim, what are we gonna do about my car? That old devil made me leave it in Cromwell."

"For chrissakes, Tug, shut up, will you? Just shut up!"

On the second floor, Tilghman found the Third District courtroom. Down the hall, he turned into a passageway that led to the chambers of Judge George Crump. That morning, when he'd called for an appointment, the secretary had told him court was not in session and the judge would be happy to see him. She greeted him now with a warm smile.

"Yes, of course, Marshal Tilghman. The judge is expecting you."

She ushered him into an office paneled in dark wood. One wall was floor to ceiling bookshelves, lined with rows of legal tomes. Before a window overlooking the courthouse lawn was a massive desk, inlaid with mahogany and rosewood. The man behind the desk was in his early fifties, tall and straight, with piercing eyes. A leonine shock of salt-and-pepper hair crowned his head, and he conveyed an impression of suppressed power. He rose with a disarming smile.

"Marshal Tilghman," he said with a solid handshake. "One of the Three Guardsmen, in the flesh. An honor, sir."

"You make me feel my age, Judge. Those days are long gone."

"I beg to differ, sir. Lawmen of your caliber were never needed more. We live in sordid times."

Crump waved him to a wingback chair. After they were seated, the jurist assessed him with an eager look. "I was never more delighted than when the governor informed me of your appointment. I consider you a godsend, Marshal."

"That's high praise," Tilghman said, hooking his hat

over a bent knee. "I've been called lots of things, but never a godsend."

"You are that indeed, believe me. So now tell me about your first day in Cromwell."

Tilghman briefly related the events of the past twenty-four hours. When he finished, Crump stared at him with open marvel. "You actually floored one of Hammer's thugs?"

"A knot on the head might teach him some manners."

"And you arrested Jim Bradley's nephew?"

"Delivered him just a while ago. The sheriff and me came to an understanding. No more deputies assigned to Cromwell."

"A brilliant start," Crump announced vigorously. "You've certainly wasted no time, Marshal."

"Still a long ways to go," Tilghman said. "Cromwell would put Sodom and Gomorrah to shame."

"The same might be said for the whole of Seminole County."

"Governor Trapp tells me you're the only honest man in the courthouse. How deep does the corruption go?"

Judge Crump recounted a tale of integrity gone askew. Seminole County was farm country, and for the most part, the people as well as public officials were honest and hardworking. But the oil strike brought vast amounts of money into play, and morality fell victim to the temptation of cold cash. The gangsters who ran Cromwell followed the practice that worked so well in Chicago and New York. They made public officials their partners in crime.

"A sad spectacle," Crump concluded. "Good men, essentially honest men, brought down by greed. Far all practical purposes, Jake Hammer runs Seminole County."

"So everybody says." Tilghman sounded doubtful. "You believe in hunches, Judge?"

"I place more faith in facts. Why do you ask?"

"A lawman learns to trust gut instinct. Lots of times it's all that kept me from gettin' killed."

Crump looked at him speculatively. "And what does your gut instinct tell you?"

"Hammer's a thug." Tilghman rubbed the bridge of his nose. "From all I've seen, he uses muscle instead of brains. He's an enforcer, not a planner."

"I'm not sure I follow you."

"Let me give you an example. Yesterday, I found out there's lots of dope being sold in Cromwell. All the dope trade comes out of Mexico, and that takes planning. Not as simple as running booze in by truck."

"Drugs," Crump said with a heavy sigh. "I had no idea it had gone that far. Are you talking about the logistics of the operation?"

"Yeah, that's part of it. Things are a little too well organized in Cromwell. Doesn't strike me as Hammer's style."

"But that is still conjecture, isn't it?"

"Maybe not altogether."

Tilghman outlined his earlier conversation with the sheriff. He explained how Bradley's anger had resulted in a slip of the tongue. A tipoff of sorts.

"Way it sounded," he went on, "Bradley was about to call Hammer a stooge of some kind. A flunky."

"I wish I'd been there to hear it for myself. What conclusion do you draw?"

"I've got a hunch Hammer's just a front man. I think somebody's pullin' his strings."

Crump's brow furrowed. "You think Hammer's a . . . puppet?"

"Just gut instinct," Tilghman allowed. "All the same, I'd bet he's not the kingpin. There's somebody else callin' the shots."

"You're talking about an overlord. Someone who runs things from the shadows."

"Let's just say I wouldn't be surprised."

"And suppose you are correct. How do you propose

to catch him? So far, we don't even have anything on Hammer.''

''There' always a weak link. I'll have to poke around and find it.''

''Bring me the proof,'' Crump said with a determined edge to his voice. ''I'd like nothing better than to convene a grand jury and hand down indictments. Seminole County needs a thorough housecleaning.''

Tilghman nodded. ''Any chance we'll get some help from the federal men? Who's the Prohibition agent for the district?''

''A man named Wiley Lynn. I doubt he'll be of any great assistance.''

''Has he made cases against anyone in Cromwell?''

''Like most Prohibition agents, he makes a case now and then just for the record. He's arrested a few small-time bootleggers.''

''Do you think he's on the take?''

''I'm not sure it matters. The public wants its liquor, and Prohibition will never change that. Nor will an army of Prohibition agents.''

''Likely not,'' Tilghman agreed. ''We've got bigger fish to fry anyway. Jake Hammer's first on the list.''

Crump looked at him. ''Where will you start?''

''Kick in some doors,'' Tilghman said with a dry chuckle. ''See what happens.''

''I hope you find that weak link, Marshal.''

''Never seen it to fail yet. Somebody always talks.''

Crump saw him to the door. After Tilghman went out, the judge returned to his chair, staring out across the courthouse lawn. He was impressed by the ageless vitality of the man, the raw sense of strength. A bulldog with a badge.

He thought Jake Hammer was in for a rough time.

CHAPTER 11

Hammer answered the phone on the first ring. "Yeah."

"Good afternoon, Jake."

The calls always disconcerted Hammer. He was not allowed to use the other man's name, for fear of being overheard by telephone operators. Yet his name, which was equally well known, inevitably entered into the conversation. He thought it was a dumb rule, but he kept his opinion to himself. Orders were orders.

"Hello," he said, kicking the door to his office closed. "What's up?"

"What's up, indeed? I think that's my question."

"You lost me there."

"Tilghman was in Wewoka this morning."

"Yeah?"

"You failed to inform me, Jake."

"What's to inform you about? I didn't know he was coming over there."

"I'm not talking about his coming here. I'm talking about the purpose of his trip."

Hammer smothered a sigh. "So what was the purpose?"

"Deputy Sanders is no longer assigned to Cromwell. Tilghman returned him to the sheriff . . . under arrest."

"What do you mean, arrest? Arrest for what?"

"Drunk and disorderly. Tilghman used it to intimidate

Bradley. No other deputies will be assigned to Cromwell.''

''I'll be a sonofabitch! And Bradley caved in?''

There was an ominous silence. ''You miss the point, Jake. How is it you didn't know about this?''

''How would I know about it? He didn't tell nobody over here.''

''Your job is to keep tabs on everything he does. Were you aware he had Sanders locked in the drunk tank last night?''

''Hey, c'mon, how would I've got wind of a thing like that? Look in my crystal ball?''

''Watch your tone of voice, Jake. I don't care for sarcasm.''

''I didn't mean nothing by it. Just pissed at Tilghman, that's all.''

''That was another reason I called. I understand he worked over one of your men.''

''Uhh, yeah.'' Hammer's forehead beaded with perspiration. ''Old bastard's got some balls on him. He put Milligan down and out for the count.''

''How did he manage that?''

''Whopped Turk over the head with his gun. Knocked him cold as a cucumber.''

''Why wasn't I informed?''

''Well—'' Hammer faltered, tried to collect wits. ''Didn't want to bother you. What's to tell?''

''You told our friend the sheriff. Why wouldn't you call me?''

''Like I said, figured it wasn't worth the bother.''

''Why don't I believe you, Jake? Why do I think you're making plans on your own?''

''What kind of plans? I've got no plans.''

''Listen to me very closely. You're pissed about Milligan, and I know that temper of yours. I don't want to hear that Tilghman disappeared or had an accident.''

''Christ, I wouldn't do nothing like that! Not without your okay.''

"You wouldn't do it unless I ordered it done. Isn't that what you meant to say?"

"Well, yeah, sure thing. You're the boss."

A moment elapsed, the only sound a hum of static on the line. "I'm disappointed in the way you've handled this. We've lost our plant in Tilghman's office, and he's made you look bad in front of the town. Why did he coldcock Milligan?"

Hammer licked his lips. "Well, I just sent him a little message. No harm in that."

"And Milligan delivered the message?"

"Yeah, why not? Turk told him to haul ass. Get lost."

"Or?"

"Well, you know . . . get out or get worked over."

"Never underestimate your opponent, Jake. A man like Tilghman doesn't scare. You should have known that."

"Gotta admit, he's a tough old geezer."

"I don't want there to be a next time. When I decide to send a message, I'll tell you. Understand?"

"Why are you so touchy about Tilghman?"

"You seem to forget he was sent there by the governor. Would you like the National Guard camped outside your club?"

"I don't think that'll happen."

The phone crackled with anger. "You're not paid to think! You're paid to do what you're told. Nothing more, nothing less. Got it?"

"Hey, it won't happen again. All right?"

"From now on, you let me worry about Tilghman. I'll tell you when to make a move."

"Good by me. I'll just tend to business."

"One other thing."

"Yeah?"

"A shipment is coming in tonight. Be at the airfield."

"Depend on it, boss. I'll be there."

The line went dead. Hammer hung up, aware that his shirt was clammy with sweat. He liked to think that he feared no man, but he knew better. He'd just spoken with Mr. Death himself, and the message still rang in his ears. Follow orders or else . . .

Hammer walked through the club. His mind was on other matters, and he scarcely noticed the gaming tables or the men at the bar. He halted at the windows, staring across the street, just as the old Ford pulled into the curb. He watched as Tilghman stepped out of the car.

One day, he told himself, his mouth set in a tight line. One day soon.

Tilghman sat down at his desk. All in all, he was pleased with the morning's excursion to Wewoka. By canning Tug Sanders he had put the sheriff, as well as the mob element, on notice. Yet he felt there was more to be done.

On the drive back, he had hatched a plan. He somehow had to exert greater control over Cromwell, further establish his authority. What was needed was a visible symbol of some sort, a statement to the townspeople as to who was in charge. He planned to send out a wake-up call.

The door swung open. Walter Sirmans, followed by another man, entered the office. Something about the other man struck Tilghman as unusual. He looked to be in his late twenties, with chestnut hair and eyes like snail heads. He was whipcord lean, all muscle and sinew, with a calm, assured manner. He reminded Tilghman of himself forty years ago.

"Afternoon, Marshal," Sirmans said amiably. "If you have a minute, I'd like you to meet someone. This is Hugh Sawyer."

Tilghman extended his hand. "Glad to make your acquaintance."

"Same here." Sawyer had an ore-crusher grip. "Anybody who can deck Turk Milligan gets my vote. Too bad I missed the show."

"I take it you and Milligan aren't friends."

"We tangled once over at the Sportsmen's Club."

"Let me guess," Tilghman said wryly. "Milligan took second prize."

Sawyer smiled. "I got lucky."

"Don't let him fool you," Sirmans broke in. "That's why I brought him by. He can whip any man in town."

"I'll take your word for it," Tilghman said. "But that still leaves me in the dark. What can I do for you, Walt?"

"Other way 'round, Marshal. Word's out you packed Tug Sanders off to Wewoka. Any truth to it?"

"Like they say, good news travels fast."

"Well then, you need a deputy you can trust. We'd like you to consider Hugh for the job. The Citizens Committee will gladly pay his salary."

"Why the sudden concern?"

"Well, you know . . ." Sirmans appeared embarrassed. "We're not much help to you, Marshal. Hell, we're just businessmen. Hugh's altogether another story. He could back your play."

Tilghman looked at the younger man. "What kind of work have you done before?"

"Mostly a roustabout," Sawyer said. "But I'd be willin' to learn a new trade."

"What makes you think you're cut out to be a lawman?"

"I don't cotton much to people like Hammer and his crew. Maybe I could be part of settin' things straight."

Tilghman liked his attitude. "You're handy with your fists. How are you with a gun?"

"I served with the army over in France. Got the Croix de Guerre for shootin' a bunch of Germans. I don't usually miss."

"How'd you feel about killing people?"

"Didn't like it," Sawyer said firmly. "But I didn't lose any sleep either. Figured I'd done my job."

Tilghman hired him on the spot. A man who could kill when duty demanded and take no pleasure in it was the raw stuff of a peace officer. He swore Sawyer in, and found an old badge in one of the drawers. The younger man beamed with pride.

"Something else," Sirmans said after a round of handshakes. "You might want to pay a call on Zack Mosley. He brought in the discovery well, Coffeepot Number One. Owns a whole string of wells. Twenty, maybe more."

"Wealthy man," Tilghman observed. "Why would I call on him?"

"Mosley's an outspoken opponent of Hammer and his gang. Says the mob's robbing his men blind. You might find some support there."

"Why doesn't he belong to your Citizens Committee?"

"Zack's sort of his own man. Not much of a joiner. But you might swing him around."

"Swing him around to what?"

"Well, he's got over two hundred men on his payroll. That's why Hammer doesn't mess with him. Wouldn't hurt to have him in your camp."

"You've got a point," Tilghman said. "I'll have a talk with him."

Sirmans looked pleased. "Nothing ventured, nothing gained, I always say."

"I'm of the same opinion. Matter of fact, I plan on holding a town meeting. I'd like you to spread the word, turn out a crowd."

"Why would you hold a town meeting?"

"I intend to post some ordinances. Where's a good place to hold it?"

Sirmans considered a moment. "We've only got one church in town. That would be the most likely spot."

"What's the preacher's name? I'll need to speak with him."

"Virgil Pryor," Sirmans said. "Would you mind telling me what you mean by ordinances?"

"Walt, show up and find out. You'll like what you hear."

A huge bull wheel groaned, playing out cable thick as a man's wrist over the crown block. On the derrick floor a massive beam bobbed in a teeter-totter motion, and the cable lowered a string of drilling tools deeper into the earth. A roughneck waited by a long wooden lever, ready to reverse the cable once the hole was bored another eight feet in depth. Zack Mosley stood nearby as the drilling string disappeared down the wellhead.

Tilghman and Sawyer watched the operation some yards from the derrick. The mechanics of it—wheels and cables and screeching pulleys—had never made sense to Tilghman. He understood that the drill gouged out chunks of earth, which were then bailed to the surface in a large bucket, and deposited in the slush pit. In time, at some unknown depth, there might be oil at the bottom of the hole. Beyond that it was mystery to him.

Oil exploration was still a rudimentary science. Large campanies relied on geologists, and seismographs were commonly used to map subsurface formations. But wildcatters such as Mosley still operated on the principle of creekology, searching for oil where nature left clues. Gas seeps, medicine springs, and slicks along creek banks were the spots most wildcatters spudded in wells. Mosley was fond of saying, "Only the drill finds oil," and he'd brought in the Cromwell field, and Coffeepot Number One, with old time creekology. Today, he was drilling Coffeepot Number Twenty-three.

The roughneck winched the tools out of the hole. Then he quickly engaged the band wheel, and ran his bailer into the well. When he brought the bailer out of the hole it was full of pulverized cuttings and water. Mosley inspected the cuttings, rubbing some between his fingers, smelling it, before he turned away. The roughneck dumped the cuttings into a slush pit, and readied the bailer for another trip into the hole. Mosley climbed down a ladder at the side of the rig.

A rangy man, somewhere in his late thirties, he was powerfully built from a lifetime of physical labor. He walked forward from the rig. "Sorry to keep you waiting, Marshal. Had to check the cuttings."

"I understand," Tilghman said. "Think you'll bring in another gusher?"

"Smells like paysand to me." Mosley looked at Sawyer. "See you're wearin' a badge, Hugh. Have you quit the fields?"

Sawyer grinned, a thumb hooked in his new gun belt. "Signed on today," he said. "Deputy town marshal."

Mosley just nodded. "What can I do for you gents?"

"We're holding a town meeting," Tilghman informed him. "Tomorrow night about seven or so, in the church. Hope you'll attend."

"Why would you want me there?"

"Walt Sirmans says you're opposed to Hammer and his bunch. We need more people like you to step forward."

Mosley squinted at him. "You really think you're gonna run Hammer out of Cromwell?"

"What I aim to do is put him in jail."

"Our last marshal said the same thing. What makes you think Hammer won't kill you too?"

Tilghman smiled. "Lots of folks have tried to kill me."

"So I've heard," Mosley said. "You've got guts, Marshal. I'll give you that."

"Give me some of your time. Attend the meeting."

"Hell, why not? I'm willing to listen."

When they drove off, Mosley walked back to the rig. As he mounted the ladder, he recalled hearing that Tilghman was pushing seventy. He wondered why a gray-haired gunman of the old school would take on a pack of gangsters.

Cromwell seemed to him the wrong place to pick a fight. The wrong place and the wrong time.

CHAPTER 12

Early the next morning Tilghman and Sawyer met for breakfast. They took a table by the window of a cafe upstreet from the jail. Their night hadn't ended until two in the morning, and the deputy could have used another hour's sleep. Tilghman looked as though he'd just stepped from a cold shower.

Sawyer was amazed by the older man's energy. The workday of a peace officer apparently began around seven and ended at night when the last drunk had gone home. He was no less impressed with the marshal's appetite, which would have done justice to a roustabout. Tilghman ordered buckwheat cakes, eggs sunny-side-up, and crisp bacon. He took his coffee black.

When the waitress brought their orders, Tilghman noticed the younger man glance at the load on his platter. Sawyer, who seemed more interested in a wake-up coffee, had just ordered bacon and eggs with toast. Tilghman poured sorghum on his buckwheat cakes.

"Got to stoke your engine," he said. "A law officer never knows when he'll get his next meal. Might be at noon and might not be till midnight."

Sawyer chewed thoughtfully a moment. "What's wrong with taking time out to eat?"

"Let's suppose some jaybird robbed the bank. You're

hot on his tail and gainin' ground fast. You gonna stop when the noon whistle blows?''

"You're saying we don't keep regular hours."

"I'm saying we're not like regular folks. There's no quittin' time for a man who wears a badge. He's on duty round the clock."

Sawyer understood that it was not idle conversation. He was being treated to a quick education in law enforcement. Last night, during a routine patrol of the town, Tilghman had explained that there were three types of drunks. A happy drunk could be coaxed into calling it a night. A reasonable drunk could be talked into heading for home. But a fighting drunk left an officer no choice. The response had to be swift, and certain.

Around one in the morning the lesson had been borne out. Two roustabouts, ossified on liquor, had caused a disturbance in Ma Murphy's dance hall. When Tilghman and Sawyer were summoned, the roustabouts turned ugly and put up a fight. Tilghman whacked one over the head with his Colt, and Sawyer decked the other one, skinning his knuckles in the process. The men were now sleeping it off in the drunk tank.

Sawyer was no slouch in a brawl. But he'd been astounded by Tilghman's economy of motion, his reflexes and speed. The Colt had appeared in his hand even as he was dodging a punch, and he'd laid out the roustabout with one blow. Tilghman referred to the technique by the old frontier term, "buffaloing a man." Later, thinking about it, Sawyer was all the more impressed that a man seventy years old was not only tough, but fast. He wasn't sure he would want to tangle with the marshal.

Tilghman paused with his fork in midair, staring out the window. Down the street a man jumped from a battered truck and ran into the jail. A moment later he hurried outside, looking up and down the street in an agitated manner. Tilghman pushed back his chair.

"Told you to catch a meal when you could. I should've told you to eat fast. We've got business."

Sawyer followed him out the door. Downstreet, as they approached the office, the man spotted them and rushed forward. His eyes were wild. "Gave me a scare, Marshal," he babbled. "Thought you'd gone off somewheres."

"You've found me," Tilghman said. "What's the problem?"

"Work for Larry Heckert. He sent me to fetch you. We've got a dead man out there."

"Out where?"

"West end of the field," Sawyer told him. "Heckert owns three wells where the field peters out."

"Never seen nothin' like it," the man ranted. "You gotta come quick."

"Slow down," Tilghman said. "Who's the dead man?"

"You got me, Marshal. I was just sent to find you."

"All right, let's have a look. We'll follow you in my car."

The truck led them west out of town.

Larry Heckert was short and heavyset, with florid features. He stood with Tilghman and Sawyer and a small crowd of roughnecks at the edge of a slush pit. The body floated on the oily surface.

"Damnedest thing," Heckert said in a low voice. "Bobbed up like a cork first thing this morning. Scared the shit outta some of the boys."

"Bobbed up?" Tilghman repeated. "You mean he was below the surface? Down in that sludge?"

"Hell, he must've been. He just popped outta there like he'd been spit up."

"What's the best way to fish him out?"

"Already thought of that. Just waited for you to get here."

Heckert began issuing orders. The roughnecks had

rigged two cable hooks on long lengths of rope. They cast the hooks out into the pit, one securing a leg and the other curled under the dead man's chest. Several roughnecks grabbed each of the ropes and began hauling in unison. The sludge fought them, reluctantly surrendering its prize, and they slowly muscled the body across the surface. A final heave brought the dead man to firm ground.

The bloated corpse was coated with thick, black sludge. Tilghman knelt down, pulling a handkerchief from his hip pocket. A shiny speck on the dead man's chest caught his eye, and he swabbed away oily muck to reveal a badge. Engraved on the metal were the words CROMWELL TOWN MARSHAL. He exchanged a look with Sawyer.

Then, unfolding the handkerchief, he placed it over the dead man's face and wiped off a slick plaster of sludge. As the features were revealed, there was a collective intake of breath from the men gathered around. He studied the face.

"How about it?" he said. "Anybody know this man?"

"Will Bohannon," Heckert muttered. "Sonsabitches killed him after all."

After a week in the slush pit, a putrid odor emanated off the body. Tilghman was about to rise when he noticed a depression in the dead man's forehead. He leaned closer, holding his breath, and dabbed oily grime off the spot. A quick inspection satisfied him that he was looking at a bullet hole. Will Bohannon had been executed.

Tilghman questioned Heckert and the roughnecks at some length. He learned that the wells were guarded at night by a watchman who spent most of his time in the tool shack. Whether Bohannon had been shot here or elsewhere seemed a moot point. The killers had dumped his body in the slush pit, probably late at night, thinking he would never be found. But nature, after bloating the body with gas, had spoiled a perfect murder. A corpse had popped to the surface.

Sawyer was left to guard the scene. After returning to town, Tilghman arranged for an undertaker to collect the body. Then, from his office he made a series of calls. The first was to Judge Crump, who volunteered to notify the governor. The second was to the sheriff, who reacted with patently bogus shock, and promised an immediate investigation. The last call was to Zoe.

"Thought I'd better call," he said, after explaining the situation. "Didn't want you to hear it on the radio."

"My God," she said in a tremulous tone. "Those people are savages."

"Helluva way to go out. No question of that."

"I wish with all my heart you'd never gone there."

"Don't worry yourself about it. I've got a deputy to watch my back."

"Just make very sure he knows to shoot first and ask questions later."

Tilghman started to laugh but then changed his mind. He told himself she might have a point.

Shortly after dark seven men straggled into the church. Virgil Pryor, the preacher, was seated in a front pew talking with Tilghman and Sawyer. They were disappointed but hardly surprised by the small turnout for the town meeting. A pervasive sense of fear had spread throughout Cromwell with word of Will Bohannon's murder.

Walter Sirmans and the three Citizens Committee members were the first to arrive. Zack Mosley wandered in next, followed by Dr. John Leonard, one of the town's three physicians. The last man was Frank Killian, a lease hound who speculated in oil rights on unexplored land. He was known to everyone in Cromwell, even though he lived in Wewoka. Sirmans introduced him to Tilghman.

Pryor welcomed the small group to his church. Then,

after turning the floor over to Tilghman, he returned to his seat. Tilghman walked to the center aisle, his expression somber. He turned to face the men.

"Looks like the news of Bohannon's death scared most folks off. That's too bad, because I wanted to talk about some town ordinances. How to make Cromwell a safer place."

The men listened as he went on to explain. Starting tomorrow, he told them, he would begin enforcing an ordinance that barred everyone except peace officers from carrying a gun within the town limits. Violators would be arrested and charged under the state law prohibiting concealed weapons. Notices would be posted around town by tomorrow night.

Sirmans raised his hand. "Does that apply to Jake Hammer and his hooligans?"

"Any man I catch with a gun will go to jail. No exceptions."

Tilghman moved on to another subject. He noted that fire was a particular hazard in an oil town, surrounded by an oil field. Starting tomorrow, he informed them, every business establishment would be required to have a water barrel outside the premises. Anyone who failed to comply would be fined one hundred dollars a day until the barrel was in place. And again, no exceptions.

"What the town really needs is a fire truck." He looked at Zack Mosley. "You're the biggest well owner in Cromwell. Any chance you'd donate a truck? We could refit it to handle fire."

Mosley got to his feet. "All this talk about guns and fire trucks is whitewash. Your job is to run Hammer and his crowd out of town. Why else were you hired?"

Tilghman fixed him with a look. "I'll tend to that in my own good time."

"Marshal, you won't last that long. Bohannon sure as hell didn't."

Mosley clamped his hat on his head and walked out the door. There was a moment of turgid silence as the men exchanged startled looks. Then the lease hound, Frank Killian, raised his hand. He was stoutly built, with wavy black hair, attired in a tweed suit. He smiled pleasantly at Tilghman.

"I applaud your efforts, Marshal. Perhaps we could start a fund drive for the fire truck. I'll kick it off with fifty dollars."

"Good idea," Tilghman said. "I appreciate your support. Might just work."

Virgil Pryor suddenly spoke out. "We all have to support Marshal Tilghman! On Sunday I will preach that very message in no uncertain terms. And I'll tell them of your generosity too, Mr. Killian."

"Thank you, Reverend," Killian said modestly. "I'm just trying to do my part. We've all got a stake in Cromwell."

The meeting ended on that note. Tilghman thought the fund drive might spark some civic spirit in the townspeople. But he was all too aware that he'd lost the opportunity to rally broader support. Zack Mosley's remarks were dead on the money.

His job—the only reason he'd been hired—was to rid the town of mobsters.

Late that night Tilghman and Sawyer were patrolling Shawnee Avenue. The crowds were thinning out, and many establishments were preparing to close. Toward the west end of town, the street was all but deserted.

Up ahead, through the window of a cafe, they saw a man with a pistol at the counter. The pistol was pointed at Jack Otis, the owner, who was behind the cash register, forking over money. The robber appeared jittery, waving the pistol and shuffling his feet in a nervous dance. Otis looked terrified.

Tilghman signaled Sawyer to take a position outside the window. Once Sawyer was in place, he drew his Colt, and gently eased open the door. He thumbed the hammer, the metallic whirr echoing like a death knell. His voice was sharp, cold.

"Drop the gun or I'll kill you. Right now!"

The robber hesitated an instant. Then, tossing the gun on the floor, he raised his hands. Tilghman moved inside, followed closely by Sawyer. He noted that the cafe was empty, and saw the short-order cook cowering at the end of the counter. Jack Otis, his features leeched of color, let out his breath.

"Godalmighty," he said hollowly. "Thought for sure I was dead."

Tilghman spun the robber around. A short, wiry man, his eyes were dull, somehow lifeless. His hands trembled, and he seemed unable to stand still. Sawyer grunted a harsh laugh.

"You've sunk pretty low, Snake. When'd you turn to holdups?"

"You know him?" Tilghman asked.

"His name's Emmett Proctor. Used to be a roustabout, till he got on dope and turned hophead. Everybody calls him Snake because he's a slimy little bastard."

Tilghman made a snap judgment. He motioned to the door, waiting until Sawyer hustled the man outside. After scooping up the robber's gun, he looked at the cafe owner. "We'll take it from here, Mr. Otis. You go on about your business."

"Whatever you say, Marshal. Thank my lucky stars you came along."

Ten minutes later Tilghman led the way into the jail. He placed the confiscated pistol in a drawer and seated himself on the edge of the desk. As Sawyer dumped their prisoner into a chair, he leaned forward, towering over the man. His expression was stony. "You're in a world of trouble, Snake. I'd say you're looking at twenty years on the rock pile."

Proctor hugged himself, tried to still the trembling. "I wouldn't've shot him. Just needed to score, that's all."

"On cocaine, are you?"

"What if I am?"

"No skin off my back," Tilghman said. "But I'll give you a choice, Snake. You can go to prison—"

"Done been there," Proctor chimed in hurriedly. "Don't wanna go back."

"Or you can turn songbird."

"And get myself killed? Forget it."

"Your choice," Tilghman said easily. " 'Course, keep in mind, there's no dope in the state pen. Lonely nights and the cold sweats . . . for twenty years."

Proctor clasped himself tighter. His features were etched with hopelessness and fear. "What've I gotta do?"

"Don't rob anybody else, and don't try to run. Just come talk to me now and then. Tell me what's what in the dope trade."

"Like who's sellin' it, you mean?"

"That would do for starters."

"And who'd know about this? I ain't lookin' to get my throat cut."

"Just the three of us," Tilghman said. "You have my word it goes no further than this room."

Proctor closed his eyes tightly, shook his head. Finally, with a deep shudder, he looked up. "I guess you got me. I'll play along."

"Let's understand one another, Snake. Snort all the snowdust you want, but don't welch on our deal. You try it, and I'll send you to prison."

"Doing time ain't for me. I'll live up to my end."

Sawyer showed him to the door. When it closed, he turned back to Tilghman. "I don't get it. You had him on armed robbery."

"All part of law enforcement," Tilghman said. "Set a weasel to catch a lion. A tradeoff of sorts."

"Little fish for a big fish, that the idea?"

"That's the idea, Hugh. The kingfish himself."

CHAPTER 13

By the next evening Tilghman decided to take action. Four days had been spent in getting the lay of the land, determining the key players in Cromwell. It was time to put the underworld crowd on notice.

The town itself had already been put on notice. That morning, after prevailing on a local printer, he'd had a batch of handbills run off. By late afternoon he and Sawyer had tacked handbills on the walls of buildings across town. The new ordinances, which mandated water barrels and banned the concealed carry of firearms, were there for everyone to read. He saw it as an opening salvo.

After supper that evening Tilghman laid out the battle plan. Seated in the office, he explained to Sawyer that they would raid three ginmills. The dives he'd selected were located on Shawnee Avenue, where the largest crowds congregated every night. He wanted to draw attention with the raids, alert everyone in town that it was no longer business as usual. Anybody who operated a honky-tonk was now at risk.

"That'll damn sure get their attention," Sawyer agreed. "You aim to make arrests, or do we just bust up the joints?"

"We'll make arrests," Tilghman said flatly. "I intend

to get the message across. Violate the law and you go to jail.''

"Some of them are liable to put up a fight. How do we handle that?''

"I've always operated on a simple rule. A man who resists gets answered in kind. Doesn't matter whether it's guns or fists.''

"Fists don't bother me,'' Sawyer said. "What's your rule on guns?''

"There's a trick to that,'' Tilghman replied. "Get the drop on a man and he'll usually come along peaceable. But some won't, and that leaves you no choice. You get him first.''

"Kill him, that's what you're saying?''

"Any man worth shooting is worth killing. Let's hope it doesn't come to that. I prefer to take them alive.''

Sawyer wondered how many men the old marshal had killed. One thought triggered another, and his expression turned quizzical. "How come we're not raiding the Sportsmen's Club? We could arrest Jake Hammer.''

"Couple of reasons,'' Tilghman said. "I want Hammer on charges of murder and running dope. One gets him state prison time. The other puts him in the electric chair.''

"Selling dope's a state offense?''

"On the books for years. Carries a minimum sentence of one year. We arrest him for gambling or liquor, and he'll likely get off with a stiff fine. That's not good enough.''

Sawyer nodded. "You said there were a couple of reasons.''

"Other one sort of baits a trap,'' Tilghman observed. "These raids will cut into his rumrunning business. I suspect that's what got Will Bohannon killed.''

"Goddamn!'' Sawyer muttered. "You're trying to bait him into coming after you?''

Tilghman smiled. "A man gets devious in his old age.''

A sudden revelation rolled over Sawyer. He told himself Bill Tilghman was more certain than the electric chair. No court trial, no judge and jury. A simple matter of justice. One man's justice.

Not quite an hour later they raided the Paradise Grill. A speakeasy in disguise, with a menu limited to sandwiches, the dive served whiskey at the bar and hostesses to entertain customers at their tables. The owner was Johnny Fallon, a man known for his ready smile and an incendiary temper. He rushed forward, trailed by the house bouncer, as Tilghman and Sawyer stormed through the door with guns drawn. His face was mottled with rage.

"Who the hell you think you are? Get outta here before I bust your chops!"

"You're under arrest," Tilghman said levelly. "Don't give me any trouble."

"You've come to the right place, granpaw. Trouble's my middle name."

Fallon started forward, his fists cocked. Tilghman thumbed the hammer on the Colt and centered a shot directly between the owner's feet. Girls screamed and men dove for cover at the roar of the pistol. Arm extended, gun leveled, Sawyer covered the bouncer. Fallon stopped, staring at the bullet hole in the floor. He was astounded.

"You don't shoot nobody over sellin' hooch. Are you nuts?"

"Crazy as a loon," Tilghman said without humor. "You still want to make trouble?"

"No, not me," Fallon said, spreading his hands. "I'll be out of the clink before you know it anyhow. Go ahead and arrest me."

Tilghman motioned to the crowd with his pistol. "I want everybody out of here in one minute. This place is closed. Let's go!"

The roustabouts and roughnecks made a rush for the door. The hostesses, eyes wide with fright, followed them out. Fallon, along with the bouncer and two bartenders, was prodded along at gunpoint. On the street everything came to a standstill, men pointing and staring, as Tilghman marched his prisoners toward the jail. Sawyer hurried behind after he'd slapped a padlock on the door.

By midnight the three raids were completed. In all, including the ginmill owners, eleven men had been arrested. Every dive in town was on a state of alert, waiting for the lawmen to crash through the door. There was talk of nothing else, and men deserted whorehouses and dance halls to watch the action. A throng of spectators lined the street as the last of the prisoners were marched off to jail.

Zack Mosley, with Josie Rodgers at his side, watched from the window of her room on the upper floor of the Sportsmen's Club. On the street below they saw Tilghman and Sawyer herd the owner of the Tivoli Gardens and two employees into the jailhouse. Neither of them spoke for a long moment, looking on in silence. At length, Mosley grunted under his breath.

"That old man's rough as a cob. But he's gonna get himself killed."

"I know," she said softly. "Jake's about to have kittens, he's so mad. I heard him shouting at Milligan and the boys in his office."

Mosley looked concerned. "You think they'll try anything tonight?"

"Honeybun, you know the answer to that. Tonight or tomorrow night, what's the difference. They'll try."

"I wish to Christ you were out of this life. But I guess that's same song, second verse. You've heard it before."

She made no comment. Their first night together, almost two months ago, she sensed Mosley had fallen for her. Since then, with increasing regularity, he paid the tab to have her to himself for the entire night. On several occasions he had proposed marriage, promising her a better life, a fine home, and all the trappings. Though she was fond of him, even tempted by images of a better life, she still thought with a whore's heart. Lonely men often made promises to girls in the trade, mistaking the rutting instinct for love. She wasn't yet sure that what he felt was the real thing.

Nor was she sure she wanted to quit the trade. She had little formal education, but she possessed an uncanny gift for seeing things as they were. She had been reared in hunger and deprivation, in a home of such poverty that a decent meal was more treasured than affection. Later, in a series of oil towns, she had experienced life at its rawest, endured nearly all the evil an evil world could inflict. Yet she had emerged not so much a cynic as a seeker.

She knew men found her attractive, even desirable. Her jet-dark hair and violet eyes, fine features and a voluptuous figure, set her apart from other girls. Yet, like all whores, she was philosophical about such things, hardened to the difference between lust and love. In a way that was elemental, she wanted a man who wanted more than a playmate. She wasn't convinced that Mosley saw her as a woman, rather than a good-time girl, and the fact that he was wealthy hardly mattered. There were worse things than hunger, and she wasn't willing to surrender her independence until she was sure it would last. She thought she might wait a while longer.

"You like Tilghman, don't you?" she asked after a prolonged silence. "I can tell by the way you talk about him."

Mosley shrugged. "Hard not to like a man who believes right's right, and to hell with in between. He's got more brass than a billy goat."

"If you feel that way, why don't you help him? You could swing all the big rig-owners onto his side of the fence."

"I might just do that, if he lives long enough. What's with all the sudden interest? I thought you never took sides."

"I'm always a soft touch for a lost cause."

"No need to look any further, then. I'm your lost cause."

"Yes," she said in a hushed voice. "Maybe you are."

Mosley took her in his arms. She slipped into his embrace, stroking the back of his neck, and kissed him on the mouth. With other men there was nothing, but with him there was always a tingle along her spine. A fire she'd never felt before.

She let herself hope he was the one.

Early the next morning Tilghman arranged breakfast for the prisoners. A nearby cafe brought in coffee, donuts, and fried-egg sandwiches. The men were bedraggled and grouchy from their overnight stay in the holding cage. They ate in sullen silence.

After the meal Sawyer escorted them one at a time to the toilet. The washroom was along the north wall, a closetlike affair with a sink and commode. There were no windows, no way out except the door, and thus no chance of escape. The men were each allowed five minutes before Sawyer took them back to the lockup.

Tilghman was seated at the desk, talking on the telephone. When he finished, Johnny Fallon moved to the front of the cage. Like the other men, his clothes were rumpled and his jawline bristled with a day-old stubble. He glowered through the bars.

"What's the deal?" he demanded. "How long you going to keep us locked in this pig pen?"

"Not long," Tilghman told him. "I just talked with the sheriff. We're transferring you to the county jail."

"Well, let's get it done, for chrissakes. The sooner we get there, the sooner we'll get out."

"What makes you think you'll get out?"

Fallon laughed. "Stick around and watch. You'll see."

The street door swung open. A tall, swarthy man in his early thirties stepped into the office. He was attired in a chalky pinstriped suit and a dove-gray fedora. His features creased in a genial smile.

"You must be Marshal Tilghman," he said, extending his hand. "I'm Wiley Lynn, federal Prohibition agent for the district."

Tilghman shook his hand. "What can I do for you, Mr. Lynn?"

"Everybody calls me Wiley," Lynn said good-naturedly. "I heard you made some arrests. Thought I'd drop by."

"We closed down three ginmills," Tilghman remarked. "Looks like we're doing your job, Mr. Lynn. You ought to come around more often."

"Cromwell's a rough town, Marshal. Try to cut off the hooch entirely and we'd have a riot on our hands. I take the slow-but-sure approach."

"Doesn't appear to be working too well. Just about every joint in town sells liquor."

"No argument there. But Prohibition's an unpopular law. You have to use common sense. Try to reason with folks."

"Common sense and reason only go so far. A law still has to be enforced."

Fred Wagner, the hardware store owner, walked through the door. He was carrying an armload of logging chain some thirty feet in length. He dumped it on the floor, grinning at Tilghman, and turned to leave. Tilghman nodded to Lynn.

"I've got prisoners to transport. You can file federal charges on them at the courthouse."

Sawyer brought the men from the cage one by one. A howl of protest went up as Sawyer clasped handcuffs on one wrist and locked the other end through a link in the logging chain. Within minutes, all eleven men were secured to the chain, separated by intervals of a few feet. Tilghman led them through the door.

Outside, the men were halted in single file. Lynn

glanced around with a puzzled expression. "Where's your truck, Marshal?"

"Don't have one," Tilghman said. "We're traveling by shank's mare."

"You're going to make them walk to Wewoka? That's fifteen miles away!"

"Nothing like an object lesson, Mr. Lynn. Makes folks sit up and take notice."

"Come on now, that has all the earmarks of a chain gang."

"Yeah, I reckon it does. Guess that's the message."

Across the way, Jake Hammer and several of his men appeared in the door of the Sportsmen's Club. All along the street people spilled out of shops and stores to watch the spectacle. At a bawdy house upstreet, girls in negligees, laughing and pointing, crowded the windows. Hammer stared on with a look of suppressed rage.

"Let's move out," Tilghman ordered. "Keep a steady pace and we'll have you in jail by sundown."

Johnny Fallon glared at him. "You goddamn old shitheel. You're gonna pay for this!"

"Save your breath, Fallon. You'll need it before the day's over."

Sawyer got them moving. Tilghman turned, looking across the street, and locked eyes with Hammer. He held the mobster's gaze a moment, then nodded with a hard smile. Satisfied the message had been delivered, he walked to his car. The engine kicked over with an explosive cough.

Out the window he saw Wiley Lynn leaning against the fender of a Studebaker open roadster. The car was sleek and glossy, with a black leather interior and a collapsible top. He wondered how a Prohibition agent could afford one of the more expensive automobiles on the road. The federal government paid its agents meager wages, and Lynn looked unusually prosperous. He put the thought in the back of his mind.

The chained prisoners trudged through the center of

town. Tilghman hooked the Ford in low gear and followed at a sedate pace. On the boardwalks, people watched the odd parade with looks of disbelief and open amusement. Sawyer herded the men east along Shawnee Avenue, to connect with the road to Wewoka. Then he moved alongside the car and climbed into the passenger seat.

Ma Murphy, her hair in curlers, stood in the doorway of her dance hall. She patted her hands in silent applause.

Tilghman tipped his hat.

CHAPTER 14

On Saturday morning Tilghman came into the office about eight o'clock. Sawyer was already there, filling the coffeepot from the tap in the washroom. As he walked back toward the stove, one look told the tale. He saw anger in the older man's eyes.

"Something wrong, Marshal?"

Tilghman pegged his mackinaw on a wall rack. "I had breakfast in that cafe next to the hotel. Good food, nice strong coffee."

"Yeah, we've eaten there before."

"Just about finished my wheatcakes, and I happened to look out the window. Guess what I saw across the street?"

"I've already seen it," Sawyer admitted. "They took the padlock off Fallon's joint."

"Helluva note," Tilghman said, seating himself behind the desk. "You arrest a man one day and two days later he's back in business. Takes the cake."

"Well, you can't say it's a surprise. Not when he got off in court."

"Didn't say it's a surprise, Hugh. I said it's a helluva note."

"We've got Wiley Lynn to thank for that."

Yesterday, in district court, they had appeared for the arraignment hearing. Two of the ginmill owners arrested the night before had been bound over for trial on federal charges. But Wiley Lynn, silent throughout the first two hearings, had interceded on behalf of Fallon. He informed the court that the government would not press charges.

Questioned by Judge Crump, Lynn cited lack of evidence. A personal inspection of Fallon's establishment, he stated, had uncovered no sign of alcoholic spirits. When Tilghman objected, Lynn invited him to have another look at the Paradise Grill. Tilghman knew then that it would be a waste of time, wasted effort. The liquor, probably carted out the back door, had long since disappeared.

"Fallon told us as much," Sawyer said. "Just flat-out boasted he'd get off. You remember?"

Tilghman nodded. "I figured it was all brag. Lots of wind and no whistle."

"You think he bribed Lynn?"

"I think Lynn's a spiffy dresser and drives a car most folks can't afford. Lives high for a Prohibition agent."

"How do we put him in bed with Fallon?"

"I'm thinking on it, Hugh. Thinking hard."

Sawyer went off on his morning rounds. Tilghman leaned back in his chair, hands locked behind his head, and stared at the ceiling. There seemed little to be gained in raiding the Paradise Grill and again arresting Johnny Fallon. The result would very likely be the same, with Fallon thumbing his nose at the law. Which left the other half of the equation.

Upon reflection, Tilghman realized that he knew virtually nothing about Wiley Lynn. The man seemed a typical bureaucrat, willing to go along to get along, and not place himself in harm's way. But there might be more beneath the personable front and genial manner than met the eye. Perhaps the federal agent was deeper than he looked, an actor of parts. A fox in the henhouse.

From the desk drawer, Tilghman pulled out paper and pen. He scribbled a salutation to the governor, and went on to review events of the past few days. In closing, he requested an investigation by the state police into the background and activities of Wiley Lynn. He asked that the investigation be conducted in secrecy, and with all possible speed. Finished, he addressed an envelope and marked it CONFIDENTIAL. He walked out the door.

Uptown, Tilghman entered the post office. He bought a stamp at the counter, pasted it on, and shoved the envelope across. The clerk noted the addressee, Governor Martin Trapp, and gave him a curious look. As he turned from the counter, he saw a woman standing before the bank of postal boxes at the end of the room. Her dress and plain woolen coat were considerably more demure than her outfit that day outside the Sportsmen's Club. He recalled that her name was Josie Rodgers.

She was struggling to unlock a postal box. Her left arm was loaded with packages, which were precariously balanced. A pocketbook dangled from her right arm, and she was trying to insert the key in the lock. One of the packages slipped, dropping to the floor, and Tilghman moved to her side. He retrieved the package from the floor.

"Let me help you, Miss Rodgers," he said. "Looks like you've got more than you can handle."

She turned, startled by his voice. "Oh, Marshal Tilghman." Another package began to slip as she juggled the load. "Well, if you don't mind . . ."

Tilghman took the packages from her arm. "Saturday your big shopping day?"

"No, not really. I'm making new curtains for my room and . . . I guess I got carried away."

"Yeah, that's easy to do. I tell my wife she ought to take along a pony. She could load one down when she gets to shopping."

"You're married?" Josie removed a single letter from the box. "I never think of police officers being married men. That's funny, isn't it?"

"The badge does it," Tilghman said with a wry smile.

"Always surprises folks that a lawman has a private life. They just see the badge."

"I never thought of it that way." She stuck the letter in her pocketbook. "Here, let me have those packages now, Marshal. Thank you for coming to my rescue."

"We're headed in the same direction. I'll carry them along for you."

"Well . . . all right—if you're sure you don't mind."

"No bother at all."

On the street they turned toward the intersection. Her closeness made Tilghman aware that she exuded a sensuality as palpable as musk. She had a way of speaking as if she were out of breath, husky and warm, somehow intimate. Over the years he had known many prostitutes, arrested more than he could remember. Yet he detected none of the whore's seductive artifice in her manner. She seemed genuine, attractive but curiously vulnerable. A woman caught in the wrong trade.

"I just thought of it," she said suddenly. "How did you know my name?"

"Asked around," Tilghman said. "First day I was in town, you saved a roustabout from gettin' stomped by Hammer's boys. I admire a woman with grit."

"Those goons make me sick! I laughed myself silly when you conked Milligan. Talk about poetic justice!"

Tilghman took a chance. "Lots of folks think Milligan—on Hammer's orders, of course—killed Marshal Bohannon. You ever hear anything about that?"

"No." She darted a glance at him, silent as they turned the corner. "I try not to hear things like that. A girl could get herself hurt . . . or worse."

"Well, if you get the notion, don't be afraid to let me know. I'd keep it strictly between us."

"Are you talking about Bohannon?"

"Anything you might want to tell me. Nobody would be the wiser."

She was quiet for a few steps. "There is one thing," she said, lowering her voice. "Some houses in town have underage girls. And I mean *girls* . . . fifteen, sixteen years old.''

''Turns your stomach,'' Tilghman grunted, sensing she was equally offended. ''Nothing worse than a white slaver.''

''I'd like to see them taken out and shot. What they do to those little girls—it's just terrible!''

''What places are we talking about?''

A guarded look touched her eyes. ''Too many people are watching a whore and the marshal walking along right now. If I tell you, somebody will put two and two together.'' She seemed to shrink from the thought. ''You'll have to find the houses for yourself.''

Tilghman decided not to press the issue. He wanted an informant inside Hammer's club, and he was wary of scaring her off. ''I'll nose around, see what I turn up. Meanwhile, I thank you for the tip.''

''Just don't tell anybody where it came from. I wouldn't last the night.''

''Like I said, my lips are sealed.''

Ahead, they saw Jake Hammer emerge from the Sportsmen's Club. He halted on the boardwalk, smoking a long, black cigar, idly scanning the street As they approached, he looked around, clearly taken aback by the sight of them together. His features set in a scowl.

''What the hell's this?'' he demanded, staring at Josie. ''You playing footsie with the law?''

''Don't jump on her,'' Tilghman said bluntly. ''I offered to carry her packages, that's all. We were headed the same way.''

''Get inside,'' Hammer told her. ''You and me, we'll have a little talk later.''

She took the packages, glancing quickly at Tilghman, then hurried through the door. Hammer wedged the cigar into the corner of his mouth, puffing furious wads of smoke. His eyes were malevolent.

''You think I'm not on to your tricks, Tilghman? Stay the hell away from my people.''

"Jake, it's not your people I want. I'm after you."

"So what's stopping you, Mr. Hotshot Marshal?"

"Just a matter of time, Jake. You can bank on it."

Tilghman left the goad hanging in the air. He turned, aware that if looks could kill, he would be dead before he crossed the street. He walked toward his office.

Saturday night was the night everyone came to town. The roughnecks and roustabouts, with a week's wages in their pockets, were ready to howl. Fast women, hard liquor, and a fling at the gaming tables acted like a magnet on metal shavings. By dark, the boardwalks of Cromwell were a circus in motion.

Late that evening Tilghman initiated the next phase of his plan. With Sawyer at his side, he strolled uptown as though out on his normal rounds. Here and there, they stopped to look in a dance hall, or casually inspect a speakeasy. But there was nothing threatening in their manner, and no one suspected anything out of the ordinary. They appeared to be on a routine patrol of the streets.

Tilghman planned to raid a gambling dive. He had purposely waited until Saturday night, when action was heaviest at the tables. Halfway down the west end of Shawnee Avenue, he and Sawyer sauntered into what seemed just another gin mill. Before the bouncer or the barmen could react, they moved to the rear of the room and pushed aside a drapery covering a hidden doorway. The click of poker chips and dice, and the rattle of a ball in a roulette wheel, filled the back room. A crowd of a hundred or more men stood ganged around the tables.

"Everybody hold it!" Tilghman shouted. "You're under arrest!"

The room went deadly still. Saul Werner, the owner, moved away from one of the dice tables. He was solidly built, with wideset muddy eyes and angular features. He hurried forward, halting in front of Tilghman. His voice was raspy, rough and curt.

"I'm running a legitimate operation here. Not a crooked table—"

"Save it for the judge," Tilghman interrupted. "I'm arresting you and your men, Werner. We're confiscating all the money on the tables as evidence."

"You dumb son of a bitch!"

Werner took a step forward, his fist cocked. Tilghman pulled the old Colt, slipping the punch, and cracked him over the head. The gambler staggered, blood spurting from his scalp, and collapsed like an accordion slowly squeezed into sections. He slumped to the floor.

The bouncer lumbered through the door. He was broad and muscular, with the pug nose and wrinkled ears of a former prizefighter. A low, ferocious sound rumbled in his throat, and his eyes were fixed directly on Tilghman. He carried a shot-loaded blackjack in his right hand.

Sawyer stuck out his foot. The bouncer was so intent on Tilghman that he was blinded to all else. He tripped over the deputy's foot and went down heavily on his hands and knees. Sawyer jabbed a pistol muzzle into the back of his neck.

"You lookin' for a fight, toughnuts?"

"Uh—" The bouncer weighed the options, then shook his head. "Not no more."

"On your belly," Sawyer ordered. "Don't move."

Tilghman cleared the room of customers. After reviving Werner, he motioned the bouncer and seven housemen into a line. Sawyer found a satchel in Werner's office and scooped all the money off the tables. As he rejoined Tilghman, who was covering the prisoners, he grinned. He hefted the satchel.

"Got to be at least ten thousand in here. Maybe more."

"Good job," Tilghman said, nodding at the bouncer. "You made short work of that gorilla."

"Take'em alive, wasn't that what you said, Marshal?"

"I believe I did. Let's get these boys locked up."

The gamblers were paraded through the center of town. On Jenkins Street, oil men lining the boardwalks hooted and jeered, shouting catcalls at the prisoners. From the Sportsmen's Club, Hammer watched as Tilghman and Sawyer escorted the men into the jailhouse. His face congealed into a look of brute fury.

A few moments later, in his office, Hammer jiggled the hook on the telephone. "Operator? Get me 2836, in Wewoka."

After three rings, a man answered. "Hello."

"Yeah, it's me. Things are gettin' out of hand over here. That old turd just raided Werner's joint."

"How many were arrested?"

"I counted nine, including Werner. Looked like he'd been worked over."

"Tilghman's a busy bee."

Hammer snorted. "Four raids in four fuckin' days! He's worse than Bohannon ever was."

"Yes." There was a long pause. "Let me give it some thought."

"The bastard braced me today. Told me I'm the one he's really after. I say we get rid of him."

"Not yet."

"Why wait any longer? Things are just gonna get worse."

"I'll tell you when, Jake."

The line went dead. Hammer slammed the receiver on the hook. He sat staring at the phone with an ugly grimace. Orders were orders, and like it or lump it, he had to go along. But he made himself a solemn promise.

Bill Tilghman was a walking dead man.

CHAPTER 15

The prisoners were held in the Cromwell lockup over the weekend. On Monday morning Tilghman made arrangements for them to be transported by truck to the county jail. Sawyer went along to formally press charges.

Tilghman was under no illusions. Gambling was a state offense that carried a fine of one hundred dollars and a maximum sentence of thirty days in jail. But the county judge, like the sheriff and other officials, was reportedly on the mob's payroll. Saul Werner and his men would almost certainly receive a fine and no jail time. They would likely be back in business by sundown.

The point was nonetheless clear. Vice would no longer be tolerated in Cromwell, and anyone involved in the rackets was subject to arrest. Liquor and dope were at the top of Tilghman's list, with gambling and prostitution close behind. He was probing for a weak link in the underground structure, looking for an informant into Hammer's organization. His plan was to keep everyone guessing where he would strike next.

Somewhere along the way he thought Hammer would strike back. He was prepared for an attempt on his life and intended to reverse the tables. Turk Milligan, or one of Hammer's thugs, charged with attempted murder, might be persuaded to turn state's evidence. Hammer, in turn, might then be convinced to reveal who gave the orders in Seminole County. For Tilghman remained confident that an overlord operated from the background.

After the prisoners were loaded into the truck, he took Sawyer aside. "I'm going to Chandler," he said. "Almost a week since I've seen my wife, and she tends to worry. I'll be back late tonight."

"I'll look after things," Sawyer assured him. "Ought to be pretty quiet tonight, anyway."

A boomtown was generally slow on Monday nights. The roughnecks and roustabouts, after a weekend of carousing, were usually broke and nursing hangovers. There was small likelihood of problems, and Tilghman felt safe in taking the day off. He gave Sawyer a warning look.

"Just keep this to yourself," he said. "I don't want anybody to know I'm gone."

"You think Hammer might try something?"

"You're a target, the same as me. I want to find you in one piece when I get back."

Sawyer grinned. "That bunch doesn't bother me. I can look after myself."

"Cocky could get you killed," Tilghman admonished. "When you make your rounds tonight, watch your backsides. Don't get careless."

"I'll keep a sharp lookout."

"I trust you will, Hugh."

The truck, borrowed from the lumber yard, drove off with Sawyer in the passenger seat. Werner and his men, handcuffed to a logging chain, were huddled on the open bed of the truck. The prisoners were soiled and unshaven after two nights in jail, and looked more like bums than boomtown gamblers. Shopkeepers and passersby paused to watch their unceremonious exit from Cromwell.

Tilghman noted that no one was watching from the Sportsmen's Club. He wondered if Hammer was still asleep or merely unwilling to witness yet another set-

back for the vice crowd. Either way, he told himself as
he crawled into the old Ford, the raids brought pressure
to bear on Hammer. Whoever gave the orders in Seminole County was certain to apply even more pressure.
Which was all part of his plan.

He drove west out of town.

Zoe bustled around the kitchen. She was busy preparing
one of his favorite meals. A pot roast was in the oven,
and apple cobbler was warming on the back of the stove.
A glance at the clock by the cupboard told her it was
almost noon. She hurried off to the bedroom.

Last night, when he called, she'd been thrilled that he
could get away from Cromwell. Though it was only for
the afternoon and the evening, it was far more than she
might have expected. Whenever he was off on a job, he
seldom let anything interfere with the assignment. Years
ago, in the days of the horseback marshals, he was often
gone for weeks at a time. She thought there was something to be said for automobiles.

In the bedroom she quickly changed into a fresh dress.
She brushed her hair until it shone, and applied the bar-
est touch of lipstick. Inspecting herself in the mirror, she
smoothed the dress over her slim waist and gave her hair
a last fluff. She realized she was acting like a schoolgirl,
all atwitter and excited, waiting for her beau to appear
at the door. But then, despite all their years together,
things hadn't changed that much. Her heart still skipped
a beat whenever he came home.

Tilghman arrived shortly after twelve o'clock. He
waved to Neal Brown, who called out from the stables,
but walked on to the house. Zoe was waiting at the door,
her features alight with happiness, and gave him no time
to shed his mackinaw. She stepped into his arms, shoving the door closed, and kissed him tenderly on the
mouth. His arms tightened around her waist.

"You know how to welcome a man home. Maybe I'll
stay away longer next time."

"Don't you dare!" she said. "A week is more than enough."

"Way I count, it's shy of a week."

"Well, it certainly seems longer. At least a month."

Tilghman was acutely aware of her closeness. Even now, for all his years, the nearness of her, the smell of her hair, still made him feel like a randy, young colt. Sometimes he surprised himself.

"What's on the stove?" he said, sniffing the air with exaggerated interest. "You fix something special?"

"Oh, nothing much," she said with a teasing smile. "Just the usual pot roast . . . and apple cobbler."

"Great God Almighty. There's not a decent meal to be had in Cromwell. Lead me to it."

"I think you only married me for my cooking."

"Yeah, that too."

Tilghman hooked his coat and hat on wall pegs beside the door. As she led him into the kitchen, he playfully swatted her on the rump. She gave a little yelp of surprise and pleasure, grabbing his hand, and got him seated at the table. While he watched, she heaped a plate with roast beef, simmering gravy, and mashed potatoes. She served coffee in steaming mugs.

"Aren't you eating?" he asked.

"Coffee's fine for now. You go ahead."

Tilghman tore into the food with relish. While he ate, Zoe chatted on about events in Chandler and the forthcoming presidential election. She studiously avoided the subject of Cromwell, apparently content to watch him enjoy the meal. When he finished a large bowl of cobbler, she poured him another mug of coffee. He patted his stomach.

"I'll have to let my belt out a notch. Hope you're not planning anything special for supper."

"You like pot roast so much, I planned to warm it up for supper. How does that sound?"

"Anything that good deserves a second trip around."

"Are you sure you can't stay the night?"

"Wish I could," Tilghman said. "But my new deputy, Hugh Sawyer . . ."

"Yes, I recall you mentioning his name."

"Good man, got his head on straight. But I don't want to leave him alone there too long. By himself, he's no match for that bunch."

She sipped coffee. "You're afraid he might end up like the other marshal?"

"I reckon anything's possible." Tilghman slowly knuckled his mustache. "Hugh's pretty handy when push comes to shove. All the same, no need to take chances."

"On the phone you never say too much. Would you mind telling me about it . . . all of it?"

Tilghman was not surprised by the question. One way or another, he knew she would work around to the matter of Cromwell. He briefly explained the raids, and his need to find a reliable informant. She listened, never interrupting, while he elaborated on his hunch about a kingpin of the rackets. He made no mention of the treats by Hammer.

"That's the size of it," he finally said. "Have to keep the heat on them till something breaks."

She was silent a moment. "Do you think this girl— Josie—will work with you?"

"I'd have to say it's a long shot. She's scared to death of Hammer. Just like everybody else in town."

"So where will you find an informant?"

Tilghman shrugged. "Hold more raids, push people to the wall. Somebody's bound to talk, leastways when I get them on serious charges. There's always a turncoat."

"All this pushing and shoving," she said. "Won't that provoke them to retaliate in some way?"

"Well, it's not much different from the old days. Horse thief or a rumrunner, they're all the same. You have to force them into a corner."

"In other words, force them to fight."

Tilghman dodged the unspoken question. "I'd sooner get the goods on them. One songbird's all I need to clean out that courthouse—and the mob."

"Yes, of course," she said, considering. "But what about this behind-the-throne kingpin? How do you expose him?"

"I just suspect Hammer or the sheriff could turn the trick. I've got an idea they both take orders from him."

"And when you get too close, won't he order them to . . . stop you?"

"Nobody's gonna stop me. Don't worry yourself on that score."

She saw it would be useless to press the issue. Nor was she willing to spoil their day together by prying further. She began clearing the table.

"Neal's dying of curiosity to hear all the gory details. Why don't you go talk to him while I do the dishes?"

"Tell you the truth, I could use a little walk. I'm stuffed as a Christmas goose."

"Just don't lose track of time. I have plans for you, Mr. Tilghman."

"Yeah, like what?"

She vamped him with a look. "Use your imagination."

Tilghman laughed, reaching for her. She eluded him with a taunting smile, collecting his plate from the table. Still chuckling, he got his hat and coat, and walked down to the stables. He found Neal Brown inside one of the rear stalls, inspecting the hoof of a brood mare. Brown quickly moved outside, closing the stall door. His expression was one of eager anticipation.

"I see you're still kickin'."

"Hello to you too, Neal."

Brown squinted at him. "Tell me everything you didn't tell the missus. Knowin' you, that's the only part worth hearing."

"Arrested a few men," Tilghman said evenly.

''Whacked a couple over the head. Not much to tell just yet.''

''What happened to the ones you arrested?''

''I doubt any of them will do jail time. They'll likely get off with stiff fines.''

''Damnation!'' Brown said testily. ''What's the world comin' to?''

''Different times,'' Tilghman allowed. ''Lots of corrupt people in high places. Not like the old days.''

''Helluva thing, that marshal gettin' killed. I read about it in the paper.''

''Still haven't turned up any leads on that. I've got a pretty fair notion who shot him. But provin' it won't be easy.''

Brown wiped his nose on a kerchief. ''What about the gang leader? Got your sights set on him?''

''After a fashion,'' Tilghman said. ''Way it looks, the headman's off in the shadows somewhere. I've got to flush him out.''

''How you aim to do that?''

''Damn good question, Neal. I'm workin' on it.''

''Well, you got time,'' Brown said. ''What the hell, you've only been there a week.''

Tilghman looked around the stables. ''How's everything here? Any problems?''

''Nothin' I can't handle. Don't fret yourself about it.''

Tilghman moved over to Copperdust's stall. He rubbed the stallion's muzzle, and talked with Brown a while longer. Finally, as the sun tilted westward, he walked back to the house. Zoe was waiting in the parlor.

The balance of the afternoon was spent in idle conversation. As though by mutual agreement, nothing more was said of Cromwell. They spoke of friends and local news and Zoe related all the latest gossip. Content to be together, they kept it in a lighthearted vein.

After supper, aroused by looks more than words, they walked arm in arm to the bedroom. They undressed in the dark and came together in a fierce embrace under the down comforter. Their lovemaking was a union of spirit as much as flesh, and they lay locked in one another's arms long into the evening. Neither of them wanted the interlude to fade.

Late that night, Tilghman prepared to leave. Zoe, wearing nothing but a housecoat, walked him to the door. She waited as he shrugged into his mackinaw and clapped on his hat. When he was ready, she slipped her arms around his waist and hugged him tightly. A tear rolled down her cheek.

"What's this?" he said, wiping away the tear. "Going sad on me?"

She smiled bravely. "I love you too much to let you go. That's always been my problem."

"I'll be back before you know it. You won't hardly have time to miss me."

"I miss you already."

She waited at the door as he drove off in the Ford. The sky was clear, flecked with stars, and the old car was visible far down the road. A wayward thought surfaced, and she wondered how many times she'd watched him ride off into the night. She heard herself say it with no word spoken.

Too many times.

CHAPTER 16

Shortly after midnight Tilghman approached the turnoff to Cromwell. The macadam highway abruptly gave way to a washboard dirt road, rutted with tire tracks. The road twisted southeasterly through rolling plains ablaze with starlight.

The visit with Zoe had left him feeling mellow. He was stuffed with pot roast and apple cobbler, and satiated with the scent of her love. Thinking about it, he told himself he was a damn fool to leave her and return to Cromwell. A smart man would have had more sense.

There were times, even at his age, when she seemed to cast a spell over him. Sometimes it was a look, or the way she moved, and anytime she touched him it never failed. He couldn't pinpoint the sensation, but it was as though he felt something shift inside himself. There was a pleasant tightness in his chest, a sudden change in heart rhythm, almost a lurch. He felt young again.

Tilghman was intrigued by the thought. As he drove through the starlit hills, he couldn't shake a sense of loss at having left her behind. There was no way to bring her along, for a boomtown filled with roughnecks and whores was no place for a lady. But nonetheless, as he approached the outskirts of the oil field, he felt separated from her by more than distance. The stark hotel room suddenly seemed a world apart.

Up ahead, Tilghman caught the outline of a truck in his headlights. As he drew closer, he saw that the truck was overloaded, the frame riding dangerously low to the ground. The slat-sided bed was covered with a heavy tarpaulin, and he noted that the truck carried Kansas license plates. He shifted into low gear as the road wound over a hill, and the truck ground to a slow, lurching crawl. The bed sank lower on the rear axle, and for a moment Tilghman thought the truck would stall. He followed a few car lengths behind.

At last, with a shuddering heave, the truck topped the hill. The driver shifted gears on the downgrade and the truck rapidly gained speed. Halfway down the slope the truck jounced through a deep rut, and the rope securing the tarpaulin at the rear snapped loose. A small crate slammed through the wooden slats, sailing out onto the road, and burst apart. Tilghman swerved sharply to miss the crate, and in the glare of headlights he saw quart bottles of liquor bouncing and shattering on the hard-packed earth. He suddenly realized he was tailing a bootlegger.

Tilghman gunned the engine. He brought the Ford alongside the truck, gas pedal pressed to the floorboard, and passed it on the bend of a curve. He spun the steering wheel sharply to the right as he cleared the truck's fender, then accelerated to avoid a collision. The truck driver swung right to clear the rear end of the Ford, his front tires jarring over cratered ruts in the road. The steering wheel jerked violently and he lost control, barreling toward the shoulder. The truck went over the edge, the front crashing downward into a shallow ditch. The rear tires rotated crazily in the air.

Farther down the road Tilghman jammed on the brakes. The Ford skidded to a dusty stop, and he quickly shifted into reverse. Gears groaning, he backed toward the truck, peering through the rear window. The headlights from the truck reflected off the wall of the ditch, casting a muslin glow up over the road. He saw two men scramble out the passenger door of the cab, and disappear from view on the opposite side of the truck. A moment later the men rose from behind the hood, silhouetted in the dull glimmer of headlights. One held a pistol, and the other a Thompson submachine gun.

Streaks of flame from the muzzle blast were followed by the booming chatter of the tommy gun. The rear window disintegrated as a maelstrom of .45 slugs tore through the Ford. Tilghman hurled himself out the door, drawing his Colt as he hit the ground. The engine stalled as his foot came off the clutch, and the car rocked to a halt. Flat on his stomach, he wormed along the ground, and took cover behind the rear tire. The night sizzled with gunfire, the pop of a pistol interspersed with the staccato roar of the tommy gun. The Ford jounced with the impact of heavy slugs.

Tilghman was trapped. The rear tire afforded some protection, but it was just a matter of time until the drumming gunfire found its mark. His only chance was to take out the major threat, the man with the tommy gun. He inched forward, waiting for a lull in the rain of bullets, and thrust the Colt around the edge of the tire. In the glare of headlights, he saw a man pause, the Thompson at his shoulder, staring intently at the car. The Colt extended, Tilghman drew a bead on the man's chest and feathered the trigger. The man staggered, arms windmilling, and the tommy gun clattered across the front of the hood. He dropped from sight behind the truck.

The second man winged a shot which ricocheted off the Ford's bumper. A moment elapsed, then Tilghman heard the sound of someone crashing through brush at the roadside. He got to his feet, still shielded by the chassis, and cautiously peered around the rear of the car. Off in the distance, he saw a man running toward the treeline of a nearby hill. Under the pale starlight his sights were faintly visible, and he tracked the man, aiming high to allow for elevation. When the Colt roared, a spurt of dust kicked up at the man's heels, and he burst into a headlong sprint. He vanished into the trees at the top of the hill.

A flash of headlights appeared on the road beyond the truck. Tilghman held his position and watched as a car slowed, then abruptly braked to a stop. The car door opened and a man jumped out, his features a blur behind the blaze of headlights. He stood for a moment, warily surveying the scene, and finally started forward. Starlight glinted off a pistol in his hand.

"Drop the gun!" Tilghman ordered. "*Drop it!*"

The man held the pistol up, flat in his hand. He stooped down, moving with exaggerated slowness, and placed the pistol on the ground. Tilghman kept the Colt trained on his chest.

"Step out in front of the car. Keep your hands in plain sight."

Hands raised, the man moved into the beam of the headlights. His features were now visible, and Tilghman recognized him as Frank Killian, the lease hound. He recalled that Killian had supported him at the town meeting, donating money for a fire truck. He eased away from the Ford.

"You're out late, Mr. Killian."

"Marshal Tilghman?"

"You always carry a gun?"

"Yes, I do." Killian seemed flustered. "Sometimes it's dangerous on the open road at night. Better safe than sorry."

Tilghman studied him. "Where've you been?"

"Shawnee," Killian said, lowering his hands. "I had business with some oil people there."

"I recollect you live in Wewoka. Took the long way around to get home."

"I made a wrong turn outside of Shawnee. When I finally woke up, I decided to go on through Cromwell. What's happened here, Marshal?"

"Bootleggers."

Tilghman walked around the back end of the truck. The man he'd shot lay sprawled in the ditch, eyes wide in a dead man's stare. He recognized Johnny Fallon, the speakeasy owner he had arrested only four nights ago. The same man Prohibition agent Wiley Lynn had released for lack of evidence. He made a mental note to talk with Lynn.

"Who is he?" Killian asked. "Did you shoot him?"

"I shot him," Tilghman said stolidly. "After he opened up on me with a tommy gun. His partner got off into the woods."

"How did you know they were bootleggers?"

"Wrong place, wrong time, leastways for them. You want to give me a hand?"

Tilghman grabbed the dead man's legs and Killian took his arms. They carried him to the Ford, opened the door, and wedged him into the back seat. After collecting the tommy gun from the road, Tilghman tossed it in with the body. Killian stood staring at the Ford, the rear end riddled with bullet holes. He shook his head.

"It's a wonder you weren't killed, Marshal."

"Guess it was my lucky night. You'd better move your car up this way."

"Why?"

"I'm fixing to burn that truck."

Killian gave him a strange look. "Won't you need the liquor as evidence? Why would you burn it?"

"So it won't get drunk."

While Killian collected his gun and moved his car, Tilghman searched the cab of the truck. He found a box of matches on the dashboard, and removed a long screwdriver from the toolbox. At the rear of the truck, he stooped down, ramming upward with the screwdriver, and punctured the gas tank. A jet of gasoline sprayed out onto the road, spilling over into the deep ruts like a stream. He walked back to the cars, noting for the first time that Killian drove a four-door Cadillac sedan. He motioned off toward Cromwell.

"Think you'd best go ahead, Mr. Killian. There's liable to be a considerable explosion."

"Whatever you say, Marshal. Glad things worked out all right."

Killian got in his car and drove away. Tilghman lit a match, dropped it in one of the ruts, and scrambled into his Ford. As the stream of gasoline ignited, he shifted gears and roared off down the road. In the rearview mirror, he saw the blaze of gasoline dart along the ground and leap toward the truck. The gas tank erupted, and an instant later the crates of liquor exploded like a chain of firecrackers. A thunderous fireball suddenly illuminated the night.

To the east, the taillights of Killian's car disappeared over a hill. Tilghman idly wondered about the Cadillac, for he'd never known a lease hound to drive such a fine car. Yet he was all the more curious about Killian taking a wrong turn and showing up on a road traveled by bootleggers. Not just showing up, but late at night and only five minutes behind the truck. Perhaps, he reflected, it was merely a matter of coincidence. Or maybe a little too coincidental. Too neat a fit.

His eyes were drawn to the rearview mirror as the fireball behind lit the countryside. He weighed the odds of coincidence.

Hugh Sawyer was still in the office. A single lamp burned over the desk, and there was no one in the holding cell. Emmett "Snake" Proctor stood in a darkened corner, nervously watching the door. He fidgeted, eyes bright, unable to stand still.

When Tilghman came through the door, Sawyer rose from behind the desk. Proctor seemed galvanized, all jerks and motions, shuffing uneasily in place. Tilghman looked from one to the other, nodding at Sawyer. "What's this?"

"Not sure," Sawyer said. "Snake slipped in here about an hour ago. Refuses to talk to anybody but you."

Tilghman's gaze swung around. "You have something for me, Emmett?"

Proctor blinked, unaccustomed to hearing his own name. He bobbed his head. "There's a roadhouse north of town. Cal Munson's roadhouse. Be worth a look."

"Are you saying they're selling dope?"

"Opium, herion, cocaine. Anything to tickle a man's fancy."

"Why'd you wait till now to tell me?"

Proctor grinned weakly. "Figgered I'd keep my part of the bargin. You pulled off them raids and you're still alive." He shrugged. "A man's gotta play the angles."

"You played the right one," Tilghman told him. "Who's Cal Munson?"

"A mean sonovabitch. He's in thick with Hammer."

"How do you know that?"

"Folks don't pay much mind to me. They figger I'm just another hophead. I hear things."

"You ever hear anything about a man named Frank Killian?"

"Don't ring no bells."

"Keep your ears open," Tilghman said. "Maybe you'll get lucky."

Proctor sidled toward the door. "Gotta be on my way. Don't want nobody seein' me in here."

"Thanks for the tip, Emmett. You're building credit in my book."

"That mean you're not gonna send me to prison?"

"Not tonight anyway."

Proctor edged out the door. When it closed, Tilghman glanced at Sawyer. "You ever been to Munson's roadhouse?"

"Just once," Sawyer said. "Little too fast for my style."

"Then it sounds worth raiding. Meantime, why don't you go wake the undertaker. He's got a client in the back of my car."

"Who?"

"Johnny Fallon," Tilghman said. "Caught him with a load of bootleg."

"Goddamn!" Sawyer blurted. "You killed Fallon?"

"Hugh, it's a long story. Just get the undertaker."

CHAPTER 17

The roadhouse was a mile north of town. A two-story structure, it was ablaze with lights and laughter. The parking lot was filled with cars.

Late the next night Tilghman turned off the road into the lot. He parked in the last row of cars, then killed the engine and switched off the lights. That morning he'd had the rear window replaced; but the Ford was still drafty from bullet holes, and he turned up the collar of his mackinaw. Sawyer was seated beside him, wearing a wool-lined jacket.

They stared through the windshield at the roadhouse. From inside, they heard the strains of a rinky-dink piano mixed with the shrill laughter of women and the gruffer tones of men. Through the ground-floor windows they saw movement, people milling about a central room, and occasional movement from the upstairs windows. Women in tight dresses mingled with roughnecks and roustabouts, some of them singing along with the music. Three bartenders manned a long mahogany bar at the far end of the room.

"Looks lively," Tilghman said, his breath spurting puffs of frost. "Something for everybody."

"Whatever you want," Sawyer observed. "Girls to take you upstairs for a price. All the hooch a man could ever ask for. And they serve pretty good food too."

"Not to mention dope. Leastways, if we're to believe our songbird."

"I tend to doubt Snake would lie about a thing like that. He's still scared green you'll put him away."

"Maybe so," Tilghman replied. "But he's a crafty devil all the same. Waited to see if somebody would punch my ticket."

"Hopheads are slick." Sawyer briskly rubbed his hands together against the cold. "Lots of people you'd never suspect are stuck on dope."

Tilghman stared at the roadhouse. From outward appearances, it was larger than the other dives they had raided. But he nonetheless thought the element of surprise was still in their favor. All the more so following the news of Johnny Fallon's death and the destruction of what was estimated to be over twenty thousand dollars in liquor. Word of the incident had spread throughout Cromwell by early morning.

The county coroner had scheduled an inquest for Tuesday afternoon. Reporters from as far away as Tulsa and Oklahoma City were clamoring for interviews, attracted by the sensational nature of the shootout. A lone marshal, confronted by a bootlegger wielding a tommy gun, was the stuff of headlines. The killing had captured everyone's attention, and no one suspected Tilghman would stage another raid tonight. Surprise was on his side.

Even Zoe was oddly taken with the gunfight. That morning, when he'd called her with the details, she had sounded somehow impressed. Her concern from the outset was that he would be overmatched against Roaring Twenties mobsters. She was still concerned, but last night's shootout had taken the edge off her fear. Her parting remark was to admonish him to get a good night's sleep, not overtax his strength. He hadn't told her about tonight's raid.

"Let's go over it once more," he said now to Sawyer. "Tell me again about the layout."

"Hallway in the front," Sawyer said, pointing through the windshield. "Off to the left there's the big room with the bar. To the right there's a smaller room with gambling tables. Stairs to the second floor are directly across from the front door."

"And the kitchen's at the back of the house?"

"Down along a hall by the stairs."

"Munson's office?"

"Just behind the gaming room. The door's on the right, halfway down the hall."

Tilghman nodded. "We'll hit his office first. He'd likely store the drugs there for safekeeping."

"Makes sense," Sawyer agreed. "Dope's a lot more valuable than whiskey."

"You say he's got ten, maybe twelve men working the place?"

"That's my best recollection."

"I'll head straight for his office," Tilghman said. "You cover my back and the hall, and let everybody see your gun. That'll make them think twice about starting any fireworks."

"Watch yourself with Munson," Sawyer cautioned. "He's a tough cookie, real tough."

"Time we made his acquaintance, then."

Tilghman led the way through the front door. His badge pinned to his mackinaw, his pistol in hand, he brushed past a man and a girl about to ascend the stairway. He heard muffled shouts from behind as he went by the gaming room and strode rapidly along the hall. Directly to his rear, Sawyer barked a harsh command, ordering men to stand fast or get shot. Ahead, he saw the entryway to the kitchen and the stunned looks on the faces of cooks and waiters. He barged through the door of the office.

Cal Munson was stocky, with quick, hard eyes and pugnacious features. He looked up from his desk as the door slammed open and started out of his chair. His mouth worked in a raspy, unintelligible curse, and his hand dipped inside his suit jacket. Tilghman earred back the hammer on his Colt.

"Hold real still," he said curtly. "Otherwise you're a dead man."

Munson stared at him, as though weighing the chances. Then he relaxed, lowering his arms to his sides. His expression was sphinxlike. "I heard you killed Johnny Fallon."

"That's a fact." Tilghman moved to the far end of the desk. He saw Sawyer posted in the doorway, covering the hall in both directions. "Fallon was short on smarts. How about you?"

"I got no worries," Munson said coarsely. "Everybody says you piss ice water, and maybe you do. But you'll never get out of here alive, old man." His eyes were like stones. "Unless you haul ass right now."

"You've got it bassackwards," Tilghman said. "Anybody gets killed, you're first in line."

"Jesus H. Christmas!" Sawyer suddenly whooped from the doorway. "All his boys are running like rats on a sinking ship. It's a regular goddamn stampede."

The rumble of car engines and squealing tires drifted in from the parking lot. Munson's features registered disbelief, and then, slowly, a look of resigned anger. Tilghman poked him in the ribs with the Colt, and relieved him of his pistol. He slumped into his chair.

A large banker's safe stood against the wall, its doors ajar. While Sawyer kept watch, Tilghman ransacked the contents of the safe. He found bags of cocaine and heroin on a lower shelf, and in a strongbox, thick bands of hundred-dollar bills. Finally, satisfied with his search, he turned back to the desk. He grinned at Munson.

"You're headed for prison, Cal. I'd say ten years minimum."

Munson grunted. "Who gives a damn what you say?"

"I just suppose you do. Course, if you were cooperative, I could ask the judge for leniency. All I need is a name, Cal. Your dope supplier."

"Fuck you!"

Tilghman backhanded him in the mouth. "I see your mother never taught you any manners. You ought to think it over a little more. It's the only deal you'll get."

"No deals, no names." Munson wiped blood from the corner of his mouth. "I'll take my chances with a jury."

"Then you're a lost soul, Cal. Next stop the state pen."

Tilghman began collecting evidence from the safe. Ten minutes later, when they emerged from office, there wasn't a bartender or a gaming table operator in sight. The girls who worked upstairs watched in dazed silence as they moved through the hallway. Munson himself looked startled when they came out of the roadhouse.

The only car in the parking lot was Tilghman's old Ford.

Late the next morning Judge George Crump convened the Third District Court. The bailiff announced the arraignment hearing of one Calvin Munson as the judge settled into his chair. He stared down from the bench.

"Are we ready to proceed, gentlemen?"

Titus Blackburn, the county attorney, rose from the prosecution table. "The people are prepared, Your Honor."

Munson and his attorney, John Newell, were seated at the defense table. Newell got to his feet. "I represent the accused, Judge. We are ready to go forward."

"Very well," Crump said. "Call your first witness, Mr. Blackburn."

"The people call Marshal William Tilghman."

Tilghman was seated by Sawyer in the front row of spectator benches. Across the aisle, Sheriff Bradley was seated on the bench behind the defense table. As Tilghman crossed to the witness stand, the door opened and Wiley Lynn sauntered into the courtroom. He moved down the aisle, nodding pleasantly to everyone, and took a seat beside Bradley. They put their heads together in whispered conversation.

From the witness stand, as he took the oath, Tilghman watched Bradley lean forward in huddled conversation with the defense attorney. Newell smiled, nodding vigorously, and turned back to his client. Tilghman was reminded that thieves stick together.

Blackburn approached the stand. "Marshal Tilghman, would you describe the events that transpired last night at Calvin Munson's so-called roadhouse?"

"Objection!" Newell bounded out of his chair. "Marshal Tilghman has no jurisdiction outside the town of Cromwell, Your Honor. We move to suppress the testimony."

Blackburn, instead of replying, offered no argument to overturn the objection. He stood watching with studied nonchalance, clearly willing to let the court dismiss the case. Judge Crump looked at Tilghman.

"Were you out of your jurisdiction, Marshal?"

"No, sir," Tilghman responded. "I am an Oklahoma State Marshal. I have arrest powers anywhere in the state."

"Objection overruled," Crump said. "You may answer the question."

"Objection!" Newell trumpeted, still on his feet. "Marshal Tilghman did not have a duly executed search warrant on the night of the incident. We move for dismissal on the grounds of illegal search and seizure."

Titus Blackburn again watched in impassive silence. The judge frowned at him. "Are you going to respond, Mr. Blackburn?"

"I fear I cannot," Blackburn said. "I have no knowledge of a search warrant, Your Honor."

Crump and Tilghman exchanged a glance. There was no longer any question that the county attorney was on the mob's payroll. Blackburn, if anything, was working in collusion with the defense attorney. The judge nodded at Tilghman.

"How about it, Marshal? Did you have a search warrant?"

"Didn't need one," Tilghman said. "Munson was openly selling liquor, running a gambling establishment, and operating a house of prostitution. I had lawful cause to raid the premises."

"That begs the point," Newell countered. "The marshal had no right to search my client's safe. He overstepped the letter of the law."

"Not in my court," Crump noted. "Any breach of the law opens the door to full search and seizure. Objection overruled."

Tilghman went on to testify. He related the details of the raid, purposely omitting any mention of an informant. Given the facts, he believed the case could be made without jeopardizing Emmett Proctor. The drugs and the cash strongbox, which were sitting on the prosecutor's desk, were entered into evidence. Blackburn was little more than a spectator during the testimony.

Newell subjected Tilghman to rigorous cross-examination. But he was unable to trap Tilghman into admission of unlawful procedure. Nor was he able to rattle Sawyer, who corroborated the particulars of the raid on direct examination. Munson, who was not required to testify, watched the procedure in glum silence. No other witnesses were called.

Judge Crump ruled separate trials on violation of the Volstead Act and on state drug charges. He set trial dates, and ordered Cal Munson held without bail. After remanding Munson to the county jail, the judge returned to his chambers. Bradley and Lynn avoided Munson's eyes as he was led from the courtroom by a deputy sheriff. Tilghman, trailed by Sawyer, moved across the aisle.

Bradley and Lynn fell silent. Tilghman nodded to the sheriff. "Hope your jail's secure," he said pointedly. "I'd hate to hear Munson escaped."

Bradley glared at him. "What makes you think Munson would escape?"

"For your sake he'd better not. I could always arrange for the state police to investigate your office."

"There you go again with threats. You've got a helluva nerve, Tilghman."

"Take it as a word to the wise, Sheriff."

Bradley stalked out of the courtroom. Tilghman turned his gaze on Lynn. "You take an unnatural interest in bootleggers, Mr. Lynn."

"Unnatural?" Lynn feigned confusion. "I don't follow you, Marshal."

"Today, you fed Munson's lawyer grounds for dismissal—"

"I didn't do anything of the kind!"

"—and you got the charges dropped against Johnny Fallon. Four nights later I caught him with a truckload of booze. You've got strange friends for a Prohibition agent."

"*Friends*?" Lynn looked shocked. "You're way out of line there, Marshal. I enforce the law when and where I can."

Tilghman laughed. "Appears to me you don't enforce it at all."

"That sounds vaguely like an accusation."

"Nothing vague about it, Mr. Lynn. I think you're crooked."

Lynn flushed. "I don't have to take that kind of talk!"

"Why not?" Tilghman said. "You afraid of the truth?"

Lynn sputtered, unable to frame a reply. He turned away, his eyes hot with hostility, and walked toward the door. Sawyer grunted, shook his head. "You made yourself an enemy there, Marshal."

"Just one on a long list, Hugh. Hold on here a minute. I want to have a word with the judge."

Tilghman found Crump in his chambers, seated at his desk. The jurist looked up with a pained expression. "What a sad state of affairs," he said solemnly. "Our prosecutor in league with the criminals. It boggles the mind."

"Maybe there's a way out," Tilghman observed. "Munson knows he'll never beat a jury trial. Not after what happened today. He might just talk."

"You mean a deal of some sort?"

"Suppose he gave us the lowdown? Hammer, the sheriff, maybe the name of the kingpin. Enough to take to a grand jury and get indictments. Would you grant him complete immunity?"

"Indeed I would," Crump said without hesitation. "Do you think he'll talk?"

"A couple of days in jail might loosen his tongue. I'll let him stew on it and drop by day after tomorrow. He could be the weak link in the chain."

"I hope you're right, Marshal. Are you still convinced there's a mastermind behind all this?"

"That'll be my second question to Cal Munson."

"What's the first?"

"Who supplies the drugs."

"Perhaps the answers are one and the same."

Tilghman smiled. "I'm taking bets on it, Judge."

CHAPTER 18

Late that night a Buick sedan pulled away from the rear entrance of the Sportsmen's Club. Jake Hammer was alone in the back seat, one hand resting lightly on top a small, black satchel. Bud Shuemacher drove, and Turk Milligan, a tommy gun cradled across his lap, occupied the passenger seat. The car turned south out of Cromwell.

Hammer lit a cigar. As the car sped toward Wewoka, he puffed smoke and considered what must be done. There was a risk entailed, for he was acting without orders, and that was a matter of no small concern. But given the circumstances, the risk of not acting seemed to him far greater. After all, he mused, if the dominoes fell, he was the first domino in line. He had a right to protect himself.

"Look at them goddamn flares," Milligan remarked, as they passed the eastern edge of the oil field. "I betcha hell wouldn't look no worse than that."

The night was dark, and the gas flares spewed jets of flame across the field. "Whyn't you ask Bohannon?" Shuemacher said with a sly smile. "Didn't look much different the night we sent him to hell. He'd know which is worst by now."

"Dead men don't tell no tales," Milligan said,

pleased with his snappy comeback. "Bohannon ain't gonna tell nobody nothin'."

"Get wise," Hammer retorted from the back seat. "He's already told them plenty. Like maybe he was murdered."

Milligan winced. "One in a million accident, boss. Just bad luck."

"Fuck luck!" Hammer snarled. "You told me he'd never come out of that slush pit. I should've known better."

"C'mon, boss, gimme a break, will you? Just a freak, that's all."

"I ought to rap you in the head. You're the only freak around here."

Milligan and Shuemacher stared straight ahead. Hammer had been in a foul mood since last night, when he'd received word of the raid on Cal Munson's roadhouse. That morning, when he heard that Munson had been bound over for trial, he had exploded in a violent outburst of rage. His temper had worsened throughout the day, and everyone in the club avoided his office. Even now, the two men still felt as though they were walking on eggshells. Neither of them was willing to further incur his wrath. They sat wrapped in stiff silence.

Some twenty minutes later the Buick turned off the road. Shuemacher pulled into a clearing along the banks of a tree-lined creek. He hooked the gearshift into reverse, doused the lights, and cut off the engine. A black Ford coupe was parked on the opposite side of the clearing, almost invisible in the dark overhang from the trees. Hammer opened the back door, leaving Milligan and Shuemacher in the car, and walked forward with the satchel. Jim Bradley stepped out of the Ford.

"Evening, Jake," Bradley said. "You're running late. Thought maybe you'd forgot."

"I don't forget nothing," Hammer said tightly. "When's the last time you didn't get yours?"

"Just making conversation, Jake. I've got no complaints."

"Damn right you've got no complaints. Here's your end."

Hammer handed over the satchel. They met once a week for payoffs from the Cromwell rackets. Bradley was the bagman for Seminole County, and he doled out the money to officials in the courthouse. The payoffs guaranteed that Cromwell would operate as an open town.

"The usual?" Bradley asked. "Five thousand?"

"You think I'd short you? Where do you get off askin' a question like that?"

"No need to get bent out of shape. I didn't mean nothing by it."

"For all the protection we get lately, you should be kissing my feet."

Hammer walked to the creek bank. He propped one hand against a tree and stood staring into the rippling water. Bradley tossed the satchel into his car, then moved to the shoreline. He sensed something different about tonight, an ominous mood he couldn't define. His features were troubled.

"I know you're ticked off," he said tentatively. "But Lynn and me did everything possible. We gave Munson's lawyer a good out for dismissal. Just didn't work."

"Nothin' works anymore," Hammer said in a surly voice. "Hasn't since the day that old fart showed up."

"Tilghman's a problem, no question about it. Thinks he's out to save the world."

"Goddamn do-gooder! I'd like to ice the son of a bitch."

Bradley looked alarmed. "That wouldn't be a wise idea, Jake. Anything happens to Tilghman, the governor would likely declare martial law—call out the National Guard."

"Yeah, yeah," Hammer said sullenly. "I've heard it before."

"Well, you ought to take it as gospel. No way we could protect you if the National Guard took over. They'd close down Cromwell."

"You're not protecting me now. All these raids make me look like some half-assed dumbbell. Why should the dives pay graft when there's no protection? You got an answer for that?"

"We're doing our best," Bradley mumbled. "But it's hands-off on Tilghman, and he's in thick with Judge Crump. We're caught between a rock and a hard place."

Hammer stared off into the dark. He was silent so long Bradley's nerves took an uptick. But then, with a heavy sigh, he looked around. "We've got another problem besides Tilghman. And it's gotta be solved tonight."

"What's that?"

"Cal Munson."

Bradley shifted uneasily. "What about him?"

"Cal's got to go," Hammer said in a stoic tone. "A man facing prison time starts to get funny ideas. We can't take a chance he'll talk."

"What's that mean—he's got to go?"

"I want him to have an accident. Tonight."

"Hold on now," Bradley said. "You talking about in my jail?"

"Whatever works," Hammer said, nodding. "Maybe he'll get shot trying to escape. You figure it out."

"I didn't sign on to—kill people."

"Well, look at it this way, Sheriff. If Munson talks, we'll all take the fall. How'd you like a stretch in the state pen?"

Bradley cleared his throat. "I thought Munson was a friend of yours."

"So what?" Hammer said brusquely. "We're tending to business here. Nothing personal involved. Cal would understand."

"I doubt he would appreciate the distinction."

"Yeah, well, I'm not worried about hurt feelings. You

want to be my bunkmate in stir? What other choice we got?''

"None, I suppose," Bradley said dully. "Have you cleared this with the big boy?"

"Got the go-ahead," Hammer lied. "He don't let nothin' stand in the way of business. You ought to know that."

"How the hell am I gonna make it look convincing? The last thing we want is another investigation."

"Hey, I got confidence in you, Jimbo. You'll think of something. Just get it done tonight."

"All right, I'll take care of it."

Bradley trudged back to his car. Hammer watched him pull out of the clearing and turn onto the road. As the sound of the engine faded, he walked toward the Buick. He was relieved but at the same time nagged by worry. A bigger problem still awaited him.

He thought it looked to be a long night.

The house was a sturdy two-story brick structure. On the outskirts of Wewoka, it was located on a quiet residential street lined with elm trees. The lawn was neatly manicured, and tall shrubs fronted the house. A shaft of light spilled through the living room window.

Shuemacher braked to a halt in the driveway. He shut off the lights and the engine, glancing out of the corner of his eye at Milligan. The cold night air on the hot engine set off a faint *tick-tick-tick* through the hood of the car. Not a word had been spoken on the way into town, and they waited now for instructions. Hammer crawled out of the back door.

"Stay in the car," he ordered. "I'll be through when I'm through."

Hammer took the walkway to the house. He stopped on the porch, adjusted his suit jacket, and pressed the door buzzer. From inside he heard the sound of footsteps, and a moment later the door opened. A petite woman in her late twenties motioned him inside. Her teeth flashed in a quick smile.

"Hello, Jake," she said, closing the door. "How's tricks?"

"Not too bad, Ruth. How about yourself?"

"Every day's a barrel of laughs. Never a dull moment."

A former chorus girl, she was attractive in a brassy sort of way. Her hair was flaming red, and she wore clothes that accentuated her stemlike waist and full breasts. Hammer thought she had the best legs he'd ever seen on a woman.

"Frank's in the living room," she said. "I'll make myself scarce while you boys talk."

"See you later, Ruth."

"Not if I see you first."

She laughed, moving off toward the rear of the house. Hammer watched the swish of her hips a moment, then caught himself. He dropped his hat on a vestibule table and walked through an arched doorway into the living room. Frank Killian was seated in an overstuffed easy chair, his feet resting on a hassock. Logs blazed in the fireplace.

"Good evening, Jake." He gestured to a sofa opposite his chair. "What's so important we couldn't discuss it on the phone?"

Killian usually arranged their meetings in out of the way places. He kept their association at arm's length, and apart from a few of Hammer's men, his identity was known only to Sheriff Bradley. All of the routine operations involving the Cromwell rackets were handled by phone. Tonight, Killian had allowed one of the rare visits to his home.

Hammer seated himself on the sofa. "I met with Bradley on the way over. Gave him the weekly grease."

"I imagine he'll retire the wealthiest sheriff in Oklahoma. But you're not here to talk about Bradley, are you?"

"Like I told you on the phone, we've got problems. I didn't want to mention a name, but you probably already guessed. It's Cal Munson."

"I thought as much," Killian said. "Bradley called me this morning after the arraignment. He was all apologies."

"Lot of good that'll do," Hammer said caustically. "Munson knows he lookin' at ten or twenty years. And by now, he's figured out we can't spring him."

"You think he'll turn state's evidence. Is that it?"

"I think it's a chance we can't afford to take."

Killian assessed him with a hard stare. "Why do I detect wheels within wheels, Jake? You're not telling me something."

"That's why I'm here." Hammer's throat suddenly felt dry. "There wasn't time to wait and talk with you. I had to get it solved tonight."

"Quit dancing around it, Jake. Get what solved?"

"Munson's gonna be put on ice tonight. I arranged it with Bradley."

Hammer held his breath. Frank Killian reported to the mob out of Kansas City. A man of intelligence and craft, he had been involved in the rackets since he was seventeen. Apart from running various operations, he was widely known as an enforcer, and was reputed to have killed a score of men. As a reward for loyal service, he had been given control of the Cromwell operation. His word was law.

Killian had selected Hammer as his lieutenant. Hammer was also part of the Kansas City mob, though at a far lower level. Cromwell was his big step upward as well, and he meant to make his name in the Oklahoma oil fields. But now, caught in Killian's cold stare, he felt like a butterfly pinned to a board. A film of sweat beaded his forehead.

"You're a lucky man," Killian said at length. "I happen to agree with you about Munson. He's a liability."

Hammer finally took a breath. "So you're not pissed

that I handled it on my own? I did the right thing."

"You did the right thing in the wrong way, Jake. You forgot I'm the one who gives the orders."

"Hey, it was as an emergency, Frank. We didn't have no time to waste."

"Let's put it this way," Killian said in an icy voice. "Forget once more and it will be your last time. Do you follow me, Jake?"

Hammer averted his gaze. The threat was thinly veiled, and he felt sweat trickle down his backbone. He dutifully bobbed his head. "I'll think twice next time, Frank. Got my word on it."

"You miss the point. I do the thinking and you follow orders. Understood?"

"Yeah—sure thing . . . whatever you say."

Killian stared at him a moment longer. "How did Tilghman find out Munson was peddling dope?"

"Somebody must've tipped him," Hammer said, relieved to change the subject. "I heard he went straight to Munson's safe, where the stuff was stored. Sounds like he had somebody on the inside."

"Check out everyone who worked for Munson. If you find an informant, I want him eliminated. Do it in a way that sends a message."

"I'll get on it first thing tomorrow. But we'd solve the whole thing by knockin' off Tilghman. He's our real problem."

"I still don't see that as a solution, Jake."

"Why not?" Hammer said reasonably. "We'll have to kill him sooner or later."

"Not necessarily." Killian looked into the fireplace, watching the flames with a contemplative expression. "How do we rid ourselves of Marshal Tilghman without forcing the governor's hand? I've been thinking about that."

"What'd you come up with?"

"We have to kill his reputation, not the man."

"You lost me there, Frank."

"Death before dishonor. Discredit him in the eyes of the public . . . and the governor."

"Discredit him?" Hammer echoed blankly. "What's that mean?"

Killian smiled. "Tarnish his sterling image."

"You got something in mind?"

"Listen closely, Jake. Here's how I want it handled."

CHAPTER 19

"Mornin', Marshal."

"Good morning, Hugh."

"How about a cup of java?"

"I never turn down coffee."

Tilghman seated himself behind the desk. As he started sorting through the morning mail, the hands on the wall clock touched eight o'clock. He noted a letter from Zoe, which he stuck in his pocket, and another with the Oklahoma state seal. He tore open the corner of the envelope.

Sawyer turned from the coffeepot on the stove and placed a steaming mug on the desk. He jerked a thumb at the holding cage. "What about the jailbirds? Feed 'em or let 'em out?"

Three roustabouts were watching from behind the bars. Arrested last night, they were disheveled and clearly suffering from hangovers. With no municipal court to fine them, the only punishment was to force them to miss a day's work. Tilghman ordered them released.

Sawyer unlocked the cage. The roustabouts filed out and started toward the door. As they trooped past the desk, Tilghman nailed them with a look. "Hope you boys learned your lesson."

"Yessir," one of them said. "You won't see us again, Marshal."

"For your sake, I'd better not. Next time you'll lose a day's wages."

The phone jangled as they went out the door. Tilghman lifted the receiver, identifying himself. A voice crackled on the line and he straigtened in his chair. He listened, saying nothing, his mouth razored in a thin line. After a minute, with the voice still talking rapid-fire, he placed the receiver on the hook. His features were stony.

"That was the sheriff," he said slowly. "Cal Munson hanged himself last night."

"*Hanged himself*!" Sawyer parroted with disbelief. "You mean he committed suicide?"

"So the sheriff says. They found him in his cell a little while ago. Used his belt as a noose."

"Sounds fishy to me. Munson wasn't the sort to hang himself. You believe it?"

"No, I don't," Tilghman said coldly. "I think somebody wanted him silenced, and suicide was the quick solution. They murdered him."

"So he wouldn't spill the beans," Sawyer added. "Have to be somebody in the sheriff's office. Nobody else could get into the county jail at night."

"I have no doubt Bradley ordered it done. But who gave Bradley his orders? That's the man I want."

"Jake Hammer?"

"Maybe." Tilghman considered a moment. "Or maybe Hammer's boss."

Sawyer nodded. "The kingfish you've been talkin' about."

"That would be my bet, Hugh. I'd even give odds."

"Looks like we've lost our pipeline to the drug trade."

"Go find Emmett Proctor. Tell him I want to hear anything he hears. Anything at all."

"Snake hears more than he lets on. I'll have a talk with him."

When Sawyer went out, Tilghman suddenly remembered the letter. He unfolded a report, signed by the state police commander, which had been channeled through the governor's office. The report, which Tilghman had requested not quite a week ago, was the result of an investigation into the background of Wiley Lynn. The state police had done a commendable job.

Wiley Lynn was originally from Marshall County, raised by an uncle following the death of his parents in a house fire. After army service during the war, he had served a five-year stint as a deputy sheriff. In March 1924, he had been hired as a Prohibition agent, headquartered in Holdenville, which was south of Wewoka. Despite his commission to wage war on illicit liquor, he was known to be a heavy drinker. He had been reprimanded three times in eight months by his superiors.

There were further revelations in the report. Lynn's uncle, and the uncle's two sons, had been arrested by the FBI only last summer. The uncle and cousins were subsequently convicted and imprisoned on charges of operating an interstate car theft ring from their Marshall County farm. The FBI suspected Lynn's involvement, though no connection had been established. Lynn was romantically involved with the madam of a brothel in Wewoka, and he was known to live beyond his means. The FBI maintained periodic observation of his activities.

Tilghman folded the report. Everything he'd read confirmed his original hunch. A Prohibition agent who drank to excess and consorted with fast women was suspect enough. The connection to a car theft ring, however tenuous, merely added coals to the fire. Confirmation by the FBI of high living, added to Lynn's loose attitude toward bootleggers, removed any lingering doubts. The Prohibition agent was definitely on the mob's payroll.

A truck braked to a halt on the street. Through the window, Tilghman saw Zack Mosley jump from the truck and walk toward the office. He hastily dropped the report in his desk drawer as Mosley came through the door. The oil man seemed in a cheery mood.

"Brought you a present," he said, pointing out the window. "You wanted a fire truck, and now you've got one. Even had the motor tuned."

Tilghman was astonished. "I thought you'd given up on civic duty. Why the turnaround?"

"Heard about that raid you pulled off last night. Anybody who goes after drugs gets my vote. So I'm donating a truck."

"I didn't know you were so set against drugs."

"Oh hell yes," Mosley told him. "Dope's a sneaky thing, lots worse than whiskey. Gets men killed on an oil rig."

"Well, I'm beholden to you, Zack. You've done right by Cromwell."

"C'mon, lemme show you the truck."

Mosley led the way outside. He explained that the truck, an ancient Ford, had seen better days. But it was still serviceable, with a good motor, and never failed to start. Tilghman walked around the truck, inspecting the tires and undercarriage, and returned to where Mosley waited. He shook his head with a grin.

"That'll sure beat water barrels. Ought to make a dandy fire truck."

"Yeah, once you get it refitted, you're in business. The town'll make you fire chief too."

"Think I'll stick with law work. Thanks all the same."

Mosley glanced past him. Josie Rodgers appeared in the window of her room on the upper floor of the Sportsmen's Club. She waved and Mosley waved back with a broad smile. He looked at Tilghman.

"I'll just say hello to Josie. Before I forget, how'd you like to see some fireworks? We're gonna shoot the well this afternoon."

Tilghman raised an eyebrow. "How do you shoot a well?"

"Come on out and see for yourself. Makes a helluva show."

Mosley hurried across the street. Tilghman waved to Josie, then mounted the boardwalk, where he stood admiring the truck. Fred Wagner, one of the Citizens Committee members, was watching from outside his hardware store. He moved downstreet, crossing the intersection, and stopped beside Tilghman. He nodded pleasantly.

"Congratulations, Marshal. The whole town's talking about your raid on Munson's roadhouse. Good riddance to bad rubbish."

"We're rid of him, all right," Tilghman said. "Munson hung himself in the county jail last night. Leastways, that's the sheriff's version."

Wagner was shocked. "Are you saying it wasn't suicide?"

"Draw your own conclusions. With Munson's lips sealed, lots of people are resting easier this morning. He won't squeal on anybody now."

"Good God, that's really cold-blooded—to hang a man."

"No argument there." Tilghman motioned into the street. "How do you like our new fire truck? Zack Mosley donated it to the town."

"Did he?" Wagner sounded impressed. "That was mighty generous of Zack. Always said he was a good man."

"Needs to be refitted with the right equipment. I'll leave that to you and the Citizens Committee. You can organize a volunteer fire department."

"Well, yes, I suppose we could. But we'll need a fire chief."

"Hold an election. You'll likely find the keys in the truck. She's all yours, Fred."

Tilghman smiled, mentally dusting his hands of the fire department. He walked back into the office.

*   *   *

Early that afternoon the shooter stepped out of his truck at the drilling site. His name was Tom Barlow, out of Ponca City, reportedly the best nitro man in Oklahoma. In the trade, he was addressed simply as Shooter, and it was a tribute of no small distinction. Everyone agreed he had steel cables for nerves.

Shooter Barlow was wide and squat, bald as a billiard ball. A taciturn man, with the rolling gait of a landlocked sailor, he wasted little time on amenities. After talking with Mosley, and inspecting the rig, he set about earning his pay. He prepared to shoot Coffeepot Number Twenty-three.

Mosley assigned his chief driller to assist in the operation. He then scrambled down the rig and walked to where Tilghman waited with the rest of the drilling crew. Their position was close to the road, selected for safety, more than a hundred yards from the derrick. No one wanted to be near a well when it was shot.

Standing apart, Mosley gave Tilghman a quick education in wildcatting. He explained that oil was embedded in sand at various depths in the earth. Above and below these beds there were formations of rock and clay, generally impregnated with water. The trick was to tap the oil at its upper level, but not to drill too deeply into the water. Late yesterday the crew had bored through the cap rock.

From there, it was a matter of cautiously drilling down foot by foot. The hole was bailed after each drilling, and every load of cuttings had shown streaks of color. By relieving the pressure of mud and slush on the paysand, the driller hoped to coax the oil to the surface. Yet the oil hadn't budged, and their quandary grew more acute the farther they drilled. A foot too deep would result in a water well rather than an oil well.

"Didn't have a choice," Mosley concluded. "I called Shooter and told him to hightail it down here. We've got to force the oil to wellhead."

"Nitro's dangerous stuff," Tilghman observed. "Not a job for fainthearts."

"Shooter's brought in more wells than you could count. All in a day's work to him."

A car passed by on the road. Tilghman and Mosley glanced around and saw Frank Killian at the wheel of his Cadillac. He waved, looking beyond them to the shooter's truck, and rolled his eyes with a knowing smile. He drove off in a cloud of dust.

"Nice car, that Cadillac," Tilghman said casually. "Frank Killian must be doing well."

Mosley shrugged. "You couldn't prove it by me."

"What do you mean?"

"For a lease hound, he's a queer bird. I hear he's only done a couple of deals since we brought in the field."

Tilghman looked at him. "Maybe they were valuable deals."

"All dusters," Mosley said. "Word gets around in the oil crowd. Killian's pretty much of a joke."

"Acts like a real go-getter, though, doesn't he?"

Mosley suddenly lost interest. "Watch close now, Marshal. Shooter's fixin' to load the hot stuff."

Shooter Barlow gingerly carried six two-gallon cans of nitroglycerin from his truck to the rig. He passed the cans up to the driller, and then returned to the truck, where he pulled out two cylindrical metal tubes. The tubes were five inches in diameter, one ten feet in length and the other four feet. When fully loaded, the larger tube would hold twenty-four quarts of nitro. He climbed the ladder to the derrick floor.

The driller set the larger tube in the wellhead hole. He held it steady while Barlow carefully poured liquid nitro from the cans. Once the tube was full, they capped it, and lowered it into the hole on a hook attached to a spool of rope. With the tube resting on the bottom, the hook was jiggled loose and the rope withdrawn. The idea was to explode the nitro, which would fracture the sub-surface formation, and free the oil from the sand. All that remained was to detonate the nitro.

Barlow stuffed the smaller tube with sticks of dynamite. On the last stick inserted into the canister, he added a long fuse. He then filled the tube with wadding, allowing the fuse to hang out, and crimped the top closed with pliers. At the wellhead, he struck a match, lit the fuse, and watched it fizzle a few seconds. Then he dropped the bomb into the hole and took off like a peppered duck. The driller was already down the ladder, barreling toward the crew. Barlow hit the ground running.

A dull whump sent tremors rippling through the earth. For a few moments there was nothing but absolute silence, and then a low rumbling filled the clearing. The noise quickened, as if gaining strength; the rig began to jounce and tremble, and the bull wheel ripped loose from its sills. The men watched, hypnotized by the sight, the wooden derrick swaying as though battered by a cyclonic force. In the next instant, a mere blink of the eye, Coffeepot Number Twenty-three was born. The well erupted with a wild, volcanic roar.

Timbers flew in a misty whirlwind. The crown block hurtled skyward as the gusher blew in over the top of the derrick. The spout climbed higher and higher, blotting out the sun, and at its crest, slowly blossomed into a gigantic black rosebud. A moment later, as if some strange squall had darkened the heavens, the downpour came, and it started to rain oil. Laughing madly, staring upward at the inky deluge, the men bellowed at the top of their lungs. Their shouts were lost in the savage howl of the gusher.

Shooter Barlow watched a while, amused by their antics. Finally, when the crew went to cap the wellhead, he trudged off toward his truck. Tilghman turned, hardly surprised by the look of fierce exultation on Mosley's face. He wrung the oil man's hand.

"Congratulations, Zack. You're got yourself a gusher."

"Twenty-three in a row!" Mosley marveled. "I'm the

luckiest son of a bitch on the face of the earth. Jumpin'
Jesus Christ!''

Tilghman was pleased for the younger man. He
thought there would be raucous celebration on the streets
of Cromwell tonight. But in the same instant a fleeting
image of Frank Killian passed through his mind. A lease
hound who brought in dusters. A joke among the oil
crowd.

A man who traveled the roads late at night.

CHAPTER 20

The sun went down in a splash of orange and gold. All the color was leeched from the sky as a quick autumn twilight settled over the town. With the oncoming dark, the gas flares from the wells cast a ghostly aura on the horizon. The glow rose like a shroud over the tops of buildings.

Tilghman sat at a window table in the Bon Ton Cafe. Just before sunset he'd left Sawyer to watch the office while he took a supper break. The cafe served a passable meat loaf, with mashed potatoes and gravy and canned string beans. His appetite was off and he attributed that to the death of Cal Munson. He forced himself to pick at the food on his platter.

The cafe was filled with roughnecks and roustabouts. Outside, the crowds were starting to gather along the boardwalks of Shawnee Avenue. He watched them with detached interest, lost in his own ruminations. Of all the men he'd arrested, Munson had seemed the most likely to turn informant. But the roadhouse owner was dead, and for all practical purposes, he was back where he had started. He felt himself at an impasse.

The situation brought to mind a jigsaw puzzle. The pieces were represented by Hammer and Bradley, with Wiley Lynn and various county officials on the outer edge. All of these were relatively simple to fit together, and they formed a logical, if somewhat disjointed, pattern. But the missing piece, the axis of the jigsaw, was the man who exerted control over all the others. A man he was still convinced operated from the shadows, an enigma. Until he found an informant, he would never solve the puzzle.

Through the window, he saw Mosley and the drilling crew enter a speakeasy across the street. A ritual of sorts, one he'd witnessed before. The men who brought in the well would be treated to a night of drunken revelry. Yet he was reminded not of the gusher, or Shooter Barlow's deft touch with the nitro, but rather of his earlier conversation with Mosley. A short, though somewhat revealing conversation about Frank Killian.

Tilghman idly munched a chunk of meat loaf. He disliked riddles, and yet he was forced to consider Killian in that light. On the one side, Killian was clearly a man of means, always nattily attired, able to afford the latest-model Cadillac. On the other side, he was a lease hound in perpetual motion, popping up night and day, but one who made few deals. Something was skewed, not as it appeared, and Tilghman still had reservations about their chance meeting the night he'd forced the bootleggers off the road. Killian's explanation had seemed too glib, and in retrospect, perhaps short of the truth. He thought it was worth looking into.

After paying his bill, Tilghman stepped out of the cafe. He stood for a moment, watching the crowds, then turned toward the intersection. He planned to relieve Sawyer for supper, and later they'd start their evening rounds. As he approached the corner, Hollis Kriger, a houseman in Ma Murphy's dance hall, rushed across the street. Kriger's manner was agitated, his features taut.

"Marshal!" he yelled. "You gotta come quick. Ma needs you."

"What's the problem?"

"I dunno. Ma just said to find you. She's awful upset."

"Lead the way, Hollis."

Tilghman followed him across the street. Inside the dance hall, Ma Murphy was talking to her husband, who had taken over behind the ticket booth. When she saw Tilghman, she hurried forward, clutching at his arm. Her face was wreathed with apprehension.

"Thank God you're here," she said in a quavering voice. "One of my girls has locked herself in her room. I think she means to kill herself."

"Glad I was close by," Tilghman said. "What wrong with her?"

"Man trouble, what else? Her boyfriend ditched her and she's out of her mind. I tried talking to her, but she won't listen. I can't get her to open the door."

"Does she have a gun?"

"Not that I've ever seen. She'd be more likely to cut her wrists."

"What's her name?"

"Sallie. Sallie Mae Polk."

"All right, let's have a look."

Ma led him to a stairway all but blocked from view by the ticket booth. The upper floor was bisected by a corridor, with rooms on either side for the ten-cent-a-dance girls. She stopped near the end of the hall, indicating a door. Her face was a mask of anxiety.

"Sallie Mae," she called out. "Sallie Mae, honey. Somebody's here to see you."

"Go away! I don't want to see you or anybody else. Just leave me alone!"

Tilghman rapped lightly on the door. "Sallie Mae, this is Marshal Tilghman. I'd like to talk to you a minute. Just talk, nothing more than that."

"Get away! You've got no truck in this. Let me be!"

"Open up." Tilghman rattled the doorknob. "Open up or I'll kick the door down. Be sensible now."

There was a prolonged moment of silence. Than a key jiggled in the lock and the door slowly swung open. Sallie Mae was young, a busty blonde, dressed in a sheer cotton slip covering her panties and brassiere. She gave Tilghman a pathetic look.

"Come on in," she said stridently. "But I won't talk to nobody else! You keep out of here, Ma."

Tilghman exchanged a glance with Ma. She shrugged helplessly, backing off a step, and he moved into the room. Sallie Mae slammed the door, quickly twisted the key. She retreated toward the bed, kicking at her dress, which lay on the floor. A straight razor gleamed from a bedside table. She reached for it.

"You got here just in time, Marshal. You can watch me do it."

"Hold on now—"

Tilghman swiftly crossed the room. As he approached the girl, there was a loud thump on the wall from the room next door. Sallie Mae reacted with alarcity, taking him completely unawares. Quick as a cat, she flung herself on him, knocking his hat off, and dragged him down onto the bed. She wrapped her legs around him, her slip hiked up to reveal her panties, and held him on top of her. She kissed him full on the mouth.

The door burst open. A photographer stepped into the room, and there was a flash of light as he clicked the shutter. Tilghman reared back, still trapped within Sallie Mae's legs, his mouth smeared with lipstick. The photographer snapped another photo as he untangled himself from Sallie Mae and climbed off the bed. Sheriff Jim Bradley elbowed the photographer aside, moving into the doorway. His mouth curled in a gloating smirk.

"Caught you red-handed, Tilghman." He wagged his head from side to side. "Your pecker just landed you in a world of trouble."

Tilghman eyed him narrowly. "What the hell are you talking about? What's the game here?"

"No game," Bradley said smugly. "You threatened to close down Ma's dance hall unless the girl come across. We caught you in the act."

"That's right!" Sallie Mae said, jumping out of bed.

"I just went along to help Ma. He forced himself on me!"

Tilghman looked past Bradley into the hallway. His gaze fixed on Ma Murphy. "What's happening here, Ma? Are you in on this?"

"I'm sorry, Bill." Her face was livid with shame. "I didn't have any choice but to call the sheriff. You shouldn't have threatened me . . ."

Tilghman thought her voice sounded stilted, the words rehearsed. He saw in her eyes that she was frightened, and suddenly it all came clear. She had been coerced into rigging a badger game, tricking him into bed with the girl. He collected his hat off the floor.

"Bradley, I'm coming through that door," he said with cold scorn. "You'd be wise to get out of my way."

"I'm not gonna arrest you—"

"You sorry tub of guts. I wish you'd try."

"—but you better show up in court tomorrow. I'm pressing charges."

"Press your charges and be damned. Stand aside."

Bradley quickly vacated the doorway. Ma Murphy cringed underneath Tilghman's stare when he moved into the hall. He bulled past the photographer, tempted to grab the camera. But he walked instead toward the stairs.

He knew the photographs were the least of his worries.

Sawyer's mouth dropped open.

"Didn't suspect a thing." Tilghman paced to the holding cage and back. "Walked into it blind as a bat."

"Judas Priest," Sawyer said, bewildered. "I'd never have figured Ma for that kind of thing. You and her are friends."

"We *were* friends," Tilghman said with an edge in his voice. "Bradley got to her somehow. Just spun her around."

"So what are you gonna do?"

"Before I walk into that courtroom tomorrow, I've got to find out why Ma sandbagged me. Otherwise they'll hang me out to dry."

"Sounds like a tall order. I doubt you'll get anything out of Ma. Not from the way you described it."

"Yeah, she's scared stiff." Tilghman dropped into his chair, thoughtful a moment. "You know anybody that works at Ma's place?"

"I visit one of the girls now and then. Nothing serious, you understand."

"Is she sweet on you?"

Sawyer blushed. "Well, nobody ever called me Romeo. But, yeah, I suppose she's stuck on me."

"And she knows this Sallie Mae Polk? The wildcat who jumped me?"

"I'd think she does. They all live under one roof. What makes you ask?"

"Talk to your lady friend," Tilghman said with some urgency. "Have her get close to Sallie Mae and try to pump her. Might just work."

"Damn sure might," Sawyer agreed. "Never known a woman yet that could keep a secret. They do like to gossip."

"You'll have to get it done tonight."

"I'll do my level best, Marshal."

"And it's got to be done on the sly. How can you talk to your lady friend without tipping Ma or Pa?"

"Her and the other girls generally go out for a late supper after the place closes. I'll catch her on the street."

"I'm obliged," Tilghman said earnestly. "You might just pull my fat out of the fire."

Sawyer grinned. "I'll bring you something. Don't worry."

"I've got a couple of phone calls that won't wait. Go get yourself some supper. We'll talk more later."

"Whatever you say, Marshal. I won't be long."

When Sawyer went out, Tilghman sat staring at the wall a moment. He dreaded calling Zoe, but there was no way around it. By late tomorrow, the photo of him wrapped in Sallie Mae's legs would appear in every paper in Oklahoma. He gave the operator the number.

Zoe was pleasantly surprised by his call. But then, as he went on to explain the situation, she grew silent. Tilghman sensed she was angry, and he wondered if her anger was directed at him. Whatever the circumstances, the embarrassment of the photos was more than any wife should be asked to tolerate. She had a right to be angry.

"Guess you're burned up," he said, trying for levity. "I've got steam coming out of my end of the phone."

"Of course I'm mad," said in a quick voice. "But I'm not mad at you, Bill. I'm mad at those bastards in Cromwell."

Tilghman told himself she *was* steaming. She never cursed. "Nothing's too low for them, no question about that. They're a tricky bunch."

"And this Murphy woman. Ma Murphy, is that what you said? How dare her betray you!"

"Some way or another, they've got her between a rock and a hard place. I'm looking into that."

"I should think so."

"Hate to mention it," Tilghman said reluctantly. "But when those pictures hit the paper, you might want to stay home a couple of days." He hesitated. "Folks in Chandler are liable to ask you some embarrassing questions."

"Let them!" she fumed. "I'll singe a few feathers myself. Don't think I won't!"

"You always were feisty as a bulldog pup. Guess that's why I married you."

"At the time, you said I was spunky. I much prefer that to a bulldog pup."

"All boils down to the same thing. You're one of a kind."

"Which makes us a matched pair."

"Yeah, I reckon it does."

After they hung up, Tilghman got the operator back

on the line. He gave her the number of the governor's mansion in Oklahoma City. When the governor came on the phone, Tilghman apologized for calling so late, and briefly explained the situation. He ended on a cautionary note.

"I wanted to warn you before it hits the newspapers."

Governor Trapp chuckled. "On the contrary, I take it as good news."

"You might think different after you see the pictures."

"The pictures make my point. These people are trying to smear your reputation, Bill. That means you have them worried. Very worried."

"I'd say I'm on their mind. Otherwise they wouldn't have pulled this stunt."

"Do you know Edward Markham?"

"Assistant attorney general, isn't he?"

"And a real live wire, Bill. One of the sharpest litigators I've ever seen. I'm going to call him when we're through here. He will meet you at the courthouse in Wewoka tomorrow morning."

Tilghman nodded. "What've you got in mind?"

"A little surprise," Trapp said confidently. "On my order, Markham will have your hearing transferred to Judge Crump's court. That gets you out of the hands of the county judge—the one on the mob's payroll."

"Well, that'll get me a fair hearing anyway."

"Far more than a fair hearing. I guarantee Markham will draw blood in that courtroom. He goes straight for the jugular."

"I wouldn't mind a little bloodshed, myself."

"Then you're in for a treat, Bill. You'll like Markham."

"Governor, I like him already."

When they hung up, Tilghman leaned back in his chair. A slow smile creased his face, and he chuckled to himself. The idea of it appealed to him.

A man who went for the jugular.

CHAPTER 21

LAWMAN'S LOVENEST IN CROMWELL
TILGHMAN FACES ILLICIT CHARGES

The headline dominated the front page. In a lead story, the *Wewoka Sentinel* reported the details, with a lengthy quote by Sheriff James Bradley. Accompanying the article was a photo of Tilghman pushing himself off Sallie Mae Polk's bed. The girl's bare legs were clearly visible in the photo.

The news reverberated throughout Seminole County. By ten that morning, people waited in line for a seat in Judge Crump's courtroom. They were shocked and titillated and somewhat amazed the newspaper had published such a scandalous photo. But they nonetheless turned out for what promised to be a sensational preliminary hearing. The article all but tried and convicted Tilghman.

Yet there was wild speculation about the charges. The spectators were surprised to learn that the hearing had been transferred from the County Court to the District Court. Even more, they were bewildered by a rumor that the accused would be defended by the assistant attorney general of Oklahoma. The move was unprecedented, and word spread that the governor had intervened due to the political overtones of the case. There was talk that Tilghman had been framed.

When court convened, Tilghman was charged with licentious behavior, solicitation of bribes, and extortion. He sat at the defense table with Edward Markham, the assistant attorney general. Markham was tall, in his early thirties, with piercing eyes and sharp, angular features. Earlier that morning, in a strategy session, he had listened with open interest as Tilghman related details of the incident. He was particularly intrigued by the results of Sawyer's investigation late last night. He planned to use it at the appropriate moment.

Sheriff Bradley was the opening witness. Titus Blackburn, the county attorney, led him through an accounting of the incident. On cross-examination, Markham confined his questions to matters of law enforcement in Seminole County. The sheriff grudgingly admitted that, previous to last night, his office had never conducted a raid in Cromwell. He denied any animosity toward Tilghman.

Blackburn then called Florence "Ma" Murphy to the stand. Under oath, she testified that Tilghman had become obsessed with one of her dance hall girls, Sallie Mae Polk. She went on to state that Tilghman had threatened to close her down unless she arranged a "love affair" with the girl. To protect her business, as well as Sallie Mae, she had called the sheriff after agreeing to Tilghman's demands. The sheriff had then organized a trap to catch Tilghman in the act.

After Blackburn completed direct examination, Markham approached the stand. He pinned Ma with a hard look. "Do you operate a house of prostitution?"

"No!" Ma sounded offended. "I run a respectable dance hall. Everybody knows that."

"Yet you convinced a young girl to prostitute herself for your benefit. Isn't that your testimony?"

"I did no such thing. Sallie Mae was just playacting, that's all. She led him along."

Markham produced a copy of the *Wewoka Sentinel*. He shook it in her face. "Do you call that playacting? I see bare legs and underdrawers. Isn't that carrying the role a little too far, Mrs. Murphy?"

"I don't know what you mean."

"I mean you could have trapped Marshal Tilghman in conversation. Have the sheriff hidden in a closet or somewhere, let him actually hear the extortion threat. Why was it necessary to go—" he rattled the newspaper—"*this* far?"

"I did what I was told," Ma said sheepishly. "The sheriff wanted it that way."

"I submit you lured Marshal Tilghman to that room. You led him to believe the girl was about to commit suicide, didn't you?"

"I never said any such thing."

"You were selected for this put-up job because of your long-standing friendship with Marshal Tilghman. Isn't that true?"

"I told you how it was."

"You were selected because Marshal Tilghman would never suspect you of betraying him—isn't that so?"

"No."

"You were coerced and threatened and forced to betray Marshal Tilghman, weren't you?"

"You've got it all wrong."

"Quite the contrary, Mrs. Murphy. I have it on good authority. Tell me about Turk Milligan."

A look of desperation came over Ma's face. Her eyes skittered around the courtroom, and finally came to rest on Sheriff Bradley. He stared at her with a stone-cold expression.

"Answer the question," Markham ordered roughly. "You know Turk Milligan, don't you?"

"Yes."

"And he works for a man named Jake Hammer, correct?"

"Yes."

"And night before last Milligan came to your dance hall. He was seen there, talking to you. Isn't that true?"

"I—I don't remember."

"How could you forget? Milligan threatened your life, threatened to kill you and your husband. Didn't he?"

"Objection!" Blackburn bellowed. "Counsel is badgering the witness, Your Honor!"

"Overruled," Judge Crump said. "Witness may answer the question."

"Speak up," Markham demanded. "Milligan threatened you unless you went along with the scheme against Marshal Tilghman. You solicited the help of Sallie Mae Polk. You told her of the threat—didn't you?"

Tilghman almost felt sorry for her. Ma's gaze went to the girl, who was seated in the front row of spectators. Sallie Mae looked stunned, and Ma's eyes welled over with tears. She knotted her hands together.

"I—" She took a shuddering breath. "I just don't remember."

"You've told us quite enough, Mrs. Murphy. No further questions for the witness."

Ma Murphy walked from the courtroom, her features stark. Blackburn hesitated, glancing at the sheriff in a quandary, and getting no help. With obvious reluctance, he called Sallie Mae Polk to the stand. Her voice tremulous, she answered his questions, repeating the story as though schooled in her responses. She kept darting glances at Markham, clearly frightened of what was to come. Blackburn ended the examination as quickly as possible.

Markham savaged her. In a hectoring tone, he went over her testimony again and again, trapping her in inconsistencies. Finally, when he reminded her of the penalty for perjury, she broke. Under his relentless questioning, she admitted that Ma Murphy had told her of the threat by Milligan. She had agreed to the scheme, she testified pitifully, because Ma and Pa Murphy were like family. She believed they might be killed if she refused, and she'd gone along. She left the stand in a state of shock.

Judge Crump dismissed the charges against Tilghman. Then, after a conference with Markham, he placed the girl under protective custody and ordered the state police to escort her out of the county. Her testimony was hearsay, inadmissible in a jury trial; but he was nonetheless concerned for her safety. As for Turk Milligan, he expressed doubt that Ma Murphy could ever be convinced to turn state's evidence. She was clearly fearful of her own life, and rightfully so. He suggested Tilghman have a talk with her.

When the conference was over, Judge Crump walked from the bench to his chambers. Tilghman and Markham turned to find themselves in an empty courtroom. Markham shook his head with disgust.

"The sheriff didn't waste any time beating a retreat. Too bad we can't charge him with conspiracy."

"Never stick," Tilghman said. "We'd have to get Jake Hammer first."

"What about this Milligan?"

"I'd tend to agree with the judge. Ma Murphy's been around a long time. Even if she testified, they'd kill her afterward. She knows that."

"Damn shame," Markham said bitterly. "It seems you're back back to square one, Marshal."

"Things could be worse," Tilghman commented. "Except for you, I'd be facing charges myself. I appreciate your help."

"I did very little here today. Your deputy deserves all the credit. Thank God he found out about Milligan."

"Sawyer's got a way with the ladies. Handy talent to have."

"Indeed," Markham acknowledged. "You ought to promote him."

"First thing this morning, I made him chief deputy."

"How many deputies do you have?"

Tilghman smiled wryly. "Just one."

Early that afternoon Tilghman sat staring at the telephone. Twice in the last hour he'd tried to call Zoe, but there was no answer. He wanted to share the good news, and he was disappointed she had left the house. He had thought she would stay near the phone.

The office was unusually quiet. Upon returning from Wewoka, he'd given Sawyer the afternoon off. It seemed small enough reward for all the deputy had done. But now, with time on his hands, he debated whether to have a talk with Ma Murphy. He knew she wouldn't implicate Milligan, and there was no way to force her to testify. Even if he charged her with perjury, she would still refuse. He didn't blame her.

Hard as it was to admit, he couldn't protect her. He knew it, and she knew it, and certainly Jake Hammer knew it. He stared out the window at the Sportsmen's Club, and wondered what it would take to put the mobster away. Then, hardly able to credit his eyes, he sat upright in his chair. A Buick pulled in at the curb, and Zoe was at the wheel. Neal Brown was seated beside her.

Tilghman hurried out of the office. Zoe stepped from the car as he came through the door. She smiled brightly at the dumbfounded look on his face. He stopped at the edge of the boardwalk.

"What are you doing here?"

"That's a fine greeting," she said. "I thought you would be happy to see me."

" 'Course I'm happy to see you. I'm just surprised."

She took his hand, moving onto the boardwalk, and kissed him on the cheek. "How did things go in court this morning?"

"Got the charges dismissed," Tilghman said, still taken aback by the sight of her. "That lawyer the governor sent was a real stem-winder. He proved it was a pack of lies.''

"I'm sure he did. You'll have to tell me all about it.''

Neal Brown walked forward. "Howdy do, Bill.''

"Hello, Neal. You along for the ride?''

"I guess you could say that.''

Tilghman frowned. Through the windshield of the car, he saw luggage in the back seat. He looked at Zoe. "What are those bags?''

She smiled sweetly. "Oh, don't worry about those. Show me your office.''

Before he could reply, she crossed the boardwalk. Tilghman glanced at Brown, who shrugged and followed her inside. She halted beside the desk. "My goodness,'' she said, staring around. "What a dismal place.''

"Jails generally are,'' Tilghman said. "Let's talk about those bags.''

"I've come to stay with you,'' she said airily. "You need protection against scandal.''

"What kind of scandal?''

"The kind that took you to court this morning. No one will try that again with your wife here.''

"How would you being here stop them?''

"Simply being here shows I don't believe it. And if I don't believe it—who would?''

Brown paused in the doorway. When Tilghman turned with a baffled expression, he shook his head. "Don't look at me,'' he said, folding his arms across his chest. "I'm just here to take the car back home.''

Tilghman swung back to Zoe. "You should've called me. A boomtown's no place for a lady. You can't stay here.''

"Honestly, Bill.'' She gently patted his cheek. "Do you think I don't know what goes on in a boomtown? I promise I won't swoon.''

"Well, it's just not proper. You don't belong in a sinkhole like Cromwell. You belong home.''

"I belong with my husband. Now, let's not argue

about it. I'm here and I intend to stay. There's nothing more to discuss."

Tilghman knew when he was whipped. After thirty-four years together, he recognized the determined glint in her eye. "I swear to God," he said, conceding defeat. "You're the stubbornest women I ever met."

She laughed gaily. "I'd like to get unpacked and freshen up before supper. Do we have a nice hotel?"

"Four walls and a bed. All the comforts of home."

Brown moved aside to let her out. As Tilghman came through the door, Brown chortled softly. He kept his voice low. "You was outmatched from the start. Never had a chance."

"Neal, you're a day late and a dollar short."

"How's that?"

"I've been outmatched since we got hitched."

They followed Zoe to the car.

Late that evening Hammer called the number in Wewoka. "Got some news," he said, when Killian answered the phone. "Ma Murphy sold her dance hall. Do we let her go?"

"Yes, let her go. She kept her end of the deal."

"Fat lot of good it did us! Tilghman slipped off the hook."

"There's always a next time, Jake."

"Got another news flash. You ready for this?"

"Try me."

"Tilghman brought his wife to town. The night clerk at the hotel gave me the tip. Said she's not a bad lookin' broad."

"She's younger than Tilghman?"

"Lots younger, the way I hear it."

"Which means he's probably protective of her . . . and jealous."

"Are you thinkin' what I think you're thinkin'?"

"I seriously doubt it, Jake."

"Then where are you headed?"

There was a brief pause. "Here's what I want done," Killian said after a moment. "Get hold of Wiley Lynn tonight."

"Lynn?"

"It's time he began earning his pay. We'll let him be our message bearer."

"What sort of message?"

"Use your imagination, Jake. What's the message Tilghman would least want to hear . . . about his wife?"

Hammer liked it. When they hung up, he wished he'd thought of it himself. The idea was just devious enough to work.

He placed a call to Wiley Lynn.

CHAPTER 22

Zoe awoke to a bright morning sun. Streamers of light slipped through the window shade, spilling across the room. She stretched luxuriantly, and a blissful little smile played across her mouth. A warm sensation flooded her with memories of last night. She felt lazily spent from his ardor.

A swishing sound attracted her attention. She rolled over to his side of the bed and peered around the door into the bathroom. He stood before the sink, rinsing soapy whiskers off his onyx-handled straight razor. As she watched, he stroked along his jawline with the shiny blade. He was still in his undershirt, and she saw the muscles ripple along his arm. A fleeting image of last night, when she'd lay wrapped in his arms, again brought the tingling sensation. She wished it hadn't ended.

Tilghman caught her reflection in the mirror. He turned, the razor in hand, and grinned at her. "Tried not to wake you," he said. "Did you sleep good?"

She laughed a low, throaty laugh. "If I felt any better, I'd purr."

"I recollect you did a little purring last night."

"Look who's talking! You were pretty frisky yourself."

"You're a wicked woman." Tilghman laughed, turning back to the mirror. "I'll be through here in a minute."

"Oh, take your time. I can wait."

She nestled into the pillow, stretched languidly. Her eyes roamed around the room, stopping here and there to inspect the furnishings. There was a bureau with an upright mirror, positioned beside a small closet. The telephone was on the bedside table, and two straight-back wooden chairs stood against the opposite wall. The double windows overlooked Shawnee Avenue, which was already alive with the sound of trucks and motor-cars. The room was comfortable for a boomtown, though hardly home away from home. She thought a few feminine touches were desperately in order.

"All through," Tilghman said, emerging from the bathroom. "Get a move on and we'll go have breakfast."

"Yessir! Anything you say, sir. I'll just be a jiffy."

Zoe took her time. She thought it wouldn't hurt him to cool his heels her first morning in town. When she finally came out of the bathroom, her hair was brushed until it shone and a touch of makeup complemented her features. She selected a navy dress with white trim from the closet and began changing while he waited in one of the chairs. His chipper mood slowly dissolved into a solemn expression.

"Want you to watch yourself," he said soberly. "I don't keep regular hours, and this is a rough town. You'll be alone a lot."

"How quaint," she said, gently mocking him. "You're worried about me."

"Nothing to laugh about. You know the kind of thugs I'm dealing with here in Cromwell. They might try to get to me through you."

"Are you saying they would attempt to hurt me?"

"Hurt you. Abduct you." Tilghman held her gaze. "Doesn't matter that you're a woman. They don't play by the rules."

"Well, just let them try!"

She took her pocketbook off the bureau. Quickly, with practiced ease, she snapped open the clasp and pulled out a small, short-barreled revolver. She motioned with it toward the window.

"I am an excellent shot," she said, arching one eyebrow with humor. "You may recall I had a good teacher."

Tilghman couldn't argue the point. When they were first married, he'd become concerned about her being alone while he was off chasing outlaws. He had taught her the proper handling of a gun and drilled her in the quick but deliberate method of firing with accuracy. She could place six shots in a playing card at ten paces.

"Just don't get cocky," he said. "You'll remember I always say—"

"'Cocky will get you killed.' I remember everything you ever taught me. I'll be careful. I promise."

"Then put your peashooter away and let's get some breakfast. I'm half starved."

"I would think so after last night. You were *very* energetic."

"Like I said, you're a wicked woman."

She smiled pertly. "You taught me that too."

Tilghman was amused by her saucy attitude. He helped her into her coat, collected his mackinaw and hat, and escorted her downstairs. On the street, they walked to the Bon Ton Cafe and took a window table. He ordered steak and eggs, with pancakes on the side, wryly commenting that he needed to regain his strength. She ordered toast with a single scrambled egg.

But as they ate, Tilghman kept glancing out the window at the rough-clad men on the boardwalks. His concern for her safety was uppermost in mind, and he wondered how to underscore the point. Then, with a bite of steak speared on his fork, he happened to look across the street. He saw Ma Murphy and her husband climb into a car stuffed with their belongings. Last night, he'd heard that they had sold the dance hall at a bargain rate. He nodded out the window.

"See the heavyset woman and the man? Across the way there, getting into the car."

Zoe looked around, watching as an old Mercer roadster pulled away from the curb. "Who are they?"

"Flo and Del Murphy," Tilghman said. "I told you about Ma Murphy, the one that set me up on the morals charge. That's her."

"Well, she's in for a surprise! I can't wait to give her a piece of my mind."

"You won't likely get the chance. They're running for their lives."

"I don't understand," she said, glancing again at the car. "Running from what?"

"Jake Hammer," Tilghman replied. "The rackets boss here in town. Ma and Del are afraid he'll have them killed."

"Why?"

"Ma got a little tongue-tied on the witness stand. She gave the game away and spoiled Hammer's brainstorm. He's not the kind to accept excuses."

She was appalled. "And he would have them murdered . . . for a mistake?"

"Yeah, he would," Tilghman said. "That's why you have to be extra careful. He's got no more conscience than a scorpion."

"Yes, I see that now."

"Never go out on the street after dark. Not unless I'm with you."

"No, I won't"

"Keep the door locked in the hotel, and never open it for anybody you don't know—man or woman."

"I promise."

"Just so you understand," Tilghman said. "I don't want you hurt on account of me."

She ate in silence a moment. "What a dreadful place. It isn't right for people to live in fear."

"You could always go back home. Fact is, I wish you would."

"Oh no I won't! You're not getting rid of me that easy. I'll leave when you leave."

"Figured as much." Tilghman chewed thoughtfully on beefsteak. "You'll get awful lonesome in that hotel room."

"I'll stay busy," she said. "Don't worry yourself about me."

"How will you stay busy? Unless you like ginmills and gambling dives, there's not much to do here."

"Does Cromwell have a church?"

"One," Tilghman said succinctly. "Oil men aren't big on religion."

She made a face. "Any church can use volunteers."

"Not much need for charity work in a boomtown. Most everybody's in the chips."

"I'm sure the church has social programs. Don't oil men have wives and families?"

Tilghman considered a moment. She had no friends in Cromwell, and she couldn't stay locked in a hotel room all the time. So maybe the church was something to keep her occupied, a way to fill the lonely hours. She might even meet some decent women.

"Tell you what," he said. "I'll introduce you to the preacher, Virgil Pryor. He'd likely welcome a volunteer."

"There, you see?" she said, dabbing at her mouth with a paper napkin. "I knew I'd find something to do in Cromwell."

"We'll go have a talk with Pryor."

When they finished breakfast, they walked west from the cafe. The town was already bustling with activity, the workday having begun an hour earlier. Shawnee Avenue was clogged with trucks and automobiles, and the boardwalks were crowded with people who seemed in a rush to get somewhere else. Zoe felt the electric excitement peculiar to a boomtown, where oil was king and the pursuit involved the entire community. No one seemed to have a moment to spare.

At the intersection, they rounded the corner onto Jenkins Street. Josie Rodgers, walking in the other direction, practically ran into them. She had heard Tilghman's wife was in town, and she offered no sign of recognition. She thought the marshal would prefer not to acknowledge a prostitute in the presence of his wife. But Tilghman greeted her with an amiable smile.

"Good morning, Josie," he said, halting in her path. "I'd like to have you meet my wife. Zoe, this is Josie Rodgers."

"How do you do?" Zoe said pleasantly. "I'm always happy to meet a friend of Bill's."

Josie smiled awkwardly. "Pleasure's all mine, Mrs. Tilghman."

"Oh, call me Zoe, please. I much prefer it."

"Why sure, but that goes both ways. I'm just Josie."

The women examined one another with subtle looks. Some silent communion passed between them, and despite the difference in their ages, they each liked what they saw in the other. They decided on the spot to be friends.

"Well, I'll run along," Josie said. "I've got to stop by the post office and do some errands. Sure nice meeting you, Zoe."

"Thank you," Zoe said engagingly. "I hope to see you again, Josie."

"Yeah, you bet, me too. We'll bump into each other."

Josie nodded to them, still smiling, and walked on. As they turned downstreet, Tilghman saw Wiley Lynn drive past, and then slow down, looking them over. Zoe tugged at his arm.

"What a stunning girl! She's really quite pretty."

"Josie?" Tilghman said, his mind still on Lynn. "Yeah, she turns heads."

"I remember her name. You told me she works in

that gangster's club. Is she a—you know . . ."

"A fallen woman," Tilghman supplied. "But she's not what you'd call a tramp. Lot of good in Josie."

"Is there?" Zoe playfully squeezed his arm. "Are you an expert on fallen women?"

"I've known a few in my time. Strictly business, of course."

"Of course." Zoe stopped, pointing to the pharmacy on the opposite corner. "Before I forget, I want to pick up something in the drugstore. You go along and I'll meet you at your office."

"Good idea," Tilghman said. "I need a minute to check on things anyway. Then we'll go see the preacher."

They crossed to the opposite corner. When she went into the pharmacy, Tilghman turned downstreet. Ahead, he saw that Wiley Lynn had parked his Studebaker roadster in front of the office. The Prohibition agent was leaning against the fender.

Lynn shook a cigarette from a pack. He snapped open a lighter, lit up in a haze of smoke, and returned the lighter to his pocket. He nodded as Tilghman approached. "Mornin', Marshal."

"Lynn." Tilghman halted on the boardwalk. "What brings you to Cromwell?"

"We got off to a bad start," Lynn said in a genial voice. "Maybe we could patch things up and find a way to work together. No need being at loggerheads."

"You're a poor liar, Lynn. Everybody in Seminole County knows you're on the take. I don't work with crooks."

"You ought to be more reasonable, Marshal. Things would go easier."

"I'm not interested in easier. Anything else?"

Lynn exhaled a plume of smoke. "Saw you with your wife up at the corner. She's a fine-looking woman."

Tilghman stared at him. "So?"

"So you ought to be careful nothing happens to her. Cromwell's a dangerous place."

"I think you're threatening my wife, Lynn."

"Friendly advice, one law officer to another."

"I've got some advice for you too."

"What's that?"

Tilghman stepped off the boardwalk. His left hand shot out in a blur, and he slapped the cigarette from the Prohibition agent's mouth. Before Lynn could react, Tilghman pulled the Colt and clouted him across the forehead. Stunned, his legs rubbery, Lynn sagged onto the fender of the car, and Tilghman struck him again. Lynn collapsed, sliding off the car, and fell in the street. Tilghman grabbed him by the shirt collar, the Colt raised.

"Stay away from my wife," he said coldly, "or I'll kill you."

"Bill!" Zoe screamed, running along the boardwalk. "Don't hit him again, Bill. Let him go!"

Tilghman lowered his pistol. He turned, releasing Lynn, and moved away as Sawyer rushed out of the office. Zoe stopped, aware of a strange light in her husband's eyes, and looked at the bloodied man in the street. Lynn was sprawled beside the Studebaker, unconscious, his forehead laid open by a deep gash. Sawyer grunted under his breath.

"What the devil happened?"

"Lynn's got a big mouth," Tilghman said. "He threatened my wife."

"Me?" Zoe was outraged. "He threatened *me*?"

"Yeah, he did, plain as day."

"You should have hit him again, Bill. A good one!"

Sawyer chuckled to himself. Last night he'd met Zoe when Tilghman invited him to have supper with them. He remembered being impressed as much by her spirited manner as her looks. He thought now she was a match for the marshal.

"Know what I think?" he said. "Lynn was just the

messenger boy. Hammer's the one that sent him.''

"Then Hammer has his reply," Zoe said, turning up her nose at the unconscious man. "We don't scare, do we, Bill? Not even a little!"

Tilghman laughed. "You're no Ma Murphy, that's for sure."

"I would hope to say not. I'm here to stay."

Sawyer followed them into the office. At the door, he turned, glancing across at the Sportsmen's Club. He idly wondered if anyone would be sent to collect the fallen messenger. But then, deciding it didn't matter, he closed the door.

A crowd gathered on the street to inspect Wiley Lynn.

CHAPTER 23

Tilghman told her nothing of the raid.

That evening, after supper, he escorted Zoe back to the hotel. He knew she would worry unnecessarily if she even suspected what he had planned for later. Her spirits were still good, but she'd had all day to dwell on the incident that morning. She was now sobered by the threat on her life. She understood the need for caution.

So he told her nothing. He pretended it was a routine night in Cromwell and managed to keep his mood on the light side. Zoe assured him that she would keep herself occupied until it was time for bed. She had a book to read, and she was in the middle of knitting herself a sweater. He left her securely locked in the room.

Friday night was the second busiest night of the week. Oil men were at their wildest on Saturday, the end of the work week. But they usually began gearing up in advance, and Friday brought the crowds out. Every dive in town was crawling with roughnecks and roustabouts, and the boardwalks were packed with men. There was a general mood of revelry along the streets.

Tilghman walked directly from the hotel to the office. When he entered the door, Sawyer was seated behind the desk, reading the *Wewoka Sentinel*. The deputy was waiting to be relieved for his own supper break, and he got to his feet. He dropped the newspaper on the desk,

tapping an article on the front page. He shook his head
with a sardonic smile.

"Story there about your run-in with Ma Murphy and
the sheriff. Almost sounds disappointed the charges were
dismissed."

"Not surprising," Tilghman said. "The newspaper
boys feed on dirt and scandal. Spoiled their lovenest
angle."

"You'd think they would've played up the conspiracy
angle. Hardly mentioned it at all."

"We'll give them a better story for tomorrow."

"What's that?"

Tilghman hadn't yet revealed his plans for tonight. He
motioned across the street. "We're going to raid the
Sportsmen's Club."

"Holy hell!" Sawyer was astounded. "I thought you
planned to wait till we had the goods on Hammer."

"Not after this morning. Hammer has to pay the price
when he threatens a lawman's family. Time we taught
him a lesson."

"That'll set him off like a skyrocket. He's liable to
put up a fight."

"Hope he does," Tilghman said tightly. "That'd give
me an excuse to punch his ticket. I've killed men for
less."

Sawyer felt like his ears had suddenly come un-
plugged. He realized Tilghman's calm outward manner
belied the simmering anger underneath. He cocked his
head in an inquiring look. "You're declaring war, aren't
you?"

"Nobody ever threatened my wife before. I aim for
this to be the last time."

"I'd feel the same way. But you planned to use Hammer to get at the kingfish. What happens if you kill
him?"

"Hard to say," Tilghman conceded. "Maybe he'd
send somebody to replace Hammer. Or maybe we'd lose
him altogether. No way to tell."

Sawyer nodded. "But you're willin' to risk it?"

"Never said I mean to kill Hammer. Fact is, it'd work better if we take him alive. We'll let him call the tune."

"Either way, I guess it'll make your point."

"That's the general idea," Tilghman said. "You go on and get yourself some supper. I'll lay out the plan after you come back."

When Sawyer left, Tilghman walked to the gun rack on the wall. He unlocked the chain securing the weapons and took down the sawed-off shotgun. From the bottom desk drawer, he removed a box of shells and a cleaning kit. His eyes were opaque in the lamplight.

He began swabbing the barrels of the scattergun.

Shortly after ten o'clock, Tilghman led the way out of the office. Sawyer was a step behind, carrying the shotgun, his jacket pockets stuffed with shells. On the boardwalks men stopped to stare as they angled across the street. A crowd began gathering as they went through the door of the Sportsmen's Club.

Jake Hammer was nowhere in sight. The bartenders froze, and the girls seated at tables with customers watched in stunned silence as the lawmen walked toward the rear of the club. Turk Milligan stood talking with Falcon and Shuemacher, who were posted outside the door to the gaming room. They started forward, then stopped, staring into the cavernous bores of Sawyer's shotgun. Tilghman motioned with his pistol.

"I want you boys to unload your hardware. Let's not have any monkey business."

The men obediently snaked revolvers from beneath their suit jackets and dropped them on the floor. Milligan squared his shoulders, trying to look tough, and glowered at Tilghman. His voice dripped with sarcasm. "You just committed suicide, pops."

"Think so?" Tilghman said evenly. "Last time we talked you ended up with a knot on your head. Want to try for another?"

"Big man, aren't you?" Milligan said with false bravado. "You'll change your tune before the night's over."

"Here's how it works." Tilghman gestured with the snout of the Colt. "You boys lead the way through the door. Try to give anybody the high sign, and I'll start cracking skulls. Let's go."

Falcon opened the door, followed by Shuemacher and Milligan. Tilghman shoved them aside, halting just inside the gaming room, and Sawyer kicked the door shut. The tables were crowded, the rattle of dice mingling with the click of a roulette wheel. Around the room, housemen saw the guns and the badges, and the murmur of voices gradually trailed off. Tilghman rapped out a command.

"This is a raid! Everybody stand fast!"

Sawyer swept the room with his stubby scattergun. Housemen hastily raised their hands, and the roughnecks and roustabouts stood rooted to the floor. A tense silence settled over the crowd as the *click-click-click* of the roulette wheel faded to a stop. An instant later Jake Hammer burst through the door of his office on the far side of the room. A nickel-plated revolver was clenched in his hand.

"Drop it!" Tilghman ordered. "Right now!"

Hammer's eyes hooded in a scowl. He saw the Colt leveled on him, Tilghman staring down the sights. He sensed that he was a moment away from death, that the gray-haired lawman wanted a reason to kill him. A razored smile, more of a grimace, flicked across his features, and he slowly shook his head. He tossed his gun on the floor.

"Go on, have your fun," he jeered loudly. "Lotta good it'll do you in the end."

Tilghman cleared the room of oil men. Then he ordered Hammer and his hooligans to stand against the wall beside the door. After they were lined up, he moved forward, facing them, and kept them covered with his Colt. He nodded to Sawyer.

"All right, Hugh, let's get it done."

Sawyer walked to the roulette table. He shouldered the shotgun and emptied a double load of buckshot into the wheel and the baize layout. Quickly reloading, he blasted holes in first one dice table and then the other. A stench of cordite and gunsmoke filled the room as he worked his way through the slot machines, the blackjack layouts, and the poker tables. He methodically destroyed every gaming device in the club.

When he finished, he shucked empties and stuffed fresh loads in the shotgun. He rejoined Tilghman, who was locked in a staring contest with Hammer. The mobster's eyes were like fiery agates, alive with malice. His mouth quirked in an ugly rasp.

"You're a dead man, Tilghman. I guarantee it."

"Tell you what, Jake," Tilghman said in a goading voice. "Try me anytime you feel lucky. I'm always available."

"You can bet your ass on that! It's gonna happen."

"By the way, I'm not arresting you. But if you try to reopen, I'll be back. Shotgun shells are real cheap."

Hammer looked confused. "I don't get it. What's your game?"

"You figure it out."

Tilghman backed to the door. He covered Sawyer and they moved into the outer room, closing the door behind them. Zack Mosley, who had been upstairs with Josie, waited at the front of the bar. When the gunfire began, he'd hastily dressed, warning Josie to remain in her room, and then hurried downstairs. He fell in beside Tilghman.

"What the hell happened in there? You kill Hammer?"

"Nope," Tilghman said laconically. "We put him out of business."

"Well, where is he? Didn't you arrest him?"

"Not worth the trouble. Wiley Lynn wouldn't press liquor charges, and he'd get off with a fine on the gambling operation. This works better."

"Works better?" Mosley echoed as they moved out the door onto the boardwalk. "You made a fool of him in front of the whole town. He'll come after you."

"I'm depending on it," Tilghman said. "Gave him a standing invitation."

Mosley halted at the edge of the boardwalk. He watched as Tilghman and Sawyer moved through the crowd of onlookers and crossed the street. When they disappeared into the office, he was reminded of a comment he'd heard around town. One proved again here tonight.

The old man had brass balls. Too much so for his own good.

Hammer insisted that they meet in person. What he had to say was not something to be discussed on the telephone. There was a raw urgency in Hammer's voice, and Killian finally relented. He agreed to a meeting at his home.

A little after midnight Ruth answered the door. Killian was waiting in the living room, a tumbler of brandy in one hand. Hammer refused a drink, and plopped down on the sofa. Ruth left them alone.

Killian was struck by the other man's dark manner. He sensed that Hammer's explosive temper was barely under control. "I have to admit I'm surprised," he said. "I thought a threat to Tilghman's wife would bring him into line."

Hammer snorted. "The cocksucker's too dumb to scare. He beat the shit out of Lynn."

"And then retaliated by raiding your club. We apparently touched a nerve."

"You never saw anything like it. Turned the kid deputy loose with a shotgun and blew my tables apart. Sounded like a fucking war."

"I can imagine." Killian paused, sipped his brandy. "Why didn't he arrest you?"

"Hell, he did worse," Hammer growled. "He made me look like an asshole. How can I protect the other joints if I can't protect my own? Nobody'll be talkin' about anything else."

"Which makes things even more difficult, doesn't it, Jake? We can't lose control of the town."

"There's only one thing that'll put a stop to it. You've got to let me kill him."

Killian stared into his brandy glass, as though the amber liquid held some profound revelation. "I'm forced to agree," he said at length. "But you're not the one for the job."

"Why the Christ not?" Hammer demanded. "Who's got a better reason?"

"That's the whole point. After he just raided your club, everyone would know you did it. We can't risk that."

"You're still worried about the National Guard, right? We risk that no matter who kills him."

"Maybe not," Killian said. "Suppose it was made to look like a random incident? No ties to you."

"Like an accident?" Hammer asked. "His car goes off the road, or he gets run over by a truck. Something like that?"

"Lots of men walk away from accidents. It would have to be more certain . . . final."

"Yeah, like what?"

Killian drained his brandy glass. He steepled his fingers, staring off into the middle distance with a contemplative expression. For a long moment, like a philosopher analyzing some arcane mystery, he sat lost in thought. He finally nodded to himself with a faint smile. His eyes were amused.

"A fluke," he said softly. "One of life's unforeseen mishaps."

Hammer frowned. "What's that mean?"

"A quirk of fate, Jake."

Killian reached for the phone. When he got the operator, he placed a call to Ardmore, an oil town some seventy miles southwest of Cromwell. A man answered on the second ring.

"Eddie? This is Frank Killian. How you doing?"

They chatted about business for a few minutes. Then Killian got to the point. "Look, Eddie, I need a favor. Do you have a couple of good men you could loan me?"

He listened, nodding. "You've got the idea. A special job."

There was a brief pause, then he again nodded. "Sunday night's fine. Have them report to Jake Hammer at Rose Lutke's whorehouse, in Wewoka." He listened a moment, then laughed. "You're a sport, Eddie. I owe you one."

After hanging up, he looked at Hammer. "Costana's sending two men. You heard the arrangements?"

"Yeah, I heard. So what'd I do with 'em?"

"You pass them off as traveling salesmen. Here's how I want it handled."

Killian explained the plan, elaborating on details. Hammer listened attentively, bobbing his head with approval, a broad smile across his face. After a brief discussion about timing, he rose and walked to the hallway entrance. His smile widened to a grin.

"Don't give it another thought, boss. Tilghman's as good as dead."

"Just make sure you have an alibi, Jake. Lots of witnesses."

"No two ways about it. I'll cover myself."

Ruth appeared in the hallway. She showed Hammer to the door, then moved back to the living room entrance. A motor turned over outside, and the sound of a car engine faded down the street. She crossed her arms, watching Killian pour himself another brandy. Her voice was concerned.

"I have a bad feeling about this. Tilghman's different."

"You have a habit of overlooking the obvious, Ruth."

"Oh, what's that?"

Killian raised his brandy glass. "I always win."

CHAPTER 24

On Monday evening, Tilghman invited Walt Sirmans and Reverend Pryor to supper. The men left their wives at home, for there were children to tend and the purpose of the meeting was to discuss community affairs. Zoe nonetheless joined them at the Bon Ton Cafe.

The streets were quiet. After a rowdy weekend, the roughnecks and roustabouts were recuperating with a night off. There were few customers in the cafe, and Tilghman arranged a table at the rear of the room. He sat with his back to the wall, where he could watch the door and Shawnee Avenue. Given the circumstances, he thought a degree of caution was in order.

Friday night, following the raid on Hammer's club, Zoe had treated him to a stiff lecture. She was on to his tricks, and she'd known immediately why he hadn't arrested the mobster. His intention was to provoke Hammer, and while she wasn't comfortable with the tactic, she recognized that nothing would alter the situation. She admonished him instead to adopt the maxim of discretion being the better part of valor. She extracted a promise that vigilance would become his byword.

For his part, Tilghman needed little persuading. He subscribed to the theory that there were old lawmen and bold lawmen, but very few old, bold lawmen. After forty years as a peace officer, he was all too aware that caution had its place in enforcing the law. There was a time to press hard, aggressively force the troublemaker into a corner, and a time to lay back, await developments. The other fellow, acting out of anger, invariably made a mistake. So tonight, Tilghman kept one eye on the door.

As they ate, the talk centered around the raid on the Sportsmen's Club. Sirmans, who prided himself on having brought Tilghman to Cromwell, was particularly enthused. Like a bandleader with a baton, he used his fork to punctuate his point.

"No question of it," he said keenly. "Blowing those gambling tables to smithereens was a masterstroke. The whole town's talking about it."

Virgil Pryor, a lanky man with somber features, wagged his head. "The tables were a symbol," he said, looking at Tilghman. "But to me, the most impressive thing was that you belittled Hammer in the eyes of the townspeople. Was that why you didn't arrest him, Marshal?"

"Partly," Tilghman said, avoiding a direct answer. "I wanted people to understand that Hammer and his goons don't run this town. They answer to the law like anybody else."

Sirmans jabbed the air with his fork. "You certainly did that! Closing his club was much more effective than arresting him. Do you think he'll try to reopen?"

"Hard to say," Tilghman replied. "Depends on how far he wants to carry it. Guess we'll find out."

Sirmans and Pryor were novices to the game. A merchant and a preacher, like most civilians, had little insight into the nuances of law enforcement. They would have been surprised that Tilghman viewed it as something of a chess match. The way to defeat an opponent was to block his options, force him into narrow pathways of your own choosing, and spring checkmate with an unexpected move. Tilghman saw no reason to reveal tactics, particularly since the trap had yet to be sprung. He let them think it was checkers rather than chess.

"How's things with the fire department?" he said, changing the subject. "Got that truck outfitted yet?"

"Have it ready tomorrow," Sirmans said around a mouthful of steak. "Fred Wagner took charge of getting it rigged with hoses and a water tank. At least a dozen men have volunteered to man the truck."

"Glad to hear there's some civic spirit in Cromwell. Any of them volunteer to join the Citizens Committee?"

"Well, given time, I'm sure they will. You have to understand, they're still afraid, Marshal. They're waiting to see how it turns out with Hammer."

"We need to work on that," Tilghman said. "The law is what people make it. Sooner or later, they have to take a stand."

"Speaking of civic spirit," Zoe interjected. "Perhaps the church could be a rallying point. After all, religion does unite people together."

Pryor nodded wisely. "The laws of man are founded on the laws of God. One goes hand in hand with the other."

"Yes, that's true," Zoe agreed. "But first, we have to attract more people to church. Especially more women."

"Hmmm." Pryor considered a moment. "That's an interesting observation, Mrs. Tilghman. Why do you stress the need for more women?"

"Because men follow their women, at least where religion is concerned. Women are the backbone of any church."

Zoe and Tilghman had attended church services on Sunday. Pryor had a small flock of parishioners, which was not surprising in a boomtown. But Zoe was nonetheless surprised by the small number of women in the congregation. Merchants and shopkeepers were accompanied by their wives and children; but few oil men brought their women with them to the fields. Even fewer attended church services, and Zoe thought the scarcity of women was the reason.

"Hardly any oil men attend church," she said. "But we need to get them involved in community affairs if we're to win their support in cleaning up the town. A first step would be to attract them into church."

"A splendid idea," Pryor remarked. "But roughnecks and roustabouts prefer dance halls to hymn books. How do we attract them?"

"By attracting the women they socialize with. The barmaids, the dance hall girls . . . even the prostitutes."

Sirmans was nonplussed, hardly able to credit his ears. Pryor looked aghast, sputtering for words. "Are you serious?" he said haltingly. "You want to invite fallen women into my church?"

"Why not?" Zoe said reasonably. "We are all God's children, saints and sinners alike. And your business is in saving souls . . . isn't it, Reverend?"

Tilghman smothered a laugh. He thought Virgil Pryor had no more chance than a snowball in hell of outwitting Zoe. He watched with amusement as she presented her case for filling the church with whores and dance hall girls. Within a matter of minutes, she had the preacher nodding in agreement. Pryor, like an evangelist with a newfound mission, even agreed to visit the town's bordellos. He would issue the invitation personally.

For his part, Tilghman was a neutral observer. He thought Zoe's idea had merit, and he'd encouraged her to present it at the supper meeting tonight. Yet he knew from long experience that preachers and their congregations seldom made the difference. God favored the just, and the support of the community was important to any peace officer. Still, in the end, it all came down to a man with a badge, who was willing to enforce the law with a gun. Lawbreakers were ultimately converted by the terrible, swift sword.

After supper, Sirmans and Pryor said good night outside the cafe. Zoe was exhilarated by the evening's events, chattering on with bubbly animation as Tilghman escorted her back to the hotel. She kissed him at the door, and he waited in the hall until he heard the key turn the lock. Downstairs again, he walked west toward the intersection. Up ahead, he saw Sawyer round the corner and hurry forward. The deputy had the eager look of someone bearing news.

"Glad I found you," he said. "Just got a tip on a drug party. Down at the Criterion Hotel."

The Criterion was one of the town's sleazier hotels. Tilghman raised an eyebrow. "What do you mean, a drug party?"

"Way I hear it, a couple of guys took a room at the hotel. They got hold of some cocaine and hired two girls from Ida Belle's cathouse. They're gonna have an all-night party."

Ida Belle Trotter ran a brothel adjacent to the hotel. She was known to provide girls for men staying at the Criterion. Tilghman nodded, thoughtful. "Who gave you the tip?"

"One of the girls at Ida Belle's. These guys passed her over for another girl and she got ticked. Guess her feelings were hurt."

"So she volunteered the information to you?"

"Not ten minutes ago. Ducked into the office and ducked out. Told Ida Belle she'd gone to get cigarettes."

"Sounds fishy," Tilghman said skeptically. "Too quick, too easy."

Sawyer looked baffled. "She's just a whore trying to get even. Nothin' so odd about that."

"Do you trust a whore's word?"

"Guess it depends on the situation. I thought these guys might tumble to where they bought the dope. We damn sure haven't got anything out of Snake lately."

"No, we haven't," Tilghman admitted. "Did the girl give you the men's names?"

"She only heard one name. Colter or Colton, something like that. She wasn't too sure."

"All right, let's check it out."

Tilghman was vaguely uneasy. Some visceral instinct

told him that a whore trying to even the score was still not to be trusted. He thought it smelled.

A brisk wind whipped in from the west as they walked toward the corner.

The Criterion was on Jenkins Street, a block north of the jail. Flanked by a whorehouse on one side and a ginmill on the other, the hotel was seedy even by Cromwell standards. The lobby was small, lighted by a dingy overhead globe.

A night clerk was seated in a narrow cubicle behind the front desk. He looked around, his eyes magnified by thick glasses, as Tilghman and Sawyer came through the door. Thin and stoop-shouldered, he rose from a creaky chair and moved to the counter. His expression was vacant.

"Help you, Marshal?"

"Looking for someone," Tilghman said. "You've got a couple of men staying here. One's named Colter, or maybe Colton."

"Colton. The other one's named Markel. What'd they do?"

"Not sure they've done anything. You know their line of business?"

"Salesmen of some sort. Just traveling through."

"When did they check in?"

"Late this afternoon," the clerk said with a lecherous smile. "The day man told me about them. They was askin' about girls."

"Were they?" Tilghman said. "Have they got girls with them now?"

"Couple of floozies from Ida Bell's were with them. They left a while ago."

"How long ago?"

"Maybe ten minutes."

Tilghman's look betrayed nothing. "Let me see the ledger."

The clerk pulled the registration book from beneath

the counter. He opened it to the current page, and Tilghman ran his finger down the list of names. He found John Colton and Tom Markel, their place of residence noted as Tulsa. Their business listing was the Tulsa Oil & Gas Equipment Company.

Tilghman glanced up. "What room are they in?"

"One eleven. Ground floor, almost at the end of the hall."

"Much obliged."

"Anytime, Marshal. Glad to help."

Tilghman led the way down the hall. A few doors along the corridor he stopped, motioning to Sawyer. "Something stinks here," he said. "Why would they send the girls away if they meant to have a party? I don't like it."

"Don't make sense," Sawyer said. "How do we handle it?"

"Just follow my lead. Stay clear of the door and keep your gun handy. I'll do the talking."

Loud radio music blared from Room 111. Tilghman positioned himself on one side of the door and Sawyer on the other. Hugging the wall, his pistol drawn, he rapped on the door. A man's voice called out over the radio.

"Who's there?"

"Town marshal," Tilghman yelled. "Like to talk with you."

"Door's open. C'mon in, Marshal."

Tilghman turned the knob with his free hand. He shoved on the door, then quickly stepped back. A hail of gunfire erupted from within the room, bullets sizzling through the open doorway. He caught the distinct bark of two pistols, aware in the same instant that the lights were out in the room. Dropping to the floor, he edged around the door jamb, his Colt extended, and waited. Sawyer crouched at the opposite side of the door, his gunhand braced against the jamb. He fired blindly into the dark.

A muzzle flash lit the room across from the door. As a slug whistled overhead, Tilghman fired at a man momentarily revealed in the blast of light. The man grunted, stumbling back against the wall, and pitched forward on his face. Across the room, three shots ripped out as another man flung open the window. One leg over the windowsill, he was silhouetted against the glow of streetlights, and Tilghman fired twice. Frozen there, the man slowly toppled out of the window onto the floor.

Tilghman got to his feet. He eased one hand around the doorjamb, fumbling in the dark, and found the light switch. When the lights came on, one man lay facedown by the wall, soaked with blood. The other one lay sprawled beneath the window, his eyes blank, staring at the ceiling. As Tilghman moved into the room, Sawyer walked to a bedside table and turned off the radio. They stood staring down at the dead men.

"Jesus," Sawyer muttered. "It was a setup. They were waitin' on us."

Tilghman nodded. "Doesn't take a detective to figure out who arranged it."

A quick search of the room proved revealing. There was no evidence of cocaine, and the men were registered at the hotel under false names. Their driver's license cards identified them as Joseph Scalici and Robert Terrell. Neither of them had business cards or other identification related to the Tulsa Oil & Gas Equipment Company. They were from Ardmore.

In the lobby, Tilghman ordered the desk clerk to call the undertaker. Followed by Sawyer, he then stormed into Ida Belle Trotter's whorehouse. The madam, as well as the girl who had tipped Sawyer, was subjected to a rough interrogation. Neither of them deviated from their story; they insisted the men were strangers, good-time boys looking for a party. The two girls who had accompanied the men to the hotel corroborated the story. They had been paid for services rendered and sent on their way.

After almost an hour, Tilghman ended the grilling. On the street he shook his head in disgust. "They're lying," he said gruffly. "Trouble is, we'll never prove it."

"Ida Belle's scared to death," Sawyer commented. "You could see it in her face plain as day. Same thing with the girls."

"Jake Hammer and his boys are good at scaring people."

Tilghman watched as the bodies from the hotel were loaded into the undertaker's hearse. There was little likelihood that the dead men would ever be tied to Hammer. Any request for an investigation by the Ardmore police, he told himself, would be wasted motion. Like Cromwell, Ardmore was an oil town, and heavily influenced by mob money. But with or without an investigation, he knew all there was to know about the dead men.

Joseph Scalici and Robert Terrell were hired killers.

CHAPTER 25

By the next afternoon Tilghman was at a dead end. A phone call to Ardmore brought nothing more nor less than he'd expected. The town marshal there professed to have no knowledge of Scalici and Terrell, and doubted out loud that an investigation would lead anywhere. He ended with a halfhearted promise to look into the matter.

When Tilghman hung up, he knew he was stymied. There would be no investigation, and whatever the dead men's connection to the Ardmore mob, he would never trace it back to Cromwell. He had goaded Hammer to make a move, but he'd underestimated the man's cunning. Or perhaps the cunning of whoever pulled Hammer's strings. Importing hired guns was a cagey maneuver. One he hadn't expected.

Still, as he'd told Zoe last night, his instincts were as good as ever. His aim wasn't too bad either, for he had managed to kill two men in the dark. But Zoe took little comfort from his reassurances, worrying instead that there would be another assassination attempt. Though he refused to admit it, he thought she was probably right, for he had invited the attack. Which made him question his assessment of tactics, and how the other side would respond. He had to find the man who pulled the strings.

Unable to set it aside, he was preoccupied by the

thought when the door opened. A woman in her late thirties, fashionably dressed for Cromwell, stepped into the office. She was attractive, with blond hair, blue eyes, and a sad-looking smile. Tilghman rose from his chair as she closed the door.

"Afternoon," he said. "Something I can do for you?"

"Are you Marshal Tilghman?"

"Yes, ma'am."

"I'm Lucy Stover," she said. "Mrs. Lucy Stover. I hope you can help me, Marshal."

"Have a seat." Tilghman motioned her to a chair, then resumed his seat. "What seems to be the problem?"

"I'm looking for my daughter, Marian Stover. I have reason to believe she's in Cromwell."

"How old's your daughter, Mrs. Stover?"

"Sixteen," she said dully. "Marian was always a little rebellious. Young girls often are . . ."

"I take it she ran away from home?"

"Well, no, not just exactly. She answered an advertisement in the newspaper—"

"Which paper is that?"

"Oh goodness, I forgot to tell you. I'm from Kansas City, Marshal. It was the *Kansas City Star*."

Tilghman's brow furrowed. "You drove all the way from Kansas City? Where's Mr. Stover?"

"We were divorced," she said. "Three years ago this coming January. The last I heard, he's living in California."

"Guess that explains that. Tell me about your daughter."

Lucy Stover related a familiar tale. Advertisements appeared in newspapers throughout the Midwest, promising a life of adventure and big money. The ads were directed at young women, offering work as dance hall hostesses in oil towns across Oklahoma and Texas. Worded in an enticing manner, the ads made it sound glamorous and exciting. Nothing was mentioned about wages of ten-cents-a-dance.

An ad in the *Kansas City Star* had attracted Marian Stover. After being interviewed by a man at a hotel, she returned home with visions of a romantic life in the oil fields. Her mother strenuously objected, and the next day the man came to their home, trying to charm Lucy Stover into agreement. When she refused, the girl simply disappeared that night, sneaking out with a bag of clothes. She had been gone now for more than a week.

"She's just a little girl," Lucy Stover concluded, tears welling over in her eyes. "The police in Kansas City were no help, and I decided to come here myself. I have to find her and take her home."

Tilghman knuckled his mustache thoughtfully. "What makes you think she's in Cromwell?"

"Why, this man—Carl Hunt—went on and on about Cromwell. Marian had stars in her eyes before he was through."

"I just suspect he gave you a phony name. Could you describe him?"

"Oh, I certainly can! He's not much taller than me, maybe five-foot-six. Dark brown hair, combed straight back, and brown eyes. A nice-looking man, almost handsome."

"How old?"

"Probably twenty-six or twenty-seven. Somewhere in there."

"Doesn't ring any bells," Tilghman said. "How about your daughter? Describe her."

"She looks a lot like me," Lucy Stover said with a shy smile. "Slimmer, of course, but buxom for her age. A pretty girl."

"And she's sixteen?"

"A very sweet sixteen, Marshal. Innocent as a lamb."

Tilghman doubted the girl was innocent any longer. Some inner voice also led him to doubt she would be found in a dance hall. He remembered Josie Rodgers alluding to whorehouses that specialized in underage girls. He thought it more likely than not that Lucy Stover was in for a shock.

Zoe came though the door. She apologized for interrupting, starting to leave, but Tilghman wouldn't hear of it. He introduced the women, quickly explaining the situation, and asked Zoe to stay with Mrs. Stover while he went out. Sawyer was off making afternoon rounds, and he thought the deputy might recognize the description of Carl Hunt. He promised he wouldn't be long.

Outside, Tilghman started toward the uptown business district. But as he stepped off the curb, he saw Zack Mosley and Josie Rodgers come out of the Sportsmen's Club. He first wondered why Mosley would be visiting the club in the middle of the afternoon. Then, on second thought, he decided to ask Josie a few questions. At worst, he told himself, she could only say no.

Tilghman angled across the street. He caught up with them halfway along the block. "You folks out for a stroll?"

Mosley looked as though he was about to burst with pride. "Wait'll you hear this," he said, laughing. "Josie just told Hammer to go to hell, and she quit the club. We're gonna get married."

"It's true!" Josie flushed with happiness. "The big galoot finally talked me into it. I'm out of the business for good."

"Well, congratulations," Tilghman said with a wide grin. "I'm real pleased for both of you. How'd Hammer take the news?"

Josie rolled her eyes. "That's why Zack came into town. I didn't want any trouble, and Jake's always been a little afraid of him. I told him to stuff it and we walked out."

"She let him have it," Mosley said with a gruff chuckle. "He's probably back there cussing a blue streak now that we're gone. But who gives a damn?"

"Wish I'd been there." Tilghman paused, suddenly

somber. "Look here, I don't mean to rain on your parade, but I've got a problem." He glanced at Josie. "Thought maybe you could help me."

"Ask me and see," she said. "What kind of help?"

"You recollect telling me about the house with young girls?"

Her look became guarded. "I might have mentioned it."

"I've got a woman in my office. She drove all the way from Kansas City looking for her daughter. A little girl of sixteen."

"And you think somebody turned her into a whore?"

"Wouldn't surprise me," Tilghman remarked. "You know a man named Carl Hunt?"

"Oh God." She pursed her mouth. "Maybe I'm out of the business, but these people still scare me. You never heard it from me, okay?"

"You've got my word on it."

"Well, his name isn't Carl Hunt. That's the moniker he uses when he cons girls into the life. His real name is Charlie Ebersole."

"Where's the house he runs?"

Josie quickly explained the operation. At the east end of Shawnee Avenue, a woman named Mattie Jones ran what appeared to be a boardinghouse. In truth, there were no boarders, and the operation was one of Cromwell's best-kept secrets. Ebersole, who was the woman's partner, tricked the girls into coming there with promises of a dance hall job. They were held in bondage on the second floor, and never allowed out of the house. Those who frequented the place were fearful of arrest on morals charges and kept it quiet. The underworld crowd simply pretended the operation didn't exist.

"Ebersole's a bastard," Josie said plainly. "But he's no worse than Mattie Jones. They both ought to be shot."

Mosley appeared stunned. The boardinghouse was clearly a closely guarded secret, known to few in Cromwell. He looked at Tilghman. "Just ask if you want some help, Marshal. I'd be glad to lend a hand."

"I'll tend to it," Tilghman said. "You two have other things on your mind. When's the happy day?"

"Tomorrow," Mosley said with a boyish grin. "Found a justice of the peace over in Wewoka. I'm not gonna let her get away this time."

"Don't blame you a bit, Zack. You got yourself a mighty fine bride."

Josie blushed again. "You're pretty special yourself, Marshal. Good luck with Ebersole."

"I'll let you know how it works out."

Late that afternoon Tilghman and Sawyer raided the boardinghouse. Charlie Ebersole tried to bar their way to the second floor, and Sawyer decked him with one punch. Upstairs, they found five girls, ranging in age from fourteen to sixteen. The girls were held prisoner in locked rooms, dressed only in skimpy underclothes, available to customers day or night. They cowered in abject terror as the lawmen brought them downstairs. One of them was Marian Stover.

By early evening Lucy Stover had been reunited with her daughter. She wept with joy, embracing her daughter while smothering Tilghman and Sawyer with hugs. The other girls were taken under wing by Zoe and Reverend Pryor, who arranged temporary shelter with church families. Tilghman then began calling the girls' parents, advising them that their daughters had been rescued. For Charlie Ebersole and Mattie Jones, who were thrown into the holding cell, the treatment was less charitable.

Tilghman ordered bread and water for their evening meal.

Judge George Crump cleared his docket late the next morning. By then, Mattie Jones and Charlie Ebersole had been able to retain legal counsel. Tilghman, with Sawyer riding shotgun, transported them to Wewoka in his old Ford. They were marched into the courthouse in handcuffs.

In the courtroom, they were charged with violation of the Mann Act. A federal law, enacted in 1910, the Mann Act prohibited interstate transport of women for immoral purposes. Sometimes known as the White Slavery Law, the statute carried a minimum sentence of ten years in federal prison upon conviction. The customary sentence for those who dealt in underage girls was twenty years.

The prisoners looked the worse for their night in the holding cell. Charlie Ebersole, who prided himself on his natty attire, was rumpled and unshaven. His left eye, a blend of purple and black from Sawyer's punch, was swollen shut. Mattie Jones, four years older than her partner, appeared haggard, her hair a mess and her features puffy from a night with little sleep. They both pleaded not guilty to the charges.

Titus Blackburn, the county attorney, presented the case for the government. His moral code, which could be stretched to overlook bootleggers and gamblers, permitted no leniency for white slavers. His first two witnesses were Tilghman and Sawyer, who related what they had uncovered at the boardinghouse. Then he called Marian Stover, who had been selected from among the five girls. She was the oldest, somewhat more mature, and her lone appearance spared the other girls from the courtroom ordeal. Her testimony was damning.

Lucy Stover, watching from the spectator benches, wept uncontrollably during the examination. The girl spoke in a dull voice, her youthful features haunted by the story she told. She related how she and the other girls had been lured to Cromwell by false promises. Upon arrival at the boardinghouse, each of the girls had been raped by Ebersole, to "break them in" for their new life. Afterward, held prisoner in their rooms, they were each forced to entertain as many as six or seven men a day. Mattie Jones, she testified, regularly beat any of the girls who failed to satisfy a customer. They were routinely forced to engage in perverse acts of sex.

The defense attorney was no less appalled than others in the courtroom. He declined to cross-examine the girl, all too aware that further questioning would further prejudice the case. Instead, asking the court's indulgence, he went into a whispered huddle with his clients. Ebersole seemed angry, violently shaking his head, but Mattie Jones listened with rapt attention. After a heated exchange, the lawyer informed the court that Ebersole had fired him and would seek new counsel. He would, however, remain attorney of record for Mattie Jones.

Judge Crump ordered the defendants bound over for trial. Before anyone could raise the issue, he then ordered them to be held without bail. Ebersole, cursing and threatening Mattie Jones with dark looks, was led from the courtroom by a sheriff's deputy. The defense attorney, now representing only the woman, promptly offered the government a deal. In exchange for immunity, his client was willing to plead guilty and testify against Charlie Ebersole. When Crump refused, the attorney asked for a closed conference in the judge's chambers. Over Blackburn's objection, he requested that only Marshal Tilghman be allowed to attend the conference. Judge Crump agreed.

A few minutes later they gathered in the judge's chambers. The defense attorney announced that his client had something to trade, something that merited immunity. Crump was willing to listen, but he promised nothing. His decision would be based on the value of the information. The attorney nodded to Mattie Jones.

She looked directly at Tilghman. "The night you raided Cal Munson's roadhouse, you offered him a deal. He bragged about turning you down."

Tilghman's every instinct alerted. "So?"

"So you don't believe Jake Hammer's the head man in Cromwell. What if I could give you the name of his boss?"

"How do I know your information's reliable?"

"Oh, it's the straight goods! Hammer liked my little girls, liked 'em a lot. Him and Charlie got to be drinking buddies."

"I'm still listening."

"Hammer got drunk at my place one night. He spilled the beans to Charlie. Told him who really runs the rackets."

Tilghman coaxed her with a nod. "Who's that?"

"Not so quick," she said. "Cal Munson got himself hung because he *might* have talked. If I tell you, I want a safe escort out of Oklahoma. Otherwise, no deal."

Tilghman exchanged a glance with the judge. She caught the look, and rushed on. "Charlie and me knew Hammer from the old days in Kansas City. That's how we knew he was on the square. We'd heard of his boss before."

"Before?" Tilghman repeated. "Are you talking about Kansas City?"

She shrugged. "He was the mob's top enforcer. Nobody you'd want to cross."

Judge Crump cleared his throat. "I'll leave it up to you, Marshal. If you believe her, she goes free." He paused for emphasis. "If not, she goes to prison."

"All right," Tilghman said, staring at her. "Give me a name."

"Frank Killian."

A thick silence fell over the room. Tilghman continued to stare at her, searching her eyes for a flicker of deceit. She returned his stare with a faint smile, and he somehow knew he'd heard the truth. He remembered he had meant to investigate Killian and never got around to it. Nor had he been able to turn up an informant, until today. He finally nodded to the woman.

"You just bought yourself a ticket out of Oklahoma."

CHAPTER 26

The office was quiet late that afternoon. Tilghman stood at the window, staring at the Sportsmen's Club. He was aware of Sawyer watching him from a chair tilted against the wall. But his mind was on the next move, the most critical move yet in the game. He was playing it out in his head.

On balance, he estimated his chances at fifty-fifty. Even if he failed, it was still a two-way move, forcing alternatives. Given what was known, Hammer might be persuaded to talk. But if he refused, he was almost certain to seek orders, rather than act on his own. Either way it would lead to Killian.

Tilghman thought the odds were in his favor. He had always laughed at the notion of honor among thieves. In forty years of law enforcement, he had turned dozens of badmen against their confederates. Women were no exception, and he hadn't been surprised when Mattie Jones turned on her partner. His one regret was that he couldn't take her before a grand jury.

Under the law her testimony would have been ruled hearsay, and therefore inadmissible. But Hammer was a different matter altogether, an unimpeachable witness. His testimony before a grand jury would bring down the sheriff and other county officials, and more importantly,

Frank Killian. All that remained was to convince him to talk. Today seemed the perfect time.

"I'll be back directly," he said, glancing at Sawyer. "You stick close to the office."

Sawyer got to his feet. "Sure you don't want me to come along, Marshal? No need to go in there by yourself."

"Like I told you, it's better I go alone. Hammer would never talk in front of a witness."

"I still don't care much for the idea."

"Hold down the fort, Hugh. I won't be long."

Tilghman went out the door. He crossed the street, wondering what he would find inside the club. Five days after the raid, Hammer still hadn't tried to reopen for business. Which meant nothing in itself, Tilghman told himself, particularly after the shootout at the Criterion Hotel. Hammer was probably waiting for more hired guns to arrive.

Turk Milligan and the other gang members were seated around a table in the front of the club. When Tilghman came through the door, interrupting their poker game, they started to their feet. He waved them down, moving along the bar, and entered the gaming room. The debris from the raid had been cleared out, and the floor swept clean. The room was empty.

Across the way, he rapped on the door of Hammer's office. Without waiting for a response, he stepped inside and found Hammer seated behind his desk. The mobster was in the act of pouring himself a drink from a bottle of scotch. He looked up with a surprised expression, lowering the bottle. His eyes narrowed.

"How the hell'd you get in here?"

"Nothing to it," Tilghman said. "I think your boys are snake-bit, Jake. Nobody said boo."

"You're a real comic," Hammer snapped. "What d'you want?"

Tilghman took a chair in front of the desk. "Guess

you heard about the split between Ebersole and Mattie Jones. She gave me the lowdown.''

''What lowdown is that?''

''Told me you like little girls. You ought to be ashamed of yourself, Jake.''

''So I like 'em young. So what?''

''Well, that wasn't the interesting part. She told me you got drunk and spilled the beans to Ebersole. About your boss—Frank Killian.''

Hammer went still. ''I don't know what you're talking about.''

''Sure you do,'' Tilghman said amiably. ''You're just the front man for the rackets. Killian calls the shots.''

''You're whistlin' through your nose.''

''Don't get testy, Jake. I'm here to save your skin.''

''Lucky me,'' Hammer snorted. ''Who said it needs savin'?''

''No doubt about it,'' Tilghman told him. ''Killian's got you set up to be the fall guy. Just a matter of time till I nail you.''

''Christ, you really got me scared. I'm shakin' all over.''

''Yeah, I know. That's why you tried to have me killed. Or were you just following orders?''

Hammer sipped his scotch. ''Say what you came to say. I'm a busy man.''

''Let's talk a deal.'' Tilghman gestured to the whiskey bottle. ''Complete immunity on liquor, gambling, and drugs. No trial, no prison time.''

''And what'd I have to do?''

''Give me Killian.''

''Never heard of him,'' Hammer said with a wiseacre grin. ''Anything else on your mind?''

''Two counts of murder,'' Tilghman said without a trace of humor. ''Will Bohannon and Cal Munson.''

''Are you offering me immunity on murder? Not that I ever did anything, you understand.''

''You know, that's a good point, Jake. I doubt I'd

have that much pull. Guess you'll have to take Killian's place.''

''What place is that?''

Tilghman set the barb. ''In the electric chair. You ever seen a man fried, Jake? Helluva sight.''

Hammer's eyes betrayed him. He quickly tossed off his scotch. ''We're done talkin', Tilghman. Arrest me or get lost.''

''Don't worry, I'll arrest you, Jake. Sooner than you think.''

Tilghman walked out of the office. On his way through the club, he waved to Milligan and the other poker players. Outside, he crossed the street and entered the jail, nodding to Sawyer. His mustache curled in a nutcracker grin.

''Godalmighty,'' Sawyer said, watching him intently. ''Don't tell me he talked!''

''Not in so many words.''

''You lost me there, Marshal.''

''Hugh, from now on, you've only got one assignment. Keep your eye on Hammer night and day. Stick to him like glue.''

''You think he's gonna run?''

''Yeah, he'll run all right. Straight to Frank Killian.''

Tilghman was charged with energy. He had managed to spook Hammer, and it was now a whole new game. A game of fox and hound.

A game he'd mastered forty years ago.

Sawyer was hidden in an alley across from the Sportsmen's Club. A pale moon lighted the street, and he stood lost in the shadows at the rear of a building. From his position, he was able to keep watch on the entrance to the club and the back door leading to the alley. He stamped his feet in the cold night air.

Shortly after nine o'clock Turk Milligan emerged from the club and paused on the boardwalk. He stared across at the jailhouse for a moment, then slowly inspected Jenkins Street in both directions. From the alleyway, Sawyer watched as he stepped off the curb and got into Hammer's Buick sedan. The engine turned over.

Milligan backed away from the curb. He switched on the lights, hooked into low gear, and turned the corner onto the side street. At the rear of the club, he wheeled into the alley and quickly braked to a stop. He left the motor idling, the lights on, and moved through the back door of the club. Sawyer took off running for the jail.

Tilghman looked up when he burst through the door. "They're on the move," he said, catching his breath. "Milligan just pulled the car into the alley."

"No time to waste, then. Let's go."

The old Ford was parked beside the jail. Tilghman fired the engine but left the headlights off. He and Sawyer watched as the Buick backed out of the alley, turned east on the side street, then turned right at the next corner. He pulled out, shifting gears, and followed a block behind. Under the dappled moonlight, he was able to tail the other car without headlights. The Buick drove south on the road to Wewoka.

Some thirty minutes later the Buick turned off the highway. The car wound through a residential area on the outskirts of Wewoka. Tilghman, who was still running without lights, stayed at least a block to the rear. Up ahead, on a street lined with trees, he saw the Buick nose into the driveway of a brick house. Lightly tapping the brakes, he pulled over to the curb and cut the engine. He and Sawyer watched as Hammer entered the house.

"What d'you think?" Sawyer asked. "Figure that's Killian's place?"

"You stay here," Tilghman said. "I'll go scout the—"

Headlights appeared at the opposite end of the street. Tilghman fell silent, and they ducked below the dashboard as a Studebaker roadster pulled in behind the Buick. A figure emerged from the roadster, waving to the two men in the front seat of the Buick, and started up the walkway. Sawyer let out a harsh grunt.

"Either I'm going blind or that's Wiley Lynn."

"Don't leave the car, Hugh. Not unless you hear shooting."

Tilghman ghosted off into the night. He circled a house on the opposite side of the street and cut through the back yard. Wary of neighborhood dogs, he counted houses as he moved along in the silty moonlight. The brick house was seven houses down, and he saw a woman in the kitchen, placing glasses on a tray. He waited until she walked out, then he crossed the yard and skirted the corner. Lights spilled from a window at the front of the house.

The window was less than ten feet from the head of the driveway. Tilghman edged along the side of the house, alert to any noise or movement from the Buick. He stooped low, removing his hat, and slowly brought his eyes level with the windowsill. Killian was seated in an easy chair, and side by side on a sofa were Jake Hammer and Wiley Lynn. The woman, an attractive redhead, moved from man to man, serving drinks off the tray. Then, with a glance at Killian, she walked from the living room.

There was no question as to who was in charge. Killian talked, and the other two men listened attentively, sipping their drinks. Watching them, Tilghman strained to hear voices, but caught only garbled sounds through the closed window. He was nonetheless pleased, for the tone of the meeting affirmed who gave the orders in Seminole County. Still, having confirmed that, he lacked the proof to make it stick with a grand jury. Three men talking over drinks was not hard evidence.

A low growl erupted into snarling barks. Over his shoulder Tilghman saw a mongrel hound at the front corner of the house next door. The dog was stiff-legged, hackles raised, glaring at him with yellowed eyes. From the driveway, a car door opened, and he heard the sound of men's voices. He turned away from the window, moving hurriedly toward the rear of the house. He disappeared around the corner an instant before Turk Milligan stepped off the driveway. The dog continued to bark.

Milligan scanned the side of the house. After a moment, when he saw nothing suspicious, he waved at the dog. "Quit your yappin'! Go on, scram!"

The dog gave ground, retreating with a final bark. Milligan walked back to the car, crawled in beside Shuemacher. "Must've been a cat. I didn't see nothin'."

Shuemacher nodded. "Goddamn dogs will bark at anything. Wonder how long Jake's gonna be."

"Hope it ain't much longer. I'm freezin' my ass off."

"That makes two of us."

Killian swirled the brandy in his glass. Hammer and Lynn waited, watching him, neither of them willing to break the silence. He was in a dangerous mood.

"Get out the word on Mattie Jones," he said at length. "Wherever she turns up, somebody will hear about it. I want her rubbed out."

"What about Ebersole?" Hammer asked. "He's lookin' at hard time in a federal pen. Always a chance he'll talk."

"Neither of them would have talked if you hadn't gotten drunk. I ought to cut out your tongue."

"Christ, I already said I was wrong! You ever think I could've just said nothin'? And then where'd we be?"

"Where we are now," Killian retorted. "Tilghman knows who I am, and he won't stop till he gets proof. All thanks to you, Jake."

"So we stop him," Hammer said. "Wasn't that why you told me to call Wiley? What else is he here for?"

Wiley Lynn tensed. He had been asking himself the same question. Up until now he had been no part of the conversation, a reluctant observer. His stomach felt watery as Killian's gaze fixed on him.

"Wiley, you've become a problem," Killian said. "I

have a contact in the state police, and I pay him well. He tells me that Tilghman had you investigated.''

''Investigated?'' Lynn said dumbly. ''What for?''

''I suspect he's looking for an informant. He gets you to rat on Jake and Bradley, and in the end—that leads to me.''

''Hell's fire, I wouldn't talk! You know that.''

Killian just stared at him. ''What it amounts to is, I'm faced with a double liability. You and Tilghman.''

''Get rid of Tilghman, then. Turn Jake's boys loose.''

''No, I prefer that you do it, Wiley. Tilghman whipped you once in public, and I'm sure you can provoke him again. Make it look like self-defense.''

Lynn blanched. ''You want me to kill him?''

''I have to eliminate one part of the liability. Are you willing to handle it for me, Wiley?''

Unspoken, the threat was nonetheless real. If Lynn refused, he himself would be eliminated. ''I'll take care of it,'' he said, clearly shaken. ''Don't know how, but I'll figure something out.''

''I want the good news before the end of the week. Understood?''

''Yeah, I'm with you.''

Killian dismissed him with a handshake and a hard smile. When the Studebaker pulled out of the driveway, Hammer laughed. ''Maybe they'll kill each other. I've heard Lynn's not bad with a gun.''

''Two birds with one stone,'' Killian said thoughtfully. ''That's always a possibility, Jake. Perhaps we'll get lucky.''

''What if it goes the other way? Tilghman's no pushover.''

''We'll see how it plays out.''

''I'd be glad to pop the old fucker myself. All you have to do is say the word.''

''I've told you before, I don't want you involved. Besides, you'll be busy this weekend.''

''What's up?''

"A shipment's coming in Saturday night from Mexico. You be there for the airdrop."

Killian drained his brandy glass. He stared at the crackling logs in the fireplace, suddenly intrigued by another thought. One far more important than an airdrop.

Tilghman seemed to have more lives than a cat. He wondered if Wiley Lynn was up to the job.

CHAPTER 27

Zoe met Tilghman in the lobby the next day at noon. Unless duty took him elsewhere, he made it a point to be with her at mealtime. There was nothing on his calendar today.

When they entered the cafe, Zoe let out a little cry of delight. Josie and Zack Mosley were seated at a table near the window. They rose as Zoe hurried forward, and the two women hugged one another with unrestrained glee. Tilghman and Mosley exchanged a warm handshake.

"Look at you!" Zoe exclaimed. "Mr. and Mrs. Mosley."

"It's official." Josie held out her left hand, displaying a gold wedding band. "We tied the knot yesterday."

Mosley laughed. "She almost backed out at the last minute. I had to drag her to the altar."

"You did not!" Josie swatted him on the arm. "Besides, it wasn't an altar anyway. We were married by a justice of the peace."

"Good thing too," Mosley said, putting an arm around her waist. "She was so skittish, I all but had to shanghai her. Never would've got her to a church."

"Listen to them," Tilghman said with a jocular chuckle. "You sure it was only yesterday? You already sound like an old married couple."

The roughnecks and roustabouts at nearby tables were listening with open interest. Some of them were amused that the wealthiest oil man in Cromwell had married a whore. But their comments would be reserved for later, among themselves, and in private. Tough as they were, none of them cared to tangle with Zack Mosley.

"I have to ask," Zoe said with mock innocence. "Why aren't you off on your honeymoon?"

Josie blushed. "We honeymooned in Wewoka last night. Zack had to get back to business."

"You all sit down," Mosley said, indicating the table. "Welcome to have dinner with us. Matter of fact, we're neighbors now. Josie and me moved into the Regent this morning."

Tilghman glanced out the window. After the last few days, he was wary of sitting near windows, even in daylight. He passed it off with a wry smile. "You lovebirds need some time to yourselves. Maybe we'll see you at supper."

"I can't wait that long," Zoe said, with a sly wink at Josie. "I want to hear all about your wedding. Are you free this afternoon?"

"Oh, I think so," Josie said. "Zack's just itching to get back to the rigs."

"Then we'll have ourselves a nice, long talk."

"Maybe about some other things too. I heard what you and the marshal did for those little girls. I was tickled pink."

"I'll tell you all about it this afternoon."

Zoe waved and led the way to the rear of the cafe. Tilghman got her seated, then took a chair with his back to the wall. After giving the waitress their orders, she swept the room with a glance. She lowered her voice.

"Did you see the way those men were looking at Josie and Zack? I expected to hear someone snicker out loud."

"Just ignorance," Tilghman said. "History books don't teach things like that."

"Like what?"

"Lots of those boys have grandmothers who were in Josie's line of work. Some of the best families in Oklahoma got started that way."

"Are you serious?"

"Dead serious," Tilghman said with conviction. "There weren't all that many good women around in the old days. You'd be surprised the number of men that married girls on the line."

"On the line?"

"Guess that just slipped out. I hadn't thought of it in years."

"What does it mean?"

"A delicate way of saying a woman was in the trade. Folks found ways to sugarcoat it back then."

Zoe touched his hand. "You sometimes miss the old days, don't you? I see a funny look come in your eyes."

"Yeah, I do," Tilghman admitted. "Things were a damnsight simpler in those days. Not so many rules."

"You're talking about Killian, aren't you?"

Late last night Tilghman had told her about trailing Hammer to Wewoka. He was frustrated by the barking dog and being driven off without having taken action. To avoid being spotted, he and Sawyer had pushed the car around the corner before starting the engine. She knew he was still brooding on it.

"Whole different world," he said in a musing voice. "In the old days, we'd have busted in there and taken the whole bunch. Back then, you braced a man when you knew he was guilty."

"Oh, for the wild and woolly days," Zoe said, trying for a light tone. "I just imagine that's why you got in so many gunfights."

"I suppose it was a raw sort of justice. But it beat the deuce out of grand juries and a ton of evidence before a man's brought to trial. Everybody figured a murderer got what he deserved."

The waitress returned with their orders. Tilghman

lathered a biscuit with butter and cut into short ribs falling off the bone. Zoe picked at her chicken pie, moving it around on the plate with her fork. She finally looked at him with a worried expression.

"I hope I'm wrong," she said. "You aren't planning on calling Killian out, are you? Forcing him to fight?"

"What makes you ask that?"

"You seem to be dwelling on the old days, when you were young. How things were done in the Wild West."

"Those days are gone." Tilghman paused, a chunk of short rib on his fork. "Like it or lump it, a peace officer has to change with the times. Besides, it wouldn't work anyhow."

"What wouldn't work?"

"Trying to force Killian into a fight."

"Oh?" She watched his eyes. "Why not?"

"These racketeers have a yellow streak a yard wide. They'll shoot you in the back, or hire somebody to do their dirty work. But they don't have the guts to meet you face to face. Like I said—it's a different world."

"So what will you do?"

"Don't know." Tilghman chewed thoughtfully. "I tossed and turned half the night trying to figure the next move. So far, I'm just plain stumped."

Zoe sighed. "There's nothing you could arrest them on?"

"I haven't got a speck of proof against Killian. Unless I nail him, the rackets will perk right along. He's the only one that counts."

"Perhaps you're closer than you think. Otherwise, why would they make an attempt on your life? There has to be a way!"

"I've got sore-eye from lookin' in my crystal ball. I wish I saw a way."

"I know!" she said with sudden insight. "Why not have a talk with Judge Crump? After all, you respect his opinion."

"Even so, what could he tell me?"

"You remember that old adage? Sometimes you're so close to the forest you can't see the trees. Perhaps that's the case with you. He might see something you've overlooked."

Tilghman took a swig of coffee. "You're right about the forest and the trees. Anymore, I can't tell one from the other." He lowered his coffee mug. "You could be right about the judge too."

"Then you'll go see him?"

"Nothing to lose by talking. I'll drive over this afternoon."

Zoe sensed an improvement in his mood. She knew he wouldn't have agreed unless he thought the idea had merit. She hoped there was something he'd overlooked.

A way to end it without more killing.

The courthouse square was crowded. Tilghman eased into a parking space reserved for sheriffs' cars and set the hand brake. He climbed out of the Ford.

On the courthouse steps, he met Bradley coming out of the door. The sheriff gave him a baleful look, then glanced past him at the Ford. Bradley puffed up with an indignant expression.

"You'll have to get your car out of there, Tilghman. That spot's reserved for my deputies."

"I won't be long, Sheriff. Don't worry about it."

"I could have that old junk heap impounded."

"You could, but you won't. I'm here on official business."

Bradley glowered at him. "You just keep pushin' people, don't you?"

"Here and there," Tilghman said. "Charlie Ebersole hung himself yet?"

"What the hell's that supposed to mean?"

"Thought maybe you'd got a call from Killian. Aren't you under orders to hang people who could talk?"

"Hang people?" Bradley squawled in an angry voice. "Are you out of your mind?"

Tilghman laughed shortly. "Cal Munson didn't last

one night. Maybe Ebersole will have better luck.''

"I don't know what you're talking about."

"Why, sure you do, Sheriff. You just proved it."

"Proved what?"

"Oldest trick in the book," Tilghman said. "I asked you a loaded question and you jumped on it. You forgot what was important."

Bradley appeared baffled. "I still don't know what you mean."

"You didn't even blink when I mentioned Killian."

A beat of silence slipped past. Bradley looked like a schoolboy caught out in a lie. "Who's Killian?" he said, trying to recover. "I don't recognize the name."

"That's rich," Tilghman said, genuinely amused by his discomfort. "Don't try it on the grand jury."

"What grand jury?"

"The one that'll ask you about your connection to Killian. 'Course, it's not too likely you'll live to testify."

"You're talkin' riddles."

"No riddle to it. Killian couldn't trust you on a witness stand. Your life's in danger, Sheriff."

"Bullshit!"

Bradley stormed off down the walkway. Tilghman watched him a moment, then turned into the courthouse. He agreed with the sheriff that it was bullshit, for he'd been bluffing about a grand jury. But he had seized on an opportunity to plant a seed of doubt in Bradley's mind. Killian had ordered the murder of others who might provide damaging testimony. The sheriff would have to wonder about his own chances.

Upstairs, a secretary ushered Tilghman into the judge's office. Crump rose from behind his desk, hand extended. "Bill," he said warmly. "Glad you could drop by. Congratulations again on exposing Killian. Anything new?"

Tilghman accepted his handshake. "Just had a talk with the sheriff. Trapped him into halfway admitting he works for Killian. Not that it'd ever hold up in court."

"Too bad." Crump motioned him to a chair. "Do you think Bradley will report the conversation to Killian?"

"I just suspect he will. All except the part about him being snookered."

"Doesn't that place you in even greater jeopardy? You're pushing them awfully hard."

"So far, pushing them hasn't paid off. That's why I asked to see you. I'm fresh out of ideas."

"I'll do anything I can, Bill. What's the problem?"

Tilghman related the events of last night. He described trailing Hammer to Killian's home, and observing the meeting. His frustration was evident from his tone of voice.

"Had them dead to rights," he said, palms spread upward. "Killian, Hammer, and Lynn all in one room. But that and a nickel will get me a cup of coffee. Doesn't prove a thing."

"Unfortunately so," Crump acknowledged. "I commend your resourcefulness. But the meeting in itself doesn't warrant empaneling a grand jury."

"I couldn't even get a search warrant for Killian's home. Not if I understand the law."

"I'm afraid you're right. To issue a search warrant, I'd need more than supposition. Of course, you could always arrest Wiley Lynn."

"On what charge?"

"A federal Prohibition agent consorting with a known bootlegger, Jake Hammer. I seriously doubt he would wiggle free on that one."

Tilghman looked skeptical. "Even if we made it stick, he'd probably just lose his job. The justice department doesn't like to advertise its sour apples."

Crump nodded, deliberating a moment. "You've been searching for the weak link in the chain. Perhaps Lynn is your man."

"You mean turn him into an informant?"

"Well, based on what you've told me, he must have

inside knowledge. Why else would he meet with Killian?"

"Only one problem," Tilghman said. "What do I threaten him with? Loss of his job?"

"Perhaps that would be enough. What do you have to lose by trying?"

Tilghman was reminded of the state police report on Lynn. He recalled that the Prohibition agent had some unsavory relatives convicted of a federal crime. There was always a possibility, he told himself, that the man had other skeletons in his closet. Something more threatening than merely losing a job. He thought it was worth investigating.

"Well, why not?" he said at length. "Lynn's got more than dirt on his shoes. He might be our man."

Crump looked at him. "I know this must be difficult for you. To be so close to apprehending Killian, and yet so far. You're overdue for a bit of luck."

"Funny thing about luck," Tilghman observed. "Abraham Lincoln once said, 'I'm a great believer in luck, and the harder I work, the more luck I seem to have.' I've always figured it was sound advice."

"I applaud the sentiment. But you're on the job night and day. How could you work any harder?"

"I guess it's like a dog diggin' for a rabbit. I've got to scratch a little deeper."

"Perhaps you'll find Wiley Lynn at the bottom of the hole."

"I'll let you know how it works out."

On the steps of the courthouse, Tilghman thought the day somehow looked brighter. A short while ago he'd been fresh out of leads and trading insults with the sheriff. But now, after his talk with the judge, he was back on track. He reminded himself to tell Zoe she was right.

Sometimes you had to step away from the forest to see the trees.

CHAPTER 28

Tilghman drove out before sunrise the next morning. He left Sawyer in charge of the office, with instructions not to expect him back before late that night. His destination was Madill, a small town almost ninety miles south of Cromwell. He pushed the old Ford along at a rattling speed.

A latticework of highways wound through the southern part of the state, and he was able to make good time. Shortly before noon, he crossed the line into Marshall County, once part of the old Chickasaw Nation. As he roared along, watching the countryside roll past, it occurred to him that he'd been here before. A long time ago.

Thinking back, he recalled that it was the fall of 1895. From Guthrie, the capital of Oklahoma Territory, he and Heck Thomas had taken the trail of two bank robbers. The chase led them into Indian Territory, and ultimately into the Chickasaw Nation. There, at a remote cabin on Elk Creek, they had jumped the outlaws. A shootout ensued, and the robbers ended up dead. Heck Thomas had prayed over their graves.

All of it seemed like yesterday. Yet, as it played out in his mind, he realized it was almost thirty years ago. A different time, when marshals rode horseback; certainly a different brand of law enforcement. He remembered there were no arrest warrants, no court orders, just two lawmen riding into Indian Territory. Justice was swift, often harsh, and outlaws who put up a fight were buried where they fell. He longed for the old days, the long-gone ways. A time when justice was simpler served.

Early that afternoon he pulled into Madill. The town was little more than a crossroads, with a general store, one gas pump, and a few houses lining the road. Outside the store, he braked to a halt and stepped from the car. He buttoned his mackinaw, covering the badge on his shirt, then walked toward the store. He reminded himself to take it slow, play things loose and easy.

The inside of the store was a rainbow of odors. The smell of apples and tobacco mingled with the tang of coal oil and turpentine. A wizened man with the damp eyes of a sparrow and tufts of hair sprouting from his ears stood behind the counter. He nodded to Tilghman with a bright, inquisitive look. His expression was humorous.

"Hope you ain't lost. That's about the only way most folks get here."

"Just passing through," Tilghman said genially. "Thought I'd gas up and get a bite to eat."

"Got mostly dried goods. What'd you like?"

"I could make do with cheese and crackers. Maybe a soda pop."

The storekeeper opened a cracker barrel and sliced cheese off a round on the counter. He took a bottle of soda from a water cooler and popped the top. Tilghman swigged the soda, then began munching crackers and cheese. He motioned out the store window.

"I knew a fellow from here once. His name was Lynn. Horace Lynn."

"How'd you come to know Horace?"

"Motorcars," Tilghman said, deadpan. "We had business interests."

"When was this?"

"Year or so ago."

"Guess you ain't heard," the storekeeper said, watching him. "Horace and his boys are in prison. Got caught by the Feds."

Tilghman paused, the wedge of cheese halfway to his mouth. He placed the cheese and the unfinished soda on the counter. "Reckon I'll move on," he said, digging coins from his pocket. "Two bits cover the eats and drink?"

"No need to rush off. Ain't no Feds around here now."

"Maybe I'll stop again when Horace gets out of the pen."

"Long as you're here, you ought to say hello to Orville."

"Who's Orville?"

"Horace's brother. You never met Orville?"

Tilghman acted suspicious. "Never met Horace, except when we had business. I don't recollect anybody named Orville."

"Yeah, I suppose that figures, considerin' Orville's line of work. Them Lynns always was closemouthed."

"You sayin' the brother took over Horace's . . . trade?"

"Got his own trade," the storekeeper said with a crafty look. "You a drinkin' man?"

"I take a nip now and then."

"Might pay you to call on Orville. Lots less risk in what he does than—uh, you know . . . used cars."

Tilghman gave him a cagey look. "Orville makes shine, does he?"

"You didn't hear me say that. I'm just tellin' you there's money to be made with Orville. He'd likely take to a friend of Horace's."

"Well, I don't know. Prohibition agents don't look kindly on moonshiners. Sounds risky to me."

"No risk a'tall," the storekeeper said with a sly laugh. "Not when your nephew's a Fed."

"Are you sayin' . . . ?"

"I'm sayin' go meet Orville. Might just be your lucky day."

Tilghman drove off with directions. Orville Lynn, like his imprisoned brother, was a farmer with a more profitable sideline. The fact that he hadn't been mentioned in the state police report hardly surprised Tilghman. Moonshiners were far more secretive than car thieves, and of no great interest to the state police. Operating a still was now a federal offense.

A criminal enterprise regulated by Prohibition agents.

The farmhouse was a ramshackle affair. The roof sagged and one end of the porch tilted at a sharp angle. A flop-eared hound was chained near the porch, and the yard was littered with refuse and junk. A tendril of smoke spiraled skyward from the chimney.

Tilghman turned off the road. As he pulled into the yard, the hound hit the end of the chain with a wild, slobbering bark. He switched off the engine, scrutinizing the house and a weather-beaten barn off to one side, again reminding himself to proceed with caution. Moonshiners generally treated strangers like an outbreak of anthrax.

A cornfield, the stalks withered with frost, was visible behind the barn. Beyond that was a wide shelterbelt of timber, and Tilghman thought the liquor still would probably be found deep in the woods. He had raided any number of stills as a deputy U.S. marshal, and he'd learned early on that moonshiners were a dangerous breed. They were as quick to kill as any other outlaw.

The front door opened as Tilghman stepped out of the car. A barrel-gutted man, thick as a singletree through the shoulders, crossed the porch. He was dressed in overalls and a stained woolen jacket, his jaws covered with a dark stubble. He shushed the hound with a terse command.

Tilghman smelled him from ten feet away. The odor

of corn mash, peculiar to White Lightning made in a still, was something a moonshiner could never wash off. Beyond the man, behind the open door of the house, Tilghman caught the glint of light on gunmetal. A younger man, holding a shotgun, watched him through the door. His attention went back to the one in overalls.

"Howdy," he said pleasantly. "I'm looking for Orville Lynn."

"You've found him," the man said. "What's can I do for you?"

"I'm Alvin Baker," Tilghman said, inventing a name. "Your brother and me used to do business together. Before he got sent away."

"I never heard of no Alvin Baker."

"Well, I've heard of you. Horace spoke of you often."

"Where'd you know Horace from?"

"Here and there," Tilghman said with an evasive shrug. "Helped him move some goods, if you know what I mean. We were in the same line of work."

"That a fact?" Lynn inspected him up and down. "You don't look like no car thief to me, old timer. Look more like a cow rustler."

"Yeah, I was that one time too. A man has to keep up with the times though. Switched from cows to cars."

"Let's quit dancin' around. What brings you here?"

"Things got a mite too hot runnin' cars. Anymore, one of them FBI boys is liable to jump out and grab you. I'm looking for a new racket."

"What's that got to do with me?"

"Thought we could work out a deal of some sort. I've got contacts to hell and gone, and a fair-sized bankroll. I could push a lot of shine."

Lynn stared at him. "Who said anything about shine?"

"Why, Horace did," Tilghman said with artless sincerity. "Told me you make the best shine in Oklahoma."

"Did he now?"

"Bragged a lot about your operation. Even told me you've got federal protection right in the family. Near as I recollect, he said your nephew. Or was it a cousin?"

"You're full of shit as a Christmas goose, old man."

"I'm just telling you what Horace told me."

"Like hell," Lynn said bluntly. "Horace might've told you I make shine. He wouldn't've told nobody about—the other thing . . . protection."

"How'd I know about it if Horace didn't tell me? You think I'm a mind reader?"

"I think you're too slick by half."

Lynn motioned with his left hand. The man in the doorway stepped onto the porch, the shotgun tucked into his shoulder. Lynn's eyes narrowed.

"Your name's not Alvin Baker. Who are you?"

Tilghman slowly unbuttoned his mackinaw. He peeled back the lapels to reveal the badge and the holstered Colt. "Tilghman's the name," he said. "Oklahoma State Marshal."

"You just bought yourself a world of shit, old man."

"Here's the deal, Orville. I can clear leather and stop your ticker before that boy gets off the mark. Tell him to go back inside."

Lynn hesitated, weighing the odds. Then, looking deeper into Tilghman's steely gaze, he saw his own death reflected there. He turned his head slightly, glancing toward the house, and motioned with a quick gesture. The younger man lowered the shotgun, watching them a moment, and finally backed through the doorway. Lynn looked around at Tilghman.

"I won't be arrested. You try it and I'll fight."

"Nobody's gonna be arrested today, Orville. You have a telephone in the house?"

"A phone?" Lynn appeared dumbfounded. "You wanna use the phone?"

"You use it," Tilghman informed him. "Call Wiley

and tell him what happened here today. Tell him Bill Tilghman wants to talk.''

''Talk about what?''

''How he can avoid going to prison.''

Tilghman backed to the car. He kept his eyes on Orville Lynn, and the house, as he climbed into the seat. When the engine kicked over, he hooked into reverse, gunning the Ford out onto the road. He spun the wheel, shifting gears, and roared off toward Madill. A hard smile tugged at the corner of his mouth.

He thought Wiley Lynn would understand the message.

Zoe unlocked the door. She kissed him and then hopped back in bed. When he turned on the bedside lamp, she saw that his features were lined with fatigue. She glanced at the clock on top the dresser. It was after midnight.

''You look exhausted,'' she said. ''Are you all right?''

''Nothin' a good night's sleep won't cure.''

Tilghman draped his mackinaw over a chair. He sat down, tired to the bone, his rump sore from so many hours in the car. Awake now, Zoe asked about the trip, and he told her what he'd unearthed in Madill. He unstrapped his gun belt, about to release the buckle, when there was a knock at the door. He moved across the room.

''Who's there?''

''Sawyer.''

When he opened the door, Sawyer gave him an apologetic shrug. ''Sorry to bother you, Marshal. Something's come up.''

''What's the problem?''

''Snake Proctor just slipped into the office. He won't talk to anybody but you.''

''I'll get my coat.''

Zoe sat up in bed when he closed the door. ''Honestly, Bill," she said. "Couldn't this wait until morning?"

"I won't be long. You go back to sleep."

"You're the one who needs sleep."

"Keep my side of the bed warm."

Tilghman eased out the door. He locked it behind him, shrugging into his mackinaw, and followed Sawyer down the stairs. A Friday night crowd was slowly emptying from dives along the street. On the way across town, he gave Sawyer a quick account of his trip to Madill. Sawyer agreed that the uncle had probably already made the phone call. He thought it likely that Wiley Lynn would come by for a talk.

When they entered the office, Proctor stood hidden in the shadows at the rear of the room. He looked nervous and frightened, his features rubbery with strain. Tilghman nodded in the dim lamplight. "Good to see you again, Emmett. I was starting to think you'd forgotten our deal."

"Didn't forget," Proctor said, his movements jerky. "Just waited till I had something hot. I wanna make a trade."

"What sort of trade?"

"I'll give you a load of dope and that ends it. You don't make me spy for you no more."

"How much dope are we talking about?"

"Lots," Proctor said. "Week's supply, maybe even more."

Tilghman was impressed. A shipment of drugs that large might lead directly to Killian. "All right," he said soberly. "You deliver and I'll cut you loose. But it's got to be a big haul."

"Don't worry, it's big. I got it straight from the horse's mouth."

"Which horse is that?"

"Dave Falcon and Bud Shuemacher."

Proctor went on to explain. With the Sportsmen's Club closed, Hammer's gang found livelier places to party. Tonight, in a ginmill uptown, Falcon and Shuemacher shared a bottle with a couple of the dive's girls. The girls were heavy cocaine users, and the men, drunk and showing off, bragged about a large shipment coming in tomorrow night. Shuemacher let slip that the drop would be made by airplane, at an open field west of town, near some oil storage tanks. Proctor, who worked at the dive cleaning tables, had overheard the conversation. He thought the men were too drunk to invent a story about airdrops at night.

"Tomorrow night?" Tilghman asked when he finished. "Did they say what time?"

Proctor shook his head. "Wasn't nothin' said about that. Just tomorrow night."

"I'm surprised they'd run off at the mouth like that."

"Couple of drunks tryin' to impress girls and get in their pants. Happens all the time."

"Do you know this field they're talking about? Where the drop will be made?"

"Just a guess," Proctor said. "There's a bunch of oil tanks maybe two miles out of town. West of there ain't nothin' but open country."

"I think he's right," Sawyer added. "Those tanks are off the road a ways, where the derricks begin to peter out. I remember some pastureland and a stand of woods on beyond there. Be a good spot for an airdrop."

"And a good night," Tilghman said, thinking out loud. "There'll be a full moon."

Proctor looked at him. "I kept my end of the bargain. We even-steven now?"

"Your slate's wiped clean, Emmett. Try to stay out of trouble."

"I ain't anxious to go to jail. You've seen the last of me."

Proctor hurried out the door. When he was gone, Sawyer glanced around. "What do you think, Marshal?"

"I think we'll organize ourselves a greeting party."

"All that dope, they're liable to put up a fight. We'd better go loaded for bear."

"You remember that Thompson I took off the bootleggers?"

"Gadalmightybingo! You're gonna carry a tommy gun?"

Tilghman smiled. "I'll clean it first thing tomorrow."

CHAPTER 29

The streets were mobbed with a Saturday night crowd. Shortly after dark, Tilghman and Sawyer emerged from the office and turned north along Jenkins. They strolled off on a routine patrol of the town.

Tilghman wanted everything to appear normal. Anyone watching from the Sportsmen's Club would think it was business as usual. The marshal and his deputy were out making the first of many nightly rounds on a raucous Saturday night. They were soon lost in the crowds milling along the boardwalk.

A block north they passed a pool hall on the corner. Still holding to a casual pace, they turned west along a side street. At the rear of the pool hall, they ducked into the alley and doubled back, walking south. Some moments later, their pace faster, they moved through the shadows behind the jail. The old Ford was parked in the alley.

Tilghman started the engine. Sawyer walked to the edge of the building and motioned him forward. At the end of the alley, Tilghman slowed the car and Sawyer hopped into the passenger seat. They turned west on the side street, running without headlights to the corner. There, after switching on the lights, they continued parallel to Shawnee Avenue. On the outskirts of the business district, they took the road west from town.

"Nobody spotted us," Sawyer said. "I think we pulled it off."

Tilghman checked the rearview mirror. "So far, so good. I doubt anyone will miss us either."

"Not with that big of a crowd in town. Anybody gets curious, they'll figure we're out making rounds."

"Let's hope that includes Jake Hammer."

"You're still convinced he'll show?"

"I suspect Killian wouldn't trust anybody else. Dope's too valuable to leave it to some of Hammer's boys."

"Who'd have ever thought they'd drop it out of an airplane? That's a pretty slick operation."

"All ties together, Hugh. Killian's a pretty slick operator."

Some two miles west of town the oil derricks began petering out. Off to the north, beyond the last of the derricks, a row of five large storage tanks loomed against the moonlit sky. The tanks were constructed of timber, banded with steel fittings, built to hold thousands of gallons of crude oil. A dirt road angled north alongside the tanks.

Tilghman drove past the road. Earlier that day Sawyer had drawn him a map of the suspected drop site for the drugs. West of the storage tanks was an open field that appeared to be ten acres or more in size. The field was bordered on the north and the west by scattered woods, and just beyond the western stand of timber, a farm road angled north through the countryside. After studying the map, Tilghman saw that the easiest access to the field was along the road beside the storage tanks. He thought that was the road Hammer would take.

Farther along, at the western side of the field, Tilghman turned north onto the farm road. A short distance ahead they passed a farmhouse, the windows lighted by coal oil lamps. Beyond the house, Tilghman pulled off the road and drove into the woods. The trees were spread out sufficiently for a car to negotiate a serpentine path through the timber. Tilghman cut the headlights and navigated across the wooded terrain by dappled moonlight. He braked to a halt just inside the treeline, not five yards from the edge of the field. He switched off the motor.

To their direct front, east across the field, they saw the massive outline of the storage tanks. Off to their left, the northern stand of timber formed the leg of an L with the woods where they were parked. A full moon, already well above the horizon, bathed the field in a sallow glow. Farther on, beyond the row of storage tanks, flares from casinghead gas illuminated the sky. The motor cooled with a quick *tick-tick-tick* in the chill night air.

Tilghman stepped out of the car. Sawyer opened the passenger door, following him to the rear, and waited while he unlocked the trunk. He handed Sawyer a Winchester carbine, and then took out the Thompson submachine gun, which had a fifty-round drum and a fore-grip beneath the barrel. The tommy gun had been cleaned and oiled, and he'd loaded the drum to full capacity with .45 ACP cartridges. After closing the trunk, he and Sawyer got back in the car. They sat with their weapons staring out at the field.

"Cold tonight," Sawyer commented, the words spoken in puffs of frost. "Hope you're wrong about the drop being later. We're liable to freeze our tails off."

"I'd like it sooner myself," Tilghman said. "But I've got an idea the pilot will wait till the moon's out full. He needs good visibility for the drop."

"Yeah, you're probably right. They wouldn't chance dropping it in the wrong spot."

"Not with the price of dope. God knows it's more profitable than whiskey."

"Lots more," Sawyer agreed. "How else could they afford an airplane?"

"All makes sense now," Tilghman said. "Killian's got the Kansas City mob behind him, and they've got the connections. Dope's a good example."

"Why do you say that?"

"Well, for the most part, drugs are brought in through Mexico. Takes some fancy planning to distribute the stuff around the country. Nobody beats the mob when it comes to organization."

Sawyer chuffed frost. "What with runnin' whiskey, they've got plenty of experience. Guess dope's not much different."

"Easier in a way," Tilghman noted. "Smuggling drugs doesn't attract the attention of federal agents the way liquor does. So there's fewer people to bribe."

"Speakin' of federal agents reminds me. I'm surprised Wiley Lynn hasn't been around to see you."

"It's only been a day. Maybe his uncle wasn't able to get hold of him last night. Don't worry, he'll come around."

"What if he doesn't?"

"Then I'll find a way to link him with his uncle's moonshine operation. That ought to get him five or ten years."

"Even so," Sawyer said. "That wouldn't do much where Killian's concerned. You still need an informant."

Tilghman wasn't as certain as he sounded. All day he'd been waiting on the phone to ring or Wiley Lynn to walk through the door. His fear was that Lynn might have witlessly run to Killian, seeking protection. Were that the case, he thought Lynn was likely dead by now. Killian was quick to eliminate anyone who might talk.

"Maybe you've got a point," he said after a pause. "If there's shooting tonight, let's try to take somebody alive. I can't nail Killian without a songbird."

"Hammer turned you down before. What makes tonight different?"

"Anybody we catch tonight will be facing prison time. That tends to give a man second thoughts."

Sawyer looked at him. "You open up with a tommy

gun and there won't be any prisoners. That thing sprays lead in a hurry.''

"Let's hope they come along peaceable."

"I wouldn't count on it, Marshal."

Tilghman lapsed into silence. He stared out at the field, wondering if Hammer and his men might be persuaded to surrender. The chances seemed to him somewhere between slim and none.

He thought they would fight.

The moon was near its zenith. Stars winked in the sky and a silvery luminescence flooded the field. Somewhere in the distance an owl hooted, then the night was still.

Tilghman sat wrapped in his mackinaw. His ears felt brittle, and his hands were stuffed deep in the warmth of his pockets. Beside him, Sawyer huffed steam, arms hugged to his sides, the collar turned up on his coat. The minutes dragged on.

"Jesus," Sawyer said in a chilled voice. "You think they're ever gonna show?"

Tilghman pulled out his pocket watch. He held it to a shaft of moonlight, checked the time, and returned it to his vest pocket. "Eleven o'clock," he said. "I'd judge another hour."

"What happens if they're not here by midnight?"

"We wait."

Sawyer was quiet a moment. "Never told you this before. You remind me a lot of Blackjack Pershing. I saw him over in France."

Tilghman was surprised by the comparison to the allied commander. "I'm not in Pershing's class," he said. "Where was it you saw him?"

"Just before we charged the Krauts at Château-Thierry. He came walkin' along the trenches like he was out for a Sunday stroll. Never once dodged a bullet."

"Guess that's the difference between generals and lawmen. I've dodged a few in my time."

Sawyer considered it unlikely. He wanted to say that,

like everyone else in town, he thought Tilghman had brass balls. But the comment somehow seemed inappropriate. "Well, anyway," he said, motioning into the night. "I suppose this cold put me in mind of the trenches. France wasn't any picnic in the winter."

Tilghman thought the younger man had the raw stuff of a peace officer. When Cromwell was cleaned out, and he went back to the ranch, he planned to recommend Sawyer for the job of town marshal. "Law work's a little like war," he said. "Winter or summer it's the waitin' that gets—"

Headlights appeared on the road from town. A car slowed, then turned onto the dirt road that skirted the storage tanks. They watched as the car followed the road to the woods bordering the north side of the field. The driver pulled into the edge of the treeline and rolled to a stop. The headlights went out.

"You were right," Sawyer said, suddenly alert. "They took the other road."

Tilghman nodded. "That car look familiar?"

"Hammer's Buick. Plain as day in the moonlight. I'd bet on it."

"Hugh, I think you'd win the bet."

"Now all we need's an airplane."

"I doubt we've got long to wait."

Some while later they heard it. Off in the distance the drone of an airplane engine grew steadily louder. Tilghman glanced at the moon, which was directly overhead, and felt no need to consult his watch. The drop, much as he'd suspected, had been scheduled for the stroke of midnight. The pilot was right on time.

A biplane appeared out of the south. The aircraft was fast, with a double set of wings, built for maneuverability at top speed. As the plane buzzed the field, the headlights from the Buick flashed three times in quick succession. The pilot, who was visible in the open cockpit, banked sharply to the right, gaining altitude. The plane was briefly silhouetted against the moon.

After circling off to the south, the aircraft made another pass at treetop level. The wings wobbled from side to side as the pilot shoved a large bundle out of the cockpit. He put the plane into a steep climb, clearing the northern treeline, and banked east over the storage tanks. The bundle hurtled downward and bounced twice before rolling to a stop in the center of the field. The biplane roared off into the southerly sky.

In the sudden stillness, the sound of the Buick's motor turning over drifted through the night. The car edged out of the treeline, headlights darkened, and moved across the open ground. At the center of the field, the Buick braked to a halt and the rear door swung open. A man hopped out, walking swiftly to the bundle, and hefted it in his arms. He turned back toward the car.

Tilghman cranked the Ford's engine. The sound carried distinctly, and through he left the lights off, the car was visible as he pulled out of the trees. The man with the bundle glanced around, then hurriedly tossed the bundle into the Buick and leaped through the open door. Working the clutch, Tilghman shifted gears and barreled toward the center of the field. He switched on the headlights.

A man in the passenger seat of the Buick leaned out the window. He opened fire with a tommy gun and slugs peppered the earth along the right side of the Ford. With a sudden clash of gears, the Buick wheeled away, rapidly gaining speed, and angled across the field. Tilghman pushed the gas pedal to the floorboard, closing ground as the Buick thumped onto the road beside the storage tanks. Sawyer rolled down the window, thrusting his head and shoulders through the opening. He cut loose with his Winchester.

The Buick accelerated at high speed. Where the dirt road intersected the town road, the driver tried to take the turn without slowing down and lost control of the wheel. The car skidded across the intersection and slammed nose-first into a ditch on the opposite side of the road. Tilghman braked to a halt at the intersection, grabbing the tommy gun as he stepped from the Ford. Sawyer jumped out on the other side.

The doors flew open on the Buick. Milligan tumbled from the passenger seat and Shuemacher crawled out the rear door. On the other side, Hammer lurched from the rear seat and Falcon emerged from behind the steering wheel. Milligan was off balance, stumbling around in the ditch, and he fired a burst from his tommy gun that stitched holes in the radiator of the Ford. Hammer and the other men, blinded by the Ford's headlights, opened fire with pistols. Their shots went wild.

Sawyer tucked the Winchester into his shoulder, firing as fast as he could work the lever. A slug drilled through Milligan's neck, followed by another in the stomach, and he toppled face-down in the ditch. Shuemacher, struck twice in the chest, reeled backwards and collapsed. Falcon got off a second shot, then went down hard as Tilghman opened up with the tommy gun. Hammer ran east along the ditch, weaving and bobbing, firing over his shoulder. Tilghman tracked him, feathering the trigger, and the Thompson chattered a long burst. Arms pinwheeling, Hammer was driven sideways by the impact of the slugs. He dropped in a bloody heap.

The staccato roar of gunfire abruptly ceased. Hissing steam from the Ford's radiator jarred the sudden stillness. Tilghman and Sawyer walked forward, their weapons held at the ready, inspecting the bodies. Finally, satisfied that the four men were dead, they returned to the road. Sawyer shook his head.

"Damn fools," he said in a quiet voice. "Why'd they have to fight?"

Tilghman stared into the ditch. "Some men won't have it any other way."

"Well, it's too bad about Hammer. He'll never turn on Killian now."

"Maybe he's worth more dead than he was alive."

Sawyer looked bemused. "What good does he do you dead?"

"I've got an idea the news will rattle Lynn. Might convince him to sing."

"Marshal, I sure the devil hope so. You've just about run out of candidates."

Tilghman smiled. "One's all we need, Hugh. I think his name's Wiley Lynn."

CHAPTER 30

A calm seemed to have settled over Cromwell by the next evening. Everyone was talking about Hammer's death, and they celebrated the end of the mob in Seminole County. The story of the shootout was told and retold in dives across town.

On the surface everything appeared to be business as usual. Ginmills and dance halls were filled with the regular Sunday night crowds of roughnecks and roustabouts. Yet there was speculation and concern, even though Tilghman was now looked upon as the town savior. No one expected him to close down the dives, but they wondered how rigidly he would enforce the law. They were sobered by the thought.

Shortly after dark Frank Killian drove into town from the Wewoka road. He turned onto Shawnee Avenue, inspecting the throngs on the boardwalks with casual interest. His mind was on Hammer, whose death infuriated him, for he would now have to find a replacement. Even more, his thoughts centered on Tilghman, the source of his aggravation, and a problem yet to be solved. He planned to solve it tonight.

Killian found a parking spot near the main intersection. He stepped out of the Cadillac, staring upstreet a moment, then walked to a cafe. Inside, he selected a window table and took a chair with a view of the intersection. When the waitress came by, he ordered a steak dinner with fried potatoes and coffee. As she moved away he looked out the window, leisurely surveying the street, satisfied that he had a ringside seat. He wondered if Wiley Lynn would be on time.

Directly across the street, Sawyer watched as the waitress returned with Killian's coffee. He was still somewhat amazed that the mobster would have the audacity to set foot in Cromwell. In light of last night's shootout, he thought it was suspicious, a strange move. He turned, hurrying upstreet toward Sirmans Mercantile, where he'd left Tilghman a short while ago. His tour of Shawnee Avenue had been interrupted when he spotted Killian's Cadillac. He walked faster.

Walt Sirmans, like other merchants, opened for business at noon on Sunday. He rationalized commerce on the Lord's day by the fact that business dropped off to a standstill on Monday. Later, he would think it a coincidence that he and Tilghman were engaged in a conversation about Frank Killian when Sawyer rushed into the store. The deputy looked worried.

"Killian's in town," he said. "I just saw him over in the City Cafe."

Tilghman frowned. "Killian's got more brass than I gave him credit for. Why would he come to Cromwell?"

"Asked myself the same question," Sawyer said. "Damned odd he'd show up the night after Hammer gets killed. Hardly makes any sense."

"Killian doesn't do anything without a reason. You can bet he has something in mind."

"Yeah, but what?"

"Maybe it's revenge," Sirmans interjected. "He certainly has reason for that."

"Not likely," Tilghman replied. "Killian lets other people do his dirty work. He keeps his own hands clean."

"Besides that," Sawyer said, "he's over there having

supper. Doesn't sound like a man gettin' ready to pick a fight."

Tilghman considered a moment. "Hugh, I want you to keep an eye on him. Let me know the minute he makes a move."

"Where'll you be?"

"Somewhere on the street. I'll stick around the intersection."

Sawyer nodded and hurried out the door. Tilghman watched through the storefront window as he walked east along the broadwalk. A time elapsed before Sirmans finally broke the silence. His expression was quizzical.

"Why not arrest Killian on some trumped-up charge? Even if it doesn't hold, you'd have him in jail tonight."

"I'd have to release him tomorrow," Tilghman said. "Only way I'll nail Killian is through Wiley Lynn. I kept thinking he'd come by the office today."

"What if Killian had him murdered? You said yourself it's a possibility."

"Then I'm up the creek without a paddle. I've got no leverage on Bradley and that bunch in the courthouse. No reason for them to talk, and they know it."

"Their time's running out," Sirmans commented. "Even if you don't get Killian, you've put the lid on Cromwell. Next election we'll vote those crooks out of the courthouse."

"That's too late," Tilghman remarked. "Killian's probably got somebody tapped to replace Hammer next week. I don't want to do the job all over again."

"Which brings you full circle, doesn't it? You're back to Killian."

"Let's just say I'd like to lay my hands on Wiley Lynn."

Across the way, Tilghman saw Zoe emerge from the hotel with Josie and Zack Mosley. "I'll see you later, Walt." He moved toward the door. "I'm supposed to have supper with Zoe and the Mosleys."

"Keep me posted on Killian. There's something funny about him showing up tonight."

"I'll let you know when I know."

Tilghman crossed the street to the opposite corner. He met Zoe and the Mosleys in front of the Bon Ton Cafe. Zoe smiled brightly. "We were just looking for you. Aren't you the prompt one?"

"Not exactly," Tilghman said. "We've got a situation brewing. I'll have to skip supper."

"Oh? What's wrong?"

"Frank Killian's in town. Sawyer's keeping an eye on him."

Zoe looked alarmed. "Why would Killian come here? Especially after last night?"

"I don't have the least notion. We'll have to stick with him till we find out."

"Damned queer," Mosley said seriously. "You'd think he'd steer clear of Cromwell."

"Yeah, you'd think so," Tilghman agreed. "He's down at the City Cafe having supper. Showed up bold as brass."

"That frightens me," Zoe said. "He wouldn't drive all this way just to have supper. There's more to it."

"Zoe's right," Josie added. "Somebody like him always has a trick up his sleeve. I learned that with Jake Hammer."

Tilghman nodded. "We'll know before the night's out. You folks go on to supper. I'll catch up with you later."

"Would you look at that!" Mosley said, staring past them. "Wiley Lynn just rolled into town."

Tilghman turned, following the direction of his gaze. Across the street, he saw Lynn's Studebacker roadster double-parked in front of the dance hall formerly owned by Ma Murphy. Lynn was behind the wheel, talking intently to a woman in the passenger seat. Her head lolled, and she waved him off drunkenly.

"Anybody know that woman?" Tilghman asked.

"Her name's Rose Lutke," Josie said. She runs a cat-house—excuse me, Zoe . . . a house over in Wewoka. She likes to think she's Lynn's girlfriend."

Tilghman recalled the state police report on Lynn. The report had noted that Lynn kept company with the ma-dam of a Wewoka whorehouse. Why Lynn would turn up tonight with a woman was a question that bothered Tilghman. Even more, he was troubled that Lynn and Killian had arrived in Cromwell within minutes of one another. Something was not as it appeared.

Lynn stepped out of the car. He wobbled unsteadily, apparently tanked on liquor, clutching a Colt .45 auto-matic in his right hand. But he was far from drunk, his mind on Killian's threat and the troubling phone call from his uncle. He pointed the pistol at the ground and fired, kicking up a spurt of dust in the hard-packed earth of the street. The woman yelled at him, and he dismissed her with a curt gesture. He walked toward the dance hall.

"Stay here!" Tilghman ordered. "Zack, look after the women."

Tilghman hurried across the street. He pulled his pis-tol, aware of Sawyer moving quickly along the board-walk. At the door of the dance hall, he collared Lynn and spun him around. He grabbed the Prohibition agent's gun arm, wrenching it upward, and slammed it into the wall of the building. Lynn grunted, his breath sour with the smell of whiskey.

"Lemme go, goddammit. I'm here on business."

"You're under arrest." Tilghman rammed the pistol into his ribs. "Hugh, take his gun."

Sawyer twisted the automatic out of Lynn's hand. Tilghman released his hold on Lynn's arm, lowering the old Colt to his side. Lynn seemed to relax, but on the instant, as his arm dropped, he snaked a revolver from inside his waistband. He fired twice, and Tilghman, act-ing on reflex, smashed him upside the head with the Colt. Lynn went down, the revolver clattering to the boardwalk. Tilghman staggered sideways, clutching his chest.

Sawyer caught him as he fell. His weight was too much, and Sawyer gently lowered him to the boardwalk. "Oooo Jesus," Sawyer groaned, watching blood pump from the lawman's chest. He glared around at a group of roustabouts standing nearby. "Somebody get a doctor!"

Zack Mosley bulled a path through the crowd, followed by Zoe and Josie. Zoe dropped to her knees beside Tilghman, her features terrified. She brushed his hat aside, caressing his forehead. Her voice trembled.

"Bill? Bill! Do you hear me?"

Tilghman heard her. His eyes were open, and he attempted to speak, but his mouth was numb. He tried to blink his eyelids, but nothing seemed to work. He willed her to hear him.

Zoe.

"Hang on, Bill. The doctor's on his way. I love you, Bill. I love you so much."

Me too. Wish I'd told you more.

A distant shape came swimming forward in his mind. He focused on it, fascinated by its blurred image, watching it sputter and dance and splash closer. He saw that it was a flame, not bright or fiery, somehow lessening in intensity. But nonetheless a flame.

"Oh God, Bill." Zoe touched his face. "Don't leave me! Please don't leave me."

I'll never leave you.

A smile lighted his eyes. Her voice faded, but he again willed her to hear him. *Zoe. All those years . . . together . . . I . . .*

All within him went still. He watched the flame gather itself in one last spark, watched it flicker and dim. Swiftly came a mealy, weblike darkness, and the flame died. His eyes closed.

Zoe's face went ashen, drained of color. Her mouth opened in a silent scream and tears flooded her vision.

She took him by the shoulders, lifting him with sudden strength, and cradled him in her arms. She rocked back and forth, lost.

Josie knelt beside her, sobbing, unable to speak. Mosley stared down at them, a catch in his throat, his mouth dry. He glanced at Sawyer, whose eyes glistened wetly, and looked away. For a long moment, wrapped in a cone of silence, they watched Zoe rock back and forth. No one around them spoke.

Sawyer abruptly turned away. His gaze fixed on the City Cafe, and he saw Killian standing at the rear of the Cadillac. He angled across the street at a deliberate stride, his insides gone cold as ice. Killian stiffened, eyes alert, watching with a guarded look as he drew closer. Sawyer stopped, not a pace separating them, his voice calm.

"Marshal Tilghman told me you always go heeled. Defend yourself."

"I'll have to pass," Killian said without inflection. "I have no quarrel with you, deputy."

"Defend yourself or get killed. I won't tell you again."

"You'd kill me in cold blood? I don't think you've got the stomach for it."

"You sonovbitch—"

Sawyer went berzerk. His fist lashed out and drove Killian onto the trunk of the car. He pinned the mobster with his left arm and hammered him with cold ferocity. His right arm rose and fell like a piston, and he methodically beat Killian to a pulp. His face was savage.

Zack Mosley grabbed him from behind. The oil man smothered him in a bear hug and hauled him off. "Let it go," he shouted, as Sawyer struggled to break free. "You'll kill him."

"I mean to kill him. Let me loose, goddamn you!"

Mosley was too powerful, holding him off the ground in a viselock. After several moments, lunging and kicking, Sawyer went slack. His eyes cleared, and he seemed to recover himself, regain his senses. He shook free of Mosley's grip.

Killian staggered to his feet. His jaw was broken, his nose squashed, his mouth a bloody hole of missing teeth. Mosley took him by the collar, waltzed him to the car door, and flung him inside. When Killian sat there, wheezing for breath, Mosley leaned through the door. His voice was stolid, a brute promise.

"Don't come back to Cromwell. Next time we'll all kill you."

Mosley slammed the door. After a moment, Killian managed to collect himself and start the engine. His battered features dripping blood, he backed across the street, the Cadillac bucking and jumping as he clumsily worked the clutch. He finally got the car turned around, and drove off toward the Wewoka road. Mosley and Sawyer watched until his taillights disappeared. Sawyer grunted coarsely.

"You should've let me kill him."

"You're still a law officer, Hugh. What about Wiley Lynn?"

Sawyer nodded. "Let's put the bastard in jail."

They walked back toward the crowd outside the dance hall.

A late morning sun lighted the windows. Zoe snapped the clasps on her suitcase and set it beside the door. She was dressed in black, her features lined with fatigue. She returned to the bed.

His leather bag was still open, his clothes packed. Beside it on the bed lay his gun belt, his old Colt secure in the holster. She lovingly traced her fingers over the yellowed ivory grips, flooded with memories. She remembered all those years, when he would step aboard his horse, the Colt strapped around his waist, and wave to her as he rode off. How proud he'd looked!

She tried to summon her own pride. He would have wanted her to celebrate his life, not grieve his passing.

Last night, in those last moments, she knew he had spoken to her. Not with words, though she'd heard his voice, but with the fierce light in his eyes. He was telling her what he felt, even as he drew a final breath, his eyes locked on hers. She somehow sensed the force of his will, and the words. He would be with her forever.

She placed the Colt in the bag. As she buckled the straps, a knock sounded at the door. When she opened it, Neal Brown stood in the hallway. He had driven over from Chandler that morning, after being notified by telephone. His look was sorrowful, and he quickly removed his hat. He forced a smile.

"Everything's ready," he said quietly. "I've got the car out front."

"I'm ready too, Neal. Let's go home."

Brown carried the bags downstairs. As they emerged from the hotel, a hearse pulled in behind her Buick and stopped. His casket was visible through the side window of the hearse, and the sight gave her momentary pause. But then she took hold of herself, suppressing the tears, as Brown stowed the bags in the car. A small crowd was waiting on the boardwalk.

Walt Sirmans and members of the Citizens Committee offered their condolences. Virgil Pryor and Zack Mosley shook her hand, and Josie embraced her in a tight hug. Hugh Sawyer was the last in line, his face rigid with sadness and loss. Zoe opened her purse and removed the marshal's badge. A glint of sunlight reflected off the metal. She smiled, handing it to Sawyer.

"Bill would have wanted you to have his badge. He often told me you were a fine lawman."

Sawyer choked, staring at the badge. He swallowed hard. "I won't let him down, Miz Tilghman. I'll remember everything he taught me."

"I know you will, Hugh. He was very proud of you."

Brown assisted her into the car. A moment later they drove off, the hearse following closely behind. The church bell began to toll, and up ahead, the streets were lined with townspeople and oil men, even girls from the houses. All of Cromwell had turned out to pay their last respects, to honor a man of valor. They stood silent as the procession rolled past.

Outside town the road west cleaved through a forest of timbered derricks. As the Buick went by, trailed by the hearse, the roughnecks and roustabouts put aside their work and turned to face the road. The men were somber, like sentinels at attention, their hats in their hands. For the longest while, even as the procession passed their derricks, none of them moved. They stared at the hearse under a bright November sun.

Brown wagged his head. He smiled sadly, nodding to the men so still beneath the derricks. "Looks like Bill got what he wanted."

"Oh?" Zoe said, lost in her own thoughts. "What was that?"

"Tamed himself one last town."

Zoe was struck by the words. Her eyes misted with a smile as she repeated them to herself. She thought it was the most fitting eulogy anyone would ever deliver. One last town.

Her Bill would have liked that.

EPILOGUE

William Matthew Tilghman was killed the night of November 1, 1924. By executive order of the governor, his body lay in state under the capitol rotunda for two days. The Oklahoma state flag was flown at half-mast, and over ten thousand people filed past his bier. They came to mark the passage of a man as well as the end of an era. Bill Tilghman was the last of the gunfighter marshals.

Frank Killian never returned to Cromwell. He vanished from Oklahoma the night after Tilghman's death, the dethroned underworld czar of Seminole County. Some weeks later, his body was discovered on a country road outside Kansas City, a single gunshot wound in the back of his head. Law enforcement officials speculated that he had been executed by the mob, in retaliation for his mishandling of the rackets in Cromwell. No charges were ever filed in connection with his death.

Wiley Lynn was brought to trial for the murder of Bill Tilghman. He claimed self-defense, contending that Tilghman attempted to kill him during the discharge of his duties as a Prohibition agent. He produced a search warrant for the Cromwell dance hall, even though the warrant did not bear the United States Commissioner's seal as required by law. Despite overwhelming evidence of his guilt, Lynn was acquitted by the jury. Afterward, it was revealed that the first jury vote had been 11-1 for conviction. The lone dissident held out, and ultimately badgered the other jurors into reversing their vote. Prosecutors suspected jury tampering, but were unable to prove the dissident juror had been bribed. Lynn walked out of the courtroom a free man.

Zoe Tilghman, when questioned by a newspaper reporter about the verdict, replied: ''The outcome of this trial has added a supreme dishonor to the law of Oklahoma.'' Some years would pass before justice prevailed in the murder of her husband. In 1932, after arrest and conviction on various criminal charges, Wiley Lynn was shot to death during an assault on an officer of the Oklahoma State Crime Bureau. Legend records that the officer who killed him was the former marshal of Cromwell, later the sheriff of Seminole County, and ultimately appointed by the governor as a criminal investigator for the state. His name was Hugh Sawyer.

Zack Mosley became one of the wealthiest oil men in Oklahoma. His wife, Josie, gave him three sons and a daughter, and went on to attain prominence as a benefactress of the arts and a major fundraiser for various charitable organizations. Their status in the social stratosphere of Oklahoma rose to dizzying heights, and few were aware that a former whore rubbed elbows with financiers, industrialists, statesmen, and the political elite of America. In 1933, Josie and Zack Mosley attended the presidential inauguration of Franklin Delano Roosevelt. Their place in the aristocracy of Oklahoma was thereafter without parallel.

Zoe Tilghman lived out her years on the horse ranch outside Chandler. She stayed busy with church work and operating the ranch, and though admired by eligible men of position and wealth, she never remarried. She devoted her life instead to memorializing her late husband's career as a peace officer for the benefit of future generations. The biography she authored, published in 1949, was entitled *Marshal of the Last Frontier*. She gave Bill Tilghman his rightful place in history, an icon among those who brought law and order to the dusty plains of the Old West, and one last town in Oklahoma. She wrought his name for all time for what he was in his time.

A man of valor.

In 1889, Bill Tilghman joined the historic land rush that transformed a raw frontier into Oklahoma Territory. A lawman by trade, he set aside his badge to make his fortune in the boomtowns. Yet Tilghman was called into service once more, on a bold, relentless journey that would make his name a legend for all time—in an epic confrontation with outlaw Bill Doolin.

OUTLAW KINGDOM

MATT BRAUN

THE TRAIL DRIVE SERIES
by Ralph Compton
From St. Martin's Paperbacks

The only riches Texas had left after the Civil War were five million maverick longhorns and the brains, brawn and boldness to drive them north to where the money was. Now, Ralph Compton brings this violent and magnificent time to life in an extraordinary epic series based on the history-blazing trail drives.

THE GOODNIGHT TRAIL (BOOK 1)
_____ 92815-7 $5.99 U.S./$7.99 Can.
THE WESTERN TRAIL (BOOK 2)
_____ 92901-3 $5.99 U.S./$7.99 Can.
THE CHISOLM TRAIL (BOOK 3)
_____ 92953-6 $5.99 U.S./$7.99 Can.
THE BANDERA TRAIL (BOOK 4)
_____ 95143-4 $5.50 U.S./$6.50 Can.
THE CALIFORNIA TRAIL (BOOK 5)
_____ 95169-8 $5.99 U.S./$7.99 Can.
THE SHAWNEE TRAIL (BOOK 6)
_____ 95241-4 $5.99 U.S./$7.99 Can.
THE VIRGINIA CITY TRAIL (BOOK 7)
_____ 95306-2 $5.50 U.S./$6.50 Can.
THE DODGE CITY TRAIL (BOOK 8)
_____ 95380-1 $5.99 U.S./$7.99 Can.
THE OREGON TRAIL (BOOK 9)
_____ 95547-2 $5.99 U.S./$7.99 Can.
THE SANTA FE TRAIL (BOOK 10)
_____ 96296-7 $5.99 U.S./$7.99 Can.